Torn between duty and desire...

Sawyer Hunt has always been confident with his place in the world. He knows what he wants, conceals his painful truths behind a mask of cool indifference and keeps his circle small. The only person who has ever come close to smashing through his inner walls is the one person his parents will never accept.
Xavier Daniels is sick of being Hunt's dirty little secret. When he fled the ugliness of his past, he swore he would never again hide who he is. Or let anyone hurt him or make him feel ashamed. So, discovering the man he's in love with is engaged to some mystery woman devastates him. Forced into making the only decision he can, Xavier locks up his heart, determined to keep Hunt out for good.

Sydney Shaw is the bane of her father's existence. But he's finally found a way to end her rebellious streak—marry a virtual stranger or be cut off forever. Hunt could be a great husband, if he wasn't such a cold, moody jerk and she wasn't still hung up on the guy who broke her heart at fifteen.
Marrying Sydney to save his father's company is a sacrifice Hunt will make because he suspects the elite is involved, and it's up to him and his friends to stop them. With his heart also on the line, Hunt is determined to end the threat quickly or risk losing the one person he now realizes he can't live without. Consequences be damned.

Copyright © Siobhan Davis 2021. Siobhan Davis asserts the moral right to be identified as the author of this work. All rights reserved under International and Pan-American Copyright Conventions.

This is a work of fiction. Names, characters, places, incidents and dialogues are products of the author's imagination or are used fictitiously. Any resemblance to actual people, living or dead, or events is entirely coincidental.

This book is sold subject to the condition that it shall not, by way of trade or otherwise be lent, resold, hired out, or otherwise circulated without the prior written consent of the author. No part of this publication may be reproduced, transmitted, decompiled, or stored in or introduced into any information storage and retrieval system, in any form or by any means, whether electronic or mechanical, including photocopying, without the express written permission of the author.

Printed by Amazon
Paperback edition © June 2021

ISBN-13: 9798526173544

Editor: Kelly Hartigan (XterraWeb) editing.xterraweb.com
Cover design by Robin Harper wickedbydesigncovers.wixsite.com
Photographer: Wander Aguiar
Cover Model: Andrew Biernat
Formatted By CP Smith

AUTHOR'S NOTE

This romance contains MM and MF scenes in addition to some dark themes/references. It is recommended for readers aged eighteen and older.

Sawyer continues after the end of *Jackson*, but it is before *The Hate I Feel*.

RYDEVILLE ELITE BOOK SIX
SAWYER

USA TODAY BESTSELLING AUTHOR
SIOBHAN DAVIS

PROLOGUE

Sawyer

March

M<small>Y CELL VIBRATES</small> in my pocket, and I groan when I see the name flashing on the screen. I've been dodging Dad's calls all week. *Is it too much to ask to enjoy spring break without some family interference?* I have a feeling I know why he's calling, hence my hesitation to pick up. But I get my stubborn streak from my father, and I know he won't give up until he's said his piece, so I reluctantly accept his call.

"Finally. I was about to send out a search party," Dad deadpans.

"What's up, old man?" I work hard to keep my tone lighthearted.

"I need another favor."

Another groan rips from my mouth. "Dad." My tone carries warning.

"Don't Dad me." I can visualize Ethan Hunt pacing the floor of his office with a scowl on his face. "I don't ask much of you, son, but I need your help with this."

"You said it was one time."

"And that was enough back then when we were courting

several partners, but things have changed, and it's become more pressing."

"Why?" I ask, dropping onto the couch with a sigh.

"For reasons I'm not at liberty to disclose just yet, the other parties have pulled out, leaving Shaw Software as the only contender for the merger."

"I still don't get why you want to merge with another tech company. Your new security products are going to blow that market wide-open. Stock prices will shoot through the roof. Why share the profits with another company?"

"We need the investment capital," he says in a clipped tone. "And this isn't up for debate. Keeping Herman Shaw on our side is mission critical. By all accounts, Sydney Shaw was very taken with you, and Herman approves. You know how concerned he's been over his only daughter. He thinks you're a good influence on her, and it's been suggested you take her out again."

"Fuck, Dad, no. I'll do anything to help, but not that."

I'm lucky Xavier never found out about my date with Sydney the last time. Actually, luck had nothing to do with it. I made sure nothing leaked because I didn't want to hurt him. I bought every single photo taken of me with the Shaw heiress at The Met that night and wiped every mention of it online.

I probably should've told Xavier, but we weren't even officially seeing one another, and he's a total drama queen at the best of times. I know he would've made a big deal out of it. With all the other shit I had on my plate at the time, I didn't want the additional stress, so I said nothing. Quietly took the girl out and promptly forgot our date. It's not like I wanted to be there or it meant anything to me. Jackson is the only other person who knows, and that's because the asshole eavesdropped on a call with my dad and overheard the whole thing.

But things are different now. While Xavier and I still aren't official, things are more serious between us. I shouldn't have let it get this far, because there is no scenario where it ends well, but I can't turn back the clock.

Truth is, I have strong feelings for the guy. Even though he irritates the fuck out of me half the time, I care about him, and this would hurt him.

"I'm not asking, Sawyer," Dad says, using that assertive tone he deploys when he wants to get his own way. "It's already agreed. You're taking her out Saturday night. Herman is expecting you at eight o'clock sharp."

"I have plans," I hiss between gritted teeth.

"Unmake them," he shouts. "This is more important. Our entire future is hanging on the line, son. This merger needs to happen or everything I've worked for is lost."

I'm wondering if Dad's been taking lessons in melodrama from my lover. "Let's not overreact."

"Do you think I'd be forcing you into this if I had any other choice?!" he roars down the line. "Stop being a selfish punk, and think of your mother. God, anyone would think Sydney Shaw was an ogre. She's a beautiful, highly educated woman. It's not a hardship."

"One date," I growl.

"It will be as many dates as are necessary," he says in a more even-keeled voice, having calmed his temper. "Your mother and I will see you for dinner on Sunday, and I expect a full report. Enjoy your date," he adds before hanging up.

"Motherfucker!" Frustration wells inside me, and I throw my cell across the room before burying my head in my hands. *What the fuck am I going to do now?*

CHAPTER ONE

Sawyer

June of the same year

"Please tell me you're kidding." I stare at my father in shock, barely keeping my jaw from trailing the ground. First day of summer break. First day back working at Techxet and he drops the mother of all bombs on me. Couldn't he have given me a day to settle in?

"It's a good match," he replies, striding across the floor of his prestigious office, standing in front of the floor-to-ceiling windows. "You could do worse," he adds, glancing over his shoulder as I force my feet to move, slowly approaching him.

"This is the twenty-first century, Dad. Arranged marriages don't happen unless you're a member of the fucking elite," I snap, a muscle clenching in my jaw. "Last time I checked, neither you or Shaw are. I thought you despised them and everything they stood for. Yet now you're making a move straight out of their playbook?" My incredulous tone matches the incredulous expression on my face. I stare out the window at the ground far below, wondering how much it would hurt if I were to jump.

"You don't understand." He scrubs his hand over his prickly jawline, tension tight in his features.

"Because you've insisted on keeping me in the dark these past few months. If you expect me to do this—to actually *marry* Sydney Shaw—then I need to know the reason. I am not throwing my life away without understanding why it's so important I do this."

"We're ruined, son," he says, staring out the window at Central Park below us.

"What do you mean?" I frown, wondering when my father got so melodramatic.

"Let's sit down." He strides to the meeting table in the center of his spacious office on the fortieth floor, flopping down into a chair, looking utterly defeated. All the tiny hairs rise on the back of my neck, and I have a really bad feeling about this.

Pulling out a seat, I sit down, propping my elbows on the table as I stare at my father. Gray strands are threaded through his brown hair, and the lines around his eyes are more pronounced. He looks exhausted. Battle weary. Like he's close to giving up, and that is not the man I know. Things must be really shitty if he's on the verge of admitting defeat. "Tell me what's going on."

"Two years ago, I discovered a couple of employees had embezzled hundreds of millions of dollars, almost bankrupting the business."

"What the hell?" My eyes almost bug out of my head. "Why is this the first I'm hearing about this?"

"You weren't even eighteen. It was your senior year of school, and there was a lot of other stuff going down." He drills me with a knowing look, and I get it. That was when Kai, Jackson, and I moved to Rydeville to wage war against Abby and Michael Hearst. "You didn't need to be involved." He runs a hand through his hair, struggling to meet my eyes. "I pumped most of my personal finances into the business to keep it afloat, and we managed to keep the news quiet through the usual channels."

That means he removed every news story from the web and paid off the TV channels not to report it. "Please tell me you caught the guys."

He nods. "Roland Murtagh, our ex-chief financial officer is

currently serving time in the correctional facility in Otisville. Vincent Becker, the chief technology officer before Russell Chalmers, was the other guilty party. He died the previous year in a car accident. The authorities couldn't question him, but we found enough evidence to support Murtagh's claims they were coconspirators."

"And you got the money back, right?"

He shakes his head. "The money is MIA. Murtagh claims Becker was responsible for sending it offshore. I've had a secret team working to trace the funds—with no success."

"But the business is profitable. The share price is at its highest level ever, and when you announce the new security portfolio, it's going to skyrocket. So, I don't understand how we are ruined?"

"It's happened again." He buries his head in his hands, and I can almost see the stress pressing down on his shoulders.

"Are you saying someone has embezzled money again?" My brows pucker as I contemplate how the fuck anyone could do that to us. Dad has built one of the most successful, most reputable IT enterprises in the world, and our internal security systems are robust. Developed, implemented, and maintained by some of the best brains in the IT industry. My boyfriend included.

"It happened six months ago again. After the last time, we built secret warnings into the system, and it triggered an alert. We plugged the hole before they could drain us dry, but it still made a significant dent in our finances. Warren Feldman covered it with some creative accounting, and Russell Chalmers himself personally followed the trail, but he couldn't identify the hackers. None of us know how they are getting in or how they are covering their tracks so well. We can find nothing. No footprint. No evidence they were even in our systems, except for the missing zeros on our bank statement."

"It must be a disgruntled ex-employee. Someone who worked in IT, with superior skills, and an advanced knowledge of our systems."

"I agree, but we have looked at every person who was fired or who left under a cloud, and they all came up clean. Whoever this is, they are smart, and they've just attempted it again."

I curse under my breath, rubbing at the tense spot between my brows. "That's why you want a merger. You need the investment capital."

He nods. "But it's more than that. I want access to their capital, their best IT people, and we want to use their systems because ours are compromised, and if we don't take action now, soon there will be nothing left of the business I have built from scratch."

"Shit, Dad." I wet my suddenly dry lips. "You should've told me. I can help. I want to find the bastard who did this and make them pay."

"You're on the team now, and I'm making some changes. I've scheduled a meeting for next week. I'll ask Magdalena to call you with the details. We're going to meet offsite, and the number of people involved will be small and restricted to key personnel with the right skill sets. People we can trust to get to the bottom of this while maintaining complete secrecy."

"You suspect we have a mole," I surmise, staring at my father's green eyes through his black horn-rimmed glasses.

Slowly, he bobs his head. "It's the only conclusion that makes sense. Whoever is doing this has someone on the inside who is helping them."

"Have you spoken to Murtagh? Could he be the one driving this from prison?"

"He's been questioned, and he swears he knows nothing. The man is a weasel, and I don't trust him, so I won't rule out his involvement."

My brain churns thoughts and ideas, but the most pressing issue is his request I marry Sydney Shaw. "I understand why you need Shaw Software. But I don't understand why me marrying Sydney even comes into it. What don't I know?"

Our heads swivel to the door as it opens and Dad's PA steps into the room, carrying a tray with sandwiches and coffees. Magda sets it down on the table, and I notice how her hands shake and her arms buckle with the motion. Her arthritis must be acting up, and I think I need to have the retirement talk with her again before she works herself into an early grave. "Your two o'clock is here early, Mr. Hunt. I put him in one of the small meeting rooms for now."

"Thanks, Magdalena. Sawyer and I will be done in due course, and I'll meet with him then."

Magda smiles at me before exiting the room. She's been Dad's PA for years, and I'm very fond of her. When I was a kid, I spent most every afternoon at Techxet, holed up in one of the meeting rooms, doing my homework while my parents continued with their working day, oblivious to their son and his needs. Magda was always kind and attentive. She ensured I had food and drinks and helped me with homework on the rare occasions I got stuck. When I grew bored, she would sometimes sneak in a game of Scrabble with me. She's like the grandmother I never had.

"Herman Shaw might look like a jovial giant," Dad replies, pouring coffee into cups while I nab a couple of sandwiches, "but his claws are sharp, and his bite is even worse. He's a ruthless businessman, and he hasn't gotten to where he is now without doing what is necessary."

"And that's marrying his only daughter to a virtual stranger? A man she's not in love with?"

I don't know if Sydney even *likes* me. She keeps her cards pretty close to her chest. We've been out a total of four times in the past three months, and each date has stripped an extra layer off my sanity. It's a fucking miracle I have managed to hide it from Xavier. The stress of containing it, along with the overwhelming guilt for keeping it from my boyfriend, is killing me. Maybe I should have told him, but I know it'd hurt him, even if I have kept the dates strictly PG. He won't understand. It's not like either of us discuss our families. We're usually too busy arguing or fucking.

Blood rushes to my cock, and I squirm uncomfortably on my chair. At least I'm sitting down. I can hopefully wrangle the snake in my pants into behaving until it's time to leave.

"Sydney is rebellious, and Herman is worried about her future," Dad continues. "He believes marrying a good man is all she needs to settle down and achieve her potential. She's a beautiful, smart girl lacking a sense of direction. Direction you can provide."

"That is one of the most disgustingly sexist things I have ever heard," I admit, losing my appetite. "I don't know what Sydney's story is, nor have I any interest in learning it, but she is twenty-four, and her father doesn't get to dictate her life."

"But he does when she has no way of supporting herself." Dad hands me a mug of coffee.

"I still don't see why it has to be me."

Dad exhales heavily. "He's made it a condition of the merger."

"That is preposterous." I swirl my spoon faster in my cup, growing more and more angry on Sydney's behalf. "And it's not the way business transactions usually go down."

"I agree, but this is an unusual situation, and my hands are tied. Every other investor we were talking to dropped out. Shaw Software is the last man standing. We need them, and he needs you."

"Dad, I can't marry Sydney. I'm not even twenty yet, and I'm—" I stop myself before I out my relationship with Xavier. Dad is stressed to the max, and I won't add to it. He won't like it, and I have purposely not told him because I don't want it to impact Xavier's job or color the way my father sees him. Xavier is a freaking IT genius, and I know the CTO has big plans for him. I don't want to fuck that up.

"You're what?" He strains forward across the table, eyeballing me.

"Not ready to get married. Especially to someone I don't love."

"You will learn to love her."

"You don't know that!"

"Your mom and I have never had a great passionate love affair, and we've made it work."

I flop back in my chair, appetite completely vanquished now.

"Do you even love her?" I have questioned that several times. There is no denying my parents are well suited. They are both workaholics married to their jobs, and they get along well. They share similar interests, and they rarely argue. Both are immune to displays of affection, and I grew up wondering if they even loved me or each other.

"Of course, I love your mother! She's my rock, son. We might not be outwardly affectionate, but our marriage has been everything I could have hoped for when I was your age. Lust doesn't last the distance. Respect and love do. I knew that when I married Ava, and it still rings true today."

"You make it sound so clinical and cold."

"This has got nothing to do with your mother and me." Exasperation washes over his face. "Sydney is a decent match. She might be a little wild, but you'll bring her into line. I wouldn't ask this of you if I wasn't desperate." He puts his sandwich down, pinning me with pleading eyes. "We stand to lose everything, Sawyer, if this merger doesn't go through. Think of your mother. Think of the thousands of employees who will lose their jobs. This is bigger than me or you, and we can't be selfish."

The weight of his words sits on top of me like a lead balloon. I'm not the type to do something purely because someone expects it of me, but things have always been different with my parents. The sense of obligation surrounds me now, almost smothering me.

Dad is carrying the weight of the world on his shoulders, and if I can do something to ease the burden, then I must do it. "Okay. I'll do it," I croak. "When do you want me to marry her?"

CHAPTER TWO

Sawyer

It's a damn ambush, and I have walked straight into it. The exquisite ballroom in one of the most expensive five-star hotels in NYC is packed with the usual ass kissers and hobnobbers, and there is barely standing room around the myriad of tables set up for dinner. "Holy shit," Sydney exclaims, clinging more tightly to my arm. "Did you know this was our engagement party?" She stares up at me through pretty emerald eyes fanned by long thick black lashes.

"Nope," I admit, through gritted teeth, forcing a smile as I escort my fiancée through the crowded room. "Dad said we were all having dinner together to celebrate. He mentioned nothing about half of New York lying in wait to surprise us."

I need to message Xavier before someone posts something online. All week, I've been trying to pluck up the courage to tell him, but I couldn't do it. How do I tell the guy I'm dating in secret he has to become an even bigger secret because I'm marrying a woman as a favor to my father?

"Thank fuck, I dressed up and spent time on my hair and makeup." Sydney is prone to cursing. Something I'm sure my father isn't aware of because he deplores profanity. I happen to like it. And the fact she says what she thinks. I'm guessing her potty mouth and open views have gotten her into trouble a time or ten.

She beams at some old dude with a bad combover and a leery smile as we pass by. Sydney is as experienced in handling stuffy crowds as I am. It's part of life growing up in the affluent families we did.

"You look beautiful, by the way," I tell her, and it's the truth. She's wearing a figure-hugging red silk dress that molds to her envious curves like a second skin. The front dips low, showcasing creamy skin and a glimpse of her generous tits. If I wasn't already into someone, I could probably fall into something with her. But I am spoken for, and we need to set some clear ground rules for this fake marriage.

I'm under no illusion. Sydney wants this about as much as me. On all our dates, she hasn't once tried to kiss me, nor I her. It's been more like friends hanging out than two people attracted to one another on the verge of marriage.

My scowl relaxes a smidgeon as I spy the petite brunette in the dazzling purple gown heading our way. "Sydney, darling. You look stunning. Absolutely stunning. My son is a lucky man." Mom bundles her into a hug, which Sydney indulges while fixing me with an amused expression.

"And look at you." She redirects her attention to me. "You look so handsome, Sawyer." I bend down as she stretches up to kiss my cheek.

"Some warning would've been nice," I murmur so only she can hear me.

"We wanted it to be a surprise." Mom smiles, but it doesn't quite meet her eyes. Shame flashes across her face for a fleeting moment. I'm glad she's aware railroading me into a marriage I don't want and ambushing me with an engagement party I'll loathe is a low blow and extremely selfish. "We should talk later. In private." Her eyes examine mine, and I'm relieved to see concern there. To know she isn't just going along with this without acknowledging how big of a sacrifice I'm making.

"Ah, the couple of the hour." Dad arrives, placing his hand

on Mom's shoulder as he lifts Sydney's hand and brings it to his mouth. "Congratulations, Sydney. We look forward to welcoming you to the Hunt family."

"Thank you," she says, snatching a glass of champagne from a passing waiter. "It should be interesting, for sure." Her eyes scream mischief as she takes another glass, holding it out to me. "For you, darling."

I arch a brow, silently accepting the champagne, guzzling it like it's water because I need some liquid courage to survive this night.

"Sawyer. Son." Herman Shaw materializes in front of us, slapping me heartily on the back. "It's good to see you. I never thought I'd see the day where this little rascal would walk up the aisle, yet here you are." He grins and his overly white teeth almost blind me.

"It's not like I had much choice." I keep my voice low on purpose so no one outside our little group will hear.

Mom gasps, planting a hand on her chest. "Sawyer! Don't be so crass."

I shrug, glancing between Mom, Sydney, and Herman. I don't look at Dad because I already know what I'll see on his face. "I'm just telling the truth. I don't see how pretending it's otherwise, among the present company, benefits anyone."

"It is when we're in public," Herman bellows, narrowing his eyes at me. I'm tall, but he still looms over me by a few inches. With broad shoulders and a protruding belly, he's a large man, and I can see what Dad meant now. He might look like a gentle giant, but there is no mistaking the vibe he's exuding now. The man could sit on me and crush me in one fell swoop. "I won't let my daughter be disrespected."

"That won't—"

I cut across my fuming father. "I would never disrespect Sydney, but I'm not going to bullshit her either. This is exactly what it looks like on the surface."

"Well, we need to rectify that then, don't we?" Herman huffs, barely concealing his rage.

"Daddy. Don't." Sydney tosses her long blonde hair over her shoulders, beseeching her father with a warning look. "Let Sawyer and I work out the details. We're both adults. We don't need you interfering any more than you have."

Herman's nostrils flare and he turns puce in the face. Oh. He really didn't like that. Instinctively, I wrap my arm around Sydney, tugging her in close.

"We are not getting into this again," he says through clenched teeth. "Especially not here. You agreed," he adds, in a lower tone, waving and smiling at someone over our heads. "And so did you." He swivels his head in my direction, daring me to back out.

I hold my shoulders back and lift my chin. "I gave my word, and I won't renege on it, but let's keep the bullshit for the public."

"You can start now," he adds, casting a knowing glance at Dad.

All my muscles lock up. What fresh hell is this? "Come with me, you two," Dad says, curling his fingers at Sydney and me.

"Make it convincing, sweet pea." Herman leans down to kiss his daughter on the cheek.

"Dad. Please. I'm not ten years old anymore." Sydney rolls her eyes.

"You will always be my sweet pea, pumpkin," he replies, contradicting himself.

My parents steer us through the room, and Sydney and I smile and accept congratulations as we bypass people. Some I recognize as friends of my parents or coworkers from Techxet, and others are business associates I have met at previous events. I wave at Travis and Laurena Lauder—Jackson's parents—as Dad swerves right, heading toward the raised dais at the back of the room. I stifle a groan as I figure out what's going down.

Dad leads us out through a side door into a maintenance room of sorts. Extracting a box from his pants pocket, he slaps it into my hand. "You need to give that to Sydney on stage. I'll introduce you first."

"Is that really necessary?" I ask, removing my arm from

Sydney's waist. I run my fingers along the collar of my shirt, struggling to maintain a cool head. My shirt suddenly feels tight around my neck, pinching my skin and restricting my airflow. "Everyone already knows we are engaged. The big 'Happy Engagement' banners on the wall give the game away," I drawl.

"I didn't say propose," Dad snaps, looking a little gray in the face. "Give Sydney the ring and kiss her. Give everyone something to talk about. Make it look real. I'm sure you can inject some passion into the proceedings." He offers Sydney a tight smile before taking Mom's hand. Mom looks anxious, her eyes scrunched up as she examines my face, but she's not stopping it either. It serves as a timely reminder why I'm doing this.

"Okay. Just give us a few minutes to prepare." I'm not going to kiss my fiancée for the first time in front of a salivating audience of pompous pricks. And I need to message Xavier. I hope I'm not already too late.

Dad steers Mom out of the room, and I release the breath I was holding. "I just need to send a message. Give me a sec," I tell her, fingers already flying over the keypad of my phone.

We need to talk. I'll call you when I'm free. Don't look at social media. I'll explain everything later.

Pocketing my phone, I refocus my attention on Sydney. My fiancée. The woman I'll be marrying in five weeks. Fuck me. When did life get so complicated?

"I'd like to have a conversation setting out the rules and how this will work," I explain.

"That sounds serious." She shoots me a flirty look that rubs me the wrong way.

"You know this isn't real, Sydney. It won't ever be real. It's fake. As fake as the words I'll say when we get up on that stage."

She folds her arms across her chest, and the movement draws attention to her ample cleavage. I'm bisexual. She's a gorgeous woman, and my eyes are naturally drawn to her boobs, but it doesn't mean anything other than she's attractive and she's got a great rack.

"You sure about that?" Amusement underscores her tone, irritating me again.

"I'm sure," I snap, getting all up in her face. "I'm in a relationship, and this is just…duty. There will never be anything between us."

"I wasn't aware of that, and it's okay. I get it." The flirty smile slides off her face. "I'm in love with someone else."

"We are on the same page then. We'll put on a show. Do what we need to. But there will be nothing outside of that. I'm not interested in you as anything other than a friend."

"I have no romantic or sexual interest in you either."

"Good." My shoulders relax. "That should make this easier," I say before lowering my mouth to hers.

Sydney doesn't protest, kissing me back with skillful lips and a tempting tongue that teases mine in short sensual strokes. I pull back quickly, not wanting it to escalate. This already feels like the worst betrayal. Guilt hammers at my heart. I know Xavier isn't going to understand this, and I don't know what this will mean for our relationship going forward. Whether he will agree to continue or tell me to fuck off.

But I can't worry about that now. Clasping Sydney's hand firmly, I thread my fingers in hers. The sooner we get this over and done with, the better. "I'm going to go all out on stage," I warn her. "I'll dip you down low and kiss you like crazy. You okay with that?"

"It's not like I have a choice." She throws my words back at me, and a smirk tugs up the corners of my mouth.

"Touché, sweet pea. Or should I call you pumpkin?"

She groans, rolling her eyes as we make our way outside just as Dad is introducing us to the assembled crowd.

"If you must give me a term of endearment, at least pick something original and not something that reminds me of my dad," she whispers in my ear.

"Noted," I murmur, leaning down to kiss her softly as we make our way to the stage.

I fudge my way through the awkwardness of the moment,

spewing the requisite romantic words while going down on one knee and giving the ostentatious ring to Sydney. To her credit, she gives an Oscar-worthy performance, complete with fake tears. Then I grab her, dipping her low and kissing the shit out of her to the whoops and hollers of the audience.

After, we do the rounds, accepting more congratulations, until it feels like my head will explode.

Dinner is a strained affair and an exercise in fake fuckery as everyone vies to be the fakest of them all. Herman is joined by his two sons and their wives. They barely include Sydney in the conversation, and I wonder what kind of childhood she had growing up in a house full of men. Her mom died of cancer when she was five, and that must have been really tough on her. My parents laugh and joke with the Shaws as if this isn't awkward, and when I can stand it no more, I pull Sydney out onto the dance floor.

"Was that as painful for you as it was for me?" she asks as I wrap my arms around her waist and pull her in close.

"That was off the charts, but at least we did it and survived." We sway in time to the music, and I feel several sets of eyes glued to my back. "How soon do you think we can bail?"

"In a hurry to get someplace?" She toys with the fine hairs on the back of my neck.

My muscles lock up. "What are you doing?"

"Making this look real," she whispers, drilling me with a "get with the program" look.

We dance in time to the music, and I try to loosen my tense muscles, but there isn't a part of me that isn't on edge.

"Relax, Sawyer. You look like you've got a poker shoved up your ass. I know what this is. I've always known. I was under no illusion when Dad arranged our first date."

"You know why I'm doing this. Why are you?"

"I have my reasons," she cryptically replies.

I spin her around before drawing her back in close to my body. "Such as?"

"He'll cut me off unless I do this. He doesn't believe anyone will want to marry me unless they are coerced into it, so this is his solution." Unhappiness ghosts over her face. "I'd love to tell him to stick his money and his antiquated ideals and to take his interfering ass out of my life, but I don't fancy sleeping on the streets, and without his money, I'm broke."

"What about your job?" She told me on one of our first dates that she worked the reception desk in a real estate agency.

"I got fired." She shrugs, shimmying her hips as the song changes. "I'll get another one, but it's not like it'll pay enough to sustain me in independence. A degree in languages doesn't qualify me to do much. This seemed like an easier way of handling things." She presses her chest flush against mine, and if I looked down, I'd probably see all the goods. "I figure we can stick it out for a year or two and then file for divorce. I'll use the time to figure out what I want to do with my career, and with the prenup settlement, I'll be able to fly solo. Herman Shaw can suck dick for all I care."

I bark out a laugh. "How does someone who looks so elegant curse like a sailor?"

"I have two older brothers and the majority of my youth was spent around bodyguards who cussed nonstop. Practically every second word that came out of their mouths was fuck." She shrugs. "It rubbed off. Daddy hates it, so that's an added bonus." She winks, and it's hard not to appreciate how gorgeous she is.

My cell vibrates in my pocket, and an ominous sense of dread creeps up my spine.

"You should get that. Unless you're purposely going for that constipated look?" Sydney teases.

Bile swims up my throat when I see Xavier's name flashing on the screen. "I've got to take this." I slip my cell back in my pocket as I lead her off the dance floor.

"I'm cool. Go speak to your woman. I'll be at the table when you return. I'll say you needed a bathroom break."

I don't correct her assumption. "Thanks." I squeeze her hand, grateful I'm fake engaged to Sydney and not some stuck-up bitch with delusions of grandeur. Sydney knows the score. She's cool, and she's on the same page. I'm feeling more confident I can make this work.

Until I head outside and answer Xavier's call.

"You're fucking engaged?" he screeches before I've had time to get a word in. "And I had to find out via social media?"

"I told you to stay off social media!"

"If you genuinely meant that, then you shouldn't have mentioned it! Your message was like waving a red flag in my face. Don't you know me at all?"

"Don't try and turn this around on me."

"Fuck you, Sawyer. Don't you dare try to blame any of this on me. The news is everywhere and my phone's blowing up with messages from everyone." Hurt bleeds from his words, and I feel like the biggest piece of shit to walk the planet. He's right too. Xavier loves pressing my buttons. If I tell him not to do something, he is almost guaranteed to do the opposite.

"I'm sorry." I force the words from my mouth. Because I loathe them, not that I don't mean them. Those two words have got to be the most overused words in the world. Or at least some of them. I make it a point not to utter them unless they are justified.

Like now.

"Oh, look at that. The mighty Sawyer Hunt has apologized. Now I'm shitting rainbows and farting unicorns. All is right in the world because my boyfriend has finally said sorry, but you know what, Hunt? It's not fucking good enough!" he roars, and I hold the cell away from my ear. "I am sick of being treated like shit by you. This is the final straw."

"You just need to let me explain. I—"

"I don't need to let you do anything!" he yells. "I am done, Hunt. I am so fucking done. Have a nice life. Give my commiserations to Sydney. Poor bitch has no clue what she's just signed up for."

Before I can say a word, he hangs up, and I lean back against the wall, wondering how the fuck I am going to fix this.

CHAPTER THREE

Sawyer

"I'LL HAVE ANOTHER," I tell the bartender, ignoring the fuck-me eyes he levels in my direction. Sometimes, I wonder if I have bi stamped on my forehead, or if people just like the challenge I present. It's not like I deliberately look for people to hit on me. A lot of people are intimidated by the cold, guarded indifference I wear like a cloak, but there are others who are drawn to it like they can't help themselves. Human nature fascinates me as much as it aggravates me. Some days, I really hate people, and it's those days I like to lock myself away and ignore the outside world.

"Drowning your problems in whiskey won't make them go away," Jackson says, sipping the same beer he's been drinking since we arrived at the club. "I should know."

"Don't lecture me, Lauder. I'm not in the mood." I knock back my drink, enjoying the bitter warmth as it glides down my throat. I'm glad my buddy called me after his wife, Van, spotted an article online confirming the engagement. While he's currently giving me shit, I would rather not drown my sorrows alone.

"What if someone takes a pic?" Jackson asks, casting a wary look around. "The groom out drinking himself into a coma the night of his engagement party would not go down well with the folks." The first thing I did when we got here was tell Jackson everything that is happening with Techxet so he understands why I'm going through with this sham of a marriage.

I wave my hands around. "Look around. It's a dive bar. No one gives a shit who I am in here. They're too busy fucking, smoking, or drinking to notice." I'm not sure I believe my own words, but I'm not ready to leave yet. Not until I've obliterated all ability to think.

"I still can't believe it, man." Jackson shakes his head. "No wonder Xavier was upset. I was shocked as shit when I read the article."

"He wasn't just upset. He broke up with me," I say, shaking my glass at the bartender. Dude doesn't care I'm underage. He didn't even card me, but most places I go, I get away with it because I look older. Other times, I'm recognized as the only offspring of Ethan Hunt, and they just assume I'm of age. Some places know the truth, but as long as I flash them my fake ID, they're happy to turn a blind eye.

"No, he didn't." Jackson scoffs, taking another miniscule sip of his warm beer.

"I'm pretty sure 'I'm done' and him hanging up on me was proof."

"But you guys weren't even officially together."

I glare at my friend. "Why the fuck would you say that? You know he's the only one I've been fucking for the past year. Of course, it was official."

"I don't think Xavier knew that," Jackson quietly says.

"Did he need a fucking pin or a name plate?"

"Hunt, you can be a total prick, you know that?"

I shrug because tell me something I don't know.

"You know Xavier better than any of us. He needs that label. He's always been insecure when it comes to your relationship. I don't get it either. If you like him and you're dating exclusively, why hide it?"

"You know why." His image is blurry as I stare at him. "My

father."

Jackson's brows climb to his hairline. "What the fuck, man? I thought your parents were cool with your sexuality."

"On the surface, yeah, but they are traditionalists. Dad started applying subtle pressure after I graduated. Reminding me of my responsibilities as his only heir and how important perception is to the public. I can't be at the helm of Techxet without a loving wife on my arm."

"He said that?" Disbelief oozes from my buddy's tone.

Someone turns on the jukebox, and we both groan as "Hound Dog" by Elvis Presley blasts around the dingy room.

"Yep, and it's not subtle anymore." I rest my head on my hands on the counter. "Ugh. It's official. I'm a hot mess."

Jackson chuckles. "No, you're not. Sawyer Hunt is never a hot mess."

"Thanks? I think," I mumble.

"Come on. Let's get out of here before someone notices you. I'll drive you home."

I guess I pass out in the car, waking as Jackson hauls me into the elevator that leads to my penthouse apartment. He slaps me across the face. "Wake up, dude, before I have a coronary." He pants as he straightens me up. "You're fucking heavier than you look."

"Dramatic much?" I slur, shaking him off and gripping the walls of the elevator as my legs threaten to go out from under me. I guess consuming your body weight in whiskey will do that to a guy.

"Admit it. You miss me and my drama."

"Like a hole in the head, buddy." I jab my finger in his direction, and he chuckles.

"Van misses you. She was begging me to come out tonight, but I convinced her to stay home."

"How'd you manage that? Your woman is persistent when she gets her teeth into something."

"She's crazy busy organizing the apartment, and there are boxes and shit all over the place. She has plenty to keep her occupied while I'm gone. I also told her I'd let her sit on my face when I get home. She's probably swimming in a puddle of pussy juice waiting for me to return."

"And they say romance is dead," I drawl as the elevator pings, opening at the hallway of my apartment.

"I am plenty romantic," Jackson says, slinging an arm around my shoulders and propping me up as we stagger along the hallway. "There is a time and place for romance and a time and place for fucking. Tonight, I'm going to bang my woman senseless after I eat her out. She'll be screaming my name so loud she'll be hoarse for days."

"I pity your neighbors."

"We don't have any yet," Jackson confirms as we walk into the living area. "Although the building is filling up fast." Usually, Jackson lives with me during summer break, but now he's married, he bought a brand-spanking-new penthouse, also facing Central Park, and it's only a few blocks away.

"You know the developer, Bennett Mazzone, is mafia, right?" I say.

"Everyone knows who the CEO of Caltimore Holdings is. Ben is in charge of the New York mafia and the future US mafia leader. Mark my words. That man is going places, and he's one hell of a shrewd operator. Even Dad was impressed when we met him to go through the contract. I figure it can't hurt to make some new friends. We still have elite shit to deal with. Maybe Ben's contacts could come in handy."

There are a number of reasons we're top of the elite's shit list. Last year, we killed Christian Montgomery after he tried to rape Jackson's wife, Vanessa—his only daughter—and Denton Mathers after he kidnapped Van with the intention of selling her into sexual slavery. I have zero regrets for the part I played in both men's deaths. They were vile pieces of shit who deserved to die for the reign of terror they wielded over innocents for years.

We were also instrumental in bringing the elite to their knees when Parkhurst was revealed for the front it was. Of course, the elite are highly connected, and their reach extends to government and the authorities. They handed over a few scapegoats and the scandal blew over.

Kai and Rick's father, Atticus Anderson, is still a wanted criminal with an international warrant out for his arrest. No one has seen him since shit hit the fan that day in Wyoming. William Hamilton, the new elite president, wants to string us up by our balls for making his job difficult. But we have evidence that could land him in hot water, so he's forced to toe the line for now. We know he will come after us, but we're watching, and we'll be ready for him when he does.

"He's a good person to know," I agree, flopping down on the couch as Lauder walks into my kitchen. My fingers fumble over the laces as I untie my shoes, and the room spins a little. Eventually, I get my shoes off, positioning them symmetrically under the coffee table, before sitting back in my leather couch. I loosen my tie and unbutton the top few buttons of my shirt, breathing more easily now.

"Coffee is on. Drink this for now." Jackson hands me a chilled bottle of water from the fridge.

"Why do you look funny?" I ask, uncapping my bottle as I survey my friend's scrunched-up nose and puckered brow.

"This place is way too fucking clean. It's an affront to my senses. Your kitchen smells like bleach, Hunt." His nostrils twist, and he shakes his head as he examines my spotless apartment.

"This is how normal people live, Lauder. You should try not dropping your shit all over the place for a change."

"Life is too short to tidy up. There are much more enjoyable things to do with my time. Like make love to my beautiful wife." He practically sprints to the kitchen, returning in record time with a steaming mug of coffee. "Drink the water. Pop a few pain meds, and then drink the coffee. I'm going home to Nessa."

"Thanks, man."

"I've always got your back." He looks contemplative as a familiar spark glints in his eyes. "Be at our place at two tomorrow."

"Why?"

"Just be there. We'll do lunch." He backs away, smirking. "And don't bring Sydney with you!" he calls out before disappearing out of sight.

"What the fuck is he doing here?" Xavier asks, almost frothing at the mouth, when I show up at Vanessa and Jackson's new pad the next afternoon.

"You two ladies need to talk," Jackson says. "Kiss and make up."

"For the record," Van says, coming in from the outside terrace. "I told him not to interfere."

"Was that before or after he let you ride his face?" I ask, my lips twitching.

"Oh my fucking God! Jackson!" She swats him with a dish towel. "What have I told you about sharing details of our sex life with your friends?!" She crosses her arms, trying to look angry. "No sex for a week."

"Ha! Nice try, beautiful." He reels Van into his arms. "You know you won't last twenty-four hours without my cock."

"I'm leaving." Xavier glares at me, folding his arms around his upper body but not moving a muscle. "Nessa. Please inform your meddling husband he's on my shit list now. He hasn't claimed the top spot because that place is deservedly owned by that dickhead there." He jabs his finger at me like it's a loaded weapon. "Adios, amigos." He stomps toward the door, brushing against my shoulder as he moves past me.

Van drills me with a look while waving her hands in a shooing gesture, but I don't need encouragement. "Bright One. Hold up." Jackson's hysterical laughter follows me as I race after my boyfriend. I don't care if I get shit for using my pet name for him. I'm in groveling mode, and I'll do just about anything to make this right.

Xavier slams to a halt at the elevator, but he doesn't turn around. Tentatively, I touch his waist. "Don't leave. I need to explain."

Slowly he turns around, and I suck in a gasp at the wounded look in his gorgeous sage-green eyes. I hate knowing I'm the one who put it there. "Are you really engaged and marrying that woman?"

Acid churns in my gut, but I can't deny the truth. "I am, but it's fake. It's only temporary, and it's not real."

"It is to me," he chokes out, wrapping his arms around himself. "How could you do this to me, Sawyer? How could you do this to us? I thought we were finally getting somewhere, but nothing has changed." The hurt in his eyes is replaced with molten lava. "I'm still your dirty little secret, and I'm done playing that game." He presses the button for the elevator. "I promised myself when I left North Dakota I would never hide who I am for anyone ever again, and I haven't. Except for you."

A lone tear slips out of the corner of his eye, and a tight pain spreads across my chest. The pounding in my head and a dry mouth don't help either, but that's my fault for taking a swim in a bottle of JD last night. "We can still make this right. I know you're hurt, and I'm sorry. I'm really fucking sorry, Xavier. I wanted to tell you, but I didn't know how, and then Dad sprung that engagement party on me last night, and—"

"How long have you been seeing that woman?" he asks, swiping angrily at the tear streaking down his cheek.

"I'm not seeing her," I protest. "I've only been with you."

"I know you've been on dates with her. When was the first time?"

"They weren't real dates. We hadn't even kissed until last night, and—"

I stop talking when Xavier squeezes his eyes shut, and I realize the extent of the damage I've caused. I'm not sorry I admitted that, because I was going to tell him, but I am sorry for the way it came out. "Fuck, Xavier. Please. Just hear me out. Let me tell you the reason why I'm doing it, but I swear to you there is nothing going on with Sydney, nor will there be. You're the only one I want."

He opens his eyes, and I want to stab myself through the heart for the anguish I find written all over his face. "You cheated on me with her, and I had to find out via social media because you were too gutless to tell me to my face."

"I fucked up." I drag my hand through my coiffed hair, for once unconcerned if I mess it up. "I fucked up big-time, but I will make it up to you if you just give me a chance to explain."

"Do you love me, Sawyer?"

"What?" Panic bubbles up my throat.

"It's not a difficult question." A muscle ticks in his jaw. "Do. You. Love. Me?"

"Do *you* love *me*?" I throw back at him, because I'm not good with this emotional stuff.

"Yes," he says without hesitation. "I love you like I have never loved any other man in my life."

"Xavier," I whisper, grabbing his shoulders and pulling him to me. He has never admitted that to me before, and my heart is a finely strung instrument, waiting to be plucked by him.

He shoves me away. "Answer the fucking question, Hunt. Do you love me? It's a simple yes or no."

You'd think, right? I want to tell him yes, but the words won't form on my tongue. I've never been in love, and I haven't stopped to consider exactly what our relationship is. He's the one into labels, not me. I care about him. I care about him a fuck ton, but I don't know if it's love, and I'm not going to say something I might not mean. That will only make things worse. If that's even possible.

Disappointment wars with pain and resignation on his face as the elevator pings, announcing its arrival. "That's what I thought." His eyes are like stone as he steps into the elevator, staring at me as if he's staring through me. "Don't contact me again. I don't want to see you or talk to you. As far as I'm concerned, you are dead to me."

The elevator doors close, taking him away, and I slump to the floor, burying my head in my hands. He wants nothing more to do with me, and I don't blame him. If I were in his shoes, I would do the exact same. The truth is, I have never been worthy of that man.

But maybe this is for the best. I don't know that I can ever be what he needs me to be. I don't know if I have the capacity to love, and I know that's what Xavier needs. Maybe the best way I can show him I care is to let him go.

CHAPTER FOUR

Sawyer

I SHOW UP at my parents' penthouse on Monday morning, still in a foul mood. Abby called yesterday to chew me out over the phone. She's super protective of her bestie, and she didn't hold back in telling me what a piece of shit I am for the way I've treated Xavier. My finger hovered over Xavier's number so many times, but I didn't call him. I still don't know what I should do—let him go or fight for him—and I'm guessing he's still hurt and pissed, so I'm giving us both some time to process.

"You look pale," Mom says, opening the door and ushering me inside. "Are you sick?"

"Sick at the thought of marrying someone I don't love," I say because they're not the only ones who can lay the guilt trip on thick.

"I know it's not ideal, Sawyer."

Is she for real? "Not ideal?!" I stare at her like she's sprouted horns. "Mom, it's a fucking nightmare, and it's ruining my life."

"Wow. Tell me how you really feel," Sydney says, lingering in the doorway of Mom's home office.

"I didn't know you'd be here." My brow puckers as I look at Mom. "Magda sent me a message saying the meeting was happening here now."

"It is," Dad says, appearing from the direction of the kitchen. "We're getting set up in the dining room."

"Sydney and I are wedding planning," Mom explains, beaming like it's raining gold.

"Awesome," I drawl, not attempting to hide my scowl.

"Are you always this grumpy?" Sydney asks. "Because I feel it's fair I should know exactly what I'm getting myself into."

I have zero patience for this shit right now. "We already talked about this and agreed we are on the same page. If you've changed your mind, feel free to bail."

"Don't mind him." Mom loops her arm through Sydney's, shooting me a warning look. "Sawyer's not a morning person. Best to avoid him until he's finished his run and had his coffee."

I'm on the verge of telling her both those things have already happened when I spot the chastising expression on my father's face. Buttoning my mouth, I force the words back down my throat and stride toward my father.

"This will go a lot easier if you lost the attitude and made an effort," he says as we walk into the large dining room. Russell Chalmers, Techxet's chief technology officer, is seated at the top of the long walnut table, tapping away on his laptop that is presently hooked up to the large wall-mounted TV.

"I said I'll do it. Get off my case, old man."

Russell stops typing for a second, wetting his lips and looking uncomfortable.

"Sawyer." Dad's clipped tone tells me I'm treading on shaky ground, and while I'm itching for a fight, I know better than to argue in front of his employee.

"I apologize. Can we discuss this later and just focus on the business at hand?"

"Agreed. Take a seat."

I power up my tablet and busy myself responding to emails while the room slowly fills up.

"Sawyer." A familiar voice has me lifting my head.

I do a double take as I drink in the tall, dark-haired guy, wearing trendy glasses, who is standing in front of me. "Jamison?"

Disbelief oozes from my tone.

"In the flesh."

"Dude, you've been working out." As long as I've known him, Jamison was skinny as fuck, but that guy no longer exists. The man standing in front of me is broad and muscular, and he's even changed his hair, wearing it in a trendy style that is long on top and short at the sides. Jamison did some work for me last summer on the down low, and he was efficient and discreet. It's why I suggested his name when Dad asked me.

I suggested Xavier too, although I'm questioning the wisdom of it now, for purely selfish reasons. The truth is, Xavier is our best chance at finding this hacker, and we need him. Whatever personal issues we have must be set aside. This is bigger than both of us. Bigger than my parents losing the lifestyle they've grown accustomed to.

"Is everyone here?" Dad asks Russell a half hour later, when all but two chairs are occupied.

"We're waiting for one more," Russell says, rubbing the back of his neck. "Xavier Daniels." He glances at his watch, and his brow puckers.

"Is there a problem?" Dad asks.

"His boss called me last night. Said he had tried to resign, but—"

"He what?" I blurt, feeling ill because I know this is because of me.

All eyes lock on me. I clear my throat. "Xavier is a good friend, and he's one of this country's best hackers. He never mentioned this to me, and we need him."

"Which is why I'm here, *friend*," Xavier says, his tone dripping with condescension. My ex ambles into the room looking like he lost a fight with a shrub on his way here. He's missing his usual Mohawk. A mess of dark waves rests against his forehead, the ends dyed a vibrant purple color that is new.

Xavier changes his hair color as regularly as some people change their socks. Often, it's tied to his emotions, so I can't say I'm surprised. But I *am* surprised at the wrinkled blue and green shirt with the large ketchup stain on the front and the dirty black combat-style pants he is wearing with battered Chucks.

Xavier has a wacky sense of style, but he likes to look his best. It is most unlike him to turn up anywhere looking like he just crawled out of bed and pulled on the first things he found. Especially not to an important work meeting.

Add in the visible ink on both arms, the lip ring, and brow piercing, and my father has already made up his mind about him. I can almost smell Dad's distaste from here, and it rubs me the wrong way.

"Did you not look in a mirror this morning, son?" Dad says, not concealing the disdain from his voice.

"You have a problem with how I look?" Xavier skims his eyes down his body in a "I don't give a fuck" manner.

I want to speak out, but I already got criticized for mouthing off in front of the staff, so I opt for sending Xavier a "cease and desist" look instead, which he promptly ignores.

"I wasn't planning on being here," Xavier continues, eyeballing my father with a nonchalant look. "I had resigned, but the seriousness of the situation was impressed upon me, and I was asked to reconsider." He straightens up, pointedly not looking at me. "I'm sorry if my presentation isn't to your liking. I can assure you it in no way impacts my significant badassery with a computer, but it's no skin off my back if you don't want me here. If I'm in the way, you only need to say it," he adds, finally looking at me as he delivers a message to both Hunts in the room.

"It's probably for the best if you leave," Dad says because he's a bigoted idiot.

I can't hold back anymore, and it seems my father needs a little reminder of who Xavier is. My chair scrapes off the hardwood floor as I stand. "Don't move," I say to Xavier, as he turns to leave. "Dad, you remember that situation we had in Rydeville?" I'm being cryptic on purpose because we have an audience. "And the event that happened in Wyoming?"

Dad's lips pinch together as he curtly nods.

"Xavier was the man who made a lot of that happen. He has mad skills, and you need him on this team. Trust me. He is the best at what he does, and I know if anyone can help us uncover this person it's him." Dad already knows this. When I lined up the interview for Xavier in the new Boston office, I got Dad to put in a good word for him, and I told him everything last year, so this is some bullshit, and I'm not having it.

Dad payrolled a lot of the Rydeville operation because he felt an obligation to get revenge on the elite for what they'd done to Dani Lauder, Jackson's sister. Dad is best friends with Travis Lauder, and Dad's suggestion to contact Montgomery's company, when they were looking for a robotics expert to partner with them on a project, helped to set a lot of things in motion.

I know he feels huge guilt over everything that went down. It's one of his few redeeming features, but he's shitting all over it now with the way he's treating Xavier, purely because of how he looks.

"If Xavier walks, you can kiss your company goodbye." I drill a look at my father. "Who cares what he wears? He's intelligent with sharp instincts, and he's a good guy. If you want someone to vouch for him, I'll vouch for him."

"I don't need anyone to vouch for me," Xavier interrupts. "My work speaks for itself, but I won't stay where I'm not wanted."

Tension is thick in the air as we stare at one another, and his words weigh heavy on my soul. "You're wanted." I maintain eye contact, and I know he understands the double meaning.

"Very well, Mr. Daniels. It seems I'm in the wrong. Please accept my apology. We would value your input, and I thank you for reconsidering your resignation."

"You've already thanked me," Xavier says, fixing my father with a smirk. "My boss signed off on a significant increase in my salary and a six-figure performance bonus." I hope the company is still solvent to pay him his dues when the time comes. His eyes swing back around to mine. "I'm here for the money. Only the money." His dagger hits its mark as a tight pain stabs me in the chest.

"Let's get this started," the CTO says. "We have a lot of ground to cover."

Xavier takes a seat at the end of the table beside Jamison. I watch as they shake hands and make introductions, frowning at the flare of interest I spot in Jamison's eyes. I know he's bisexual, like me. Unlike me, most of his partners have been men, and I don't like the appraising way he's staring at Xavier.

"Is there a problem, Jamison?" I ask, forcing his head to lift.

He rubs the back of his neck, looking sheepish. "Sorry, Sawyer, ugh, Mr. Hunt. I was just introducing myself."

"We've had enough delays. Please focus on the reason we are here. Don't make me regret recommending you."

Jamison can't meet my gaze as Xavier drills me with a venomous look.

Dad kicks off the meeting then, and everyone is focused as he explains the situation. The CTO shares images on the screen as he talks us through the steps he, and the previous team, took to identify the culprit or culprits. The CFO shows copies of bank statements clearly showing the withdrawals. There is healthy debate over options we can explore and how we should assign duties with everyone given an opportunity to say their piece.

Three hours later, we have a plan, and everyone has been assigned tasks. Dad ends the meeting, reminding everyone of the urgency of the situation and the need to maintain complete secrecy. Work is to be done in isolation or in small groups at the apartment Techxet owns on Seventy-fifth Street. The apartment Xavier will be staying at for the duration of his time in New York.

I pull my father aside as everyone starts gathering their belongings to leave. "Dad. I would like to have a word with you and Xavier. There is another angle I think we should explore."

"Mr. Daniels," Dad calls out as Xavier and Jamison head together toward the door. "Could you stay behind. There is something additional we need to discuss."

CHAPTER FIVE

Sawyer

Xavier arches a brow in my direction, a look of shocked surprise on his face, and I know where his mind has gone. I subtly shake my head, and his expression morphs into disappointment.

We wait in awkward silence, seated at the table, for Russell to pack up his shit. Dad closes the door after him when he eventually leaves. "Okay. Let's hear it," he says as he reclaims his seat.

"I don't think we can rule out elite involvement," I say.

"This isn't their work." Dad is quick to rebuke me.

"While I hate to agree with anything your son says, I think he is right," Xavier says as sweat breaks out on my brow. I know he's hurt and angry, but if he says one word to my father about us, I will go ballistic on his ass. "That was going through my head the entire time, except I'm not aware of anyone within our known elite acquaintances who would have access to the kind of IT expertise we are dealing with."

"Their extended network could," I say, propping my elbows on the table. "We know the organization has roots all over the US. It's not unfathomable they have someone who can do this."

"Or they have partnered with a foreign entity specialized in ransomware," Xavier muses, looking deep in thought.

"But they haven't hijacked our systems or demanded a ransom," my father protests.

"Because they've already extracted their ransom without the need to render our data inaccessible," I say. "Xavier could be right. It's like reverse ransomware. Those hackers are skilled at getting into systems undetected. There are examples all over the world where these assholes were sneaking around systems for months before they made their move. We don't know that whoever this is hasn't been doing the same to us."

"So, it's not the elite," Dad says, scrubbing a hand over his smooth jawline.

"I wouldn't discount them," Xavier says. "The people behind ransomware are in it for the notoriety and the power as much as the money. This isn't their kind of MO. If they are involved, the motivation is different."

"Or it's simply an extremely lucrative job," I suggest.

"Exactly," Xavier agrees.

"Why did you say it wouldn't be the elite?" I ask, curious why Dad seemed so sure.

"Because I made my peace with them last year," he says, clasping his hands in front of him.

Silence descends, and it's not the comfortable kind. I gawk at my father, utterly shocked. "What exactly does that mean, Dad? What the hell have you done?" Prickles of apprehension sprout goose bumps on my arms.

"I did what was necessary to protect you and your mother." He stands, indicating the conversation is over.

I jump up. "I need to know. This could all be connected."

"It's not. Just drop it, Sawyer."

"Fine," I lie, watching with a growing sense of trepidation as he walks out of the room.

"That's bullshit," Xavier says when my dad is out of listening range.

"I know." I sit back down, sighing heavily.

"What are you going to do?"

"Run a little side investigation parallel to the official one."

His eyes light up. "Are we bringing the gang in?"

"If you mean Anderson and Lauder, then yeah."

"Not Drew or Charlie?" he questions, arching a brow.

"Not yet. I'd like to see what we can unearth ourselves first. If we need back up, we'll call in the cavalry."

He nods, and there is no tension on his face as his brain churns ideas and options. Without stopping to think, I stretch across the table and take his hand.

His eyes lower to where our fingers are linked, and his Adam's apple jumps in his throat. "I miss you already," I truthfully admit. "Can't we talk? See if there is any way we can make this work?"

"The marriage is tied up in all this," he surmises, piercing me with his wise eyes.

I nod. "Dad needs this merger with Shaw Software to protect the company, and Herman Shaw wants to marry his daughter off. He made it a condition of the deal." I squeeze his fingers tighter, siphoning some of his warmth and his strength. "I don't want to do it, Bright One."

"Don't call me that." He yanks his hand out of mine, averting his eyes. "Don't pour acid over everything we shared."

"I'm not. It's still appropriate on many levels." The name Xavier is a Basque-Spanish name and part of its meaning is bright. It's one of the random facts stored in his magical brain. When he told me, I knew it was the perfect term of endearment because Xavier shines in every way possible. He's incredibly bright, as in intelligent, and his presence in my life always brightened it, even on days where he was driving me to insanity and we were bickering like crazy.

"It doesn't matter anymore." He folds his arms over his chest, still refusing to meet my gaze.

"I told her I'm with someone, and she's got a guy too. We have an understanding, and we'll only need to appear to be married in public. We can still see each other. We just need to be discreet."

"Have you any idea how fucking insulting that is, Hunt?" Lifting his head, he pierces me with red-rimmed eyes. "I always come second with you, and I want to be with someone who will put me first."

"I know you do, and you deserve that. I can't give it to you now, but someday."

He snorts, looking sad as he shakes his head. "I honestly think you believe that." His features soften a little. "You're so guarded, Sawyer. So uptight and closed off. Now I've met your father, I am beginning to understand a little more. The age gap between us never bothered me previously because you have always seemed so mature, so together. But I see the truth now." He grabs his bag off the floor, slinging it over one shoulder as he stands. "You're still trying to figure out who you are and where you fit in this world, and you're scared. Scared to open yourself up. Scared to really live. Scared to love. I hate that for you, and I used to think I was the guy who could break down your walls, but you have built them so high, and I'm not strong enough to scale them."

"You mean something to me." I stand, rounding the table so I'm standing in front of him. "You're important." I reach out, cupping his cheek, hurt when he removes my hand and takes a step back.

"Not important enough, and that's the crux of the situation for me. I love you, Sawyer. I truly do, but I can't be with you. At least not now." His eyes probe mine as my internal organs feel like they're dissolving. "I don't want to break up on bad terms. We have to work closely together, and I'm going to do this. To help your dad, even though he's a giant ass. I'll do it for you and the Techxet workers because it's the right thing. Because I want justice to prevail, and despite what your dad said, I smell the elite all over this. If this is their new play, I want in."

Determination mixes with sadness in his eyes, and I can tell he has made his mind up. I respect him enough not to continue arguing. I have lost him, and I'm the only person to blame. A sudden urge to bang my head against the wall accosts me, but I clench my hands into balls at my side, ignoring the urge. "Thank you for agreeing to help. I meant what I said. We can't do this without you."

"Sawyer, sweetheart. Can you... Oh, sorry, I didn't realize you had company," Mom says, stepping into the room carrying a large folder.

"Hi." Sydney slips into the room behind Mom, and I barely smother my groan. "I'm Sydney. Sawyer's fiancée." She thrusts her hand out toward Xavier, and the giant diamond on her ring finger glistens under the bright lights of the room.

Xavier shoves his hands into the pockets of his pants, shooting her the fakest smile I've ever seen on his face. "I know who you are."

The edge drops off her smile as she lowers her arms to her sides. "Are you a friend of Sawyer's?"

"I'm Xavier." He slants her with a knowing look, and I inwardly cringe.

"Do you work with Sawyer?" She continues probing while I silently pray for divine intervention.

"Wow." Xavier twists around, staring at me with a tortured expression. "The lies just keep on coming." I never said I told her I was with him specifically. Just that I was with someone, so he's splitting hairs, but I know it's coming from a place of pain.

"I haven't lied."

"Sawyer, what's going on?" Mom asks as Sydney frowns, her shrewd gaze bouncing between my ex and me.

"Nothing, Mrs. Hunt. Forgive me," Xavier says, dramatically bowing at the waist. "I was being rude. It's a private joke. Anyhoo." He straightens up. "I better get going. We have a lot of work to do, and I need to get settled in my new apartment." He shoots me a scathing look. "I'll see you tomorrow morning."

"I apologize if I was rude," he says to Sydney. "You seem like a nice girl. Congratulations." His eyes bore a hole in the side of my face. "I hope you will both be very happy." With those awesome parting words, he leaves, and I'm stuck in a place halfway between sadness and anger.

"He's a little...odd," Mom says after Xavier has departed the room.

"I think eccentric might be a little more fitting," Sydney says, looking at me funny.

"If you are done being judgmental assholes, was there something you wanted?" I snap.

Sydney at least has the decency to look ashamed. My mother, on the other hand, is clearly missing that memo. "Sawyer, I don't know what has gotten into you lately, but you were not raised like this. Remember your manners."

"I'm not in the mood for a lecture, Mom." I rub at my throbbing temples. "What do you want?"

She slams the folder down on the table, and a muscle pops in her jaw. "We need your input on some of these options."

"I have nothing to contribute." I place my notepad and my tablet into my messenger bag. "You pick." I lift my chin, staring at Sydney. "I'm sure whatever you decide will be perfectly lovely." Sarcasm drips from my tone, and I know I'm being an asshole, but I have zero fucks to give right now.

"I ordered you a purple silk tie for Jackson's and Vanessa's wedding," Mom continues, as if I haven't spoken. "It will match the beautiful dress we've just ordered for Sydney to wear."

"Fine, whatever." I zip up my bag and straighten up, not wanting to think about the wedding.

While my friends are already married, they didn't have a traditional wedding, so they are doing the whole shebang now purely for Jackson's mom. It's happening at a hotel in The Hamptons in four weeks' time and I'm dreading it now. I'll have to face Xavier with Sydney as my date. Plus, it'll mean it's only one week until my own wedding.

"Can I talk to you for a sec?" Sydney asks as I move to brush past both women.

"Not now. I've got to get to the office."

"Well, when?"

"I'll call you later," I lie, rushing out of the room. I need to immerse myself in work, in finding this asshole who has put me in this fucking mess, and blank out all emotion. I can do it. It's an art I perfected in my youth to stop myself from hurting whenever my parents chose work instead of me.

So, this will be a cakewalk.

I'll throw myself into finding this hacker, and I'll ignore my impending wedding and the deeply wounded look in Xavier's eyes as he finally drew a line under our relationship.

CHAPTER SIX

Xavier

I KILL THE engine and park my overstuffed SUV in front of Abby and Kai's house. Sadness clings to my body like a second skin, and my heart is heavy. The front door opens, and my bestie comes into view. Abby's smile is so wide it threatens to overtake her face, and I can't help responding in kind. Climbing out of the car, I lock the door and walk toward her.

Her pretty head tilts to the side, and little creases appear in her brow as she examines my exhausted features and my slumped shoulders. It feels like I'm carrying the weight of the world, and I'm more than ready to throw the world's largest pity party for one. Or maybe two. I'm sure my best girl would indulge me.

"Come give me some lovin'," she says, opening her arms. "You look like you could use some too."

"That and a monster dick in the ass," I mumble, collapsing into her welcoming embrace. "I just need to fuck that fucktard out of my system."

"I take it things didn't go well today?" She rubs her hand up and down my spine as I cling to her like a pathetic jilted lover.

"That's the understatement of the millennium. I couldn't even resign, and now I'm going to be working with the cheating bastard for the foreseeable future." I lift my head, still clinging to her petite body like a limpet. "Do you see it? The big PGI on my forehead?"

"PGI?"

"Pathetic. Gullible. Idiot." I shrug. "It's not my best, but it's hard to be my usual genius self when my heart is shattered into itty-bitty pieces."

"Heartbreak hasn't impacted your dramatic streak in the slightest," Kaiden says, coming up behind his wife. He leans against the door frame, narrowing his eyes at us. "I'm not completely heartless," he adds. "But you've been clinging to my wife for the last four minutes, and my hands are itching to remove every part of you from her body."

"Caveman, go out and find some wild animals to wrestle with," Abby teases, glancing over her shoulder as she continues rubbing my back.

"Were you actually timing us?" I inquire, and he arches a brow. "That is super impressive. I approve." Reluctantly, I pull away from Abby because I can't glue myself to her side, no matter how much I might want to.

Kai moves back into the hallway to let us enter the house. "Are you okay?" he asks, in a more serious tone, squeezing my shoulders.

"Honestly, no." I'm not one to mince my words, and I don't see the point in lying. Everyone knows how I feel about Hunt, and everyone knows about his supposed fake marriage. "I've never felt like this before, and it sucks ass."

"I thought you liked sucking ass." Kai smirks.

"I'd like to suck your ass," I retort because this is our thing.

"In your dreams, Bright One." His smirk grows until it looks like it'll split his face in two.

"I am going to fucking kill Jackson. Right after I kill Sawyer for letting that one out of the bag."

"I think that is so sweet." Abby loops her arm in mine. "And very un-Sawyer-like."

"Can we ban his name?" I ask as we enter the large living space. "Sawyer is now Voldemort, and he's already lost all seven parts of his soul."

"I know you're pissed," Kai says, standing in the space between the living room and the kitchen, "and I don't blame you, but Hunt is still one of my best friends."

"You're taking his side?" Hurt seeps from my pores and underscores my tone.

"I'm not taking sides. And that's not just because my wife would kick my ass and cockblock me for eternity." His lips kick up at the corners.

"I so would," Abby loyally replies, squeezing my arm. "No one treats my bestie like this and gets away with it. Sawyer is on top of my shit list, and he knows it."

"I can see it from both sides," Kai adds. "Finding out the way you did was shitty, and that's on Hunt. But he's only doing this to stop Techxet from going under." It's more than that, but Sawyer obviously hasn't called Kai to talk to him about it yet. "And he cares about you, man." His sincere brown eyes level with me. "I know he struggles to articulate his feelings, but Lauder and I have seen the way he is with you. It's not that he doesn't care."

"I don't give a fuck about the reasons anymore, Kai. We've been dating for almost a year, fucking for longer, and the guy has constantly kept me at arm's length." I rub at a tense spot between my brows as my tired brain protests the agonizing internal analysis that has been repeating in my head on a loop for days. I'm even boring myself with my repetitive thoughts. "I can't do it anymore. I need to walk away for my sanity and my self-respect."

Slowly, Kai nods. Concern shimmers in his eyes, and I'm glad I decided to backtrack and stop here before returning to NYC. I needed a hug from my bestie, and I need both of them to tell me I'm doing the right thing. Because I've been swinging back and forth, my resolve weakening despite my determination. It's damn hard to voluntarily walk away from the guy you know is the love of your life.

"Want a drink?" he asks. "I have beer in the fridge or that cider you like."

"As much as I'd love one, I have to drive to New York, and I can't stay long."

"Make him that hot chocolate he likes," Abby says, tugging me down beside her on the couch. "With marshmallows."

"And chocolate sprinkles," I add. "You can't forget the chocolate sprinkles."

Kai purses his lips, fighting a grin. "Anything else, Your Highness?"

"Is ass sucking still off the table because I—"

Abby smushes her hand over my mouth, effectively silencing me. "I know you're heartsick, but you can't proposition my husband." Her eyes twinkle with mirth. "That's my job. Isn't it, baby?" she calls out as Kai wanders into the kitchen rolling his eyes. "All joking aside, how are you? Tell me what happened."

I fill her in on what went down today and how my plans to resign are in the toilet. Then I tell her about my little run-in with Sydney and Hunt's judgy mom.

"Appearances mean everything to the Hunts," Kai says, handing me a steaming mug of chocolaty goodness. Bending down, he kisses his wife on the lips before handing her a glass of crisp white wine. He flops into the recliner chair beside us, popping the cap on his beer. "I don't think they are bad people, per se, not in the way my father is, but they're selfish cunts. They were happy to toss money at Hunt, let him throw lavish parties, and basically do whatever he wanted because it meant they could focus on their work and convince themselves they were good parents because their son wanted for nothing."

"Except their love, time, and attention, it seems," Abby says.

"Correct."

"He rarely mentions them to me," I admit. "But that's not the impression he has given me about them."

"Hunt would stab himself before admitting the truth," Kai says, knocking back his beer. Man, he's a sexy fucker when he drinks. Watching his Adam's apple bob when he swallows is sexy as hell.

"Are you eye fucking my husband?" Abby asks.

Kai spits beer all over his lap.

"Oops. Was I?" I waggle my brows, not even pretending to be sorry. "I can appreciate a sexy guy even if he is taken by the best woman to ever walk the earth."

"You are forgiven, but only just."

"I need to get laid stat. Over and over and over again. Find some big stud with a giant rectal wrecker to drill every memory of Hunt's cock from my ass."

Kai almost chokes this time, and Abby stretches over, rubbing his back as her mouth twitches.

"Would that really help?" she softly asks as I sip my hot chocolate. "I know you're hurting, and you're single now, so there's nothing stopping you from getting back in the saddle, but I know you. You mask your pain with humor. Finding a fuck buddy might give you some temporary respite, but it won't heal the cracks in your heart."

"Why do I always fall for men who will never love me back?" I croak as tears sting the backs of my eyes. "I swore after the last time this happened I'd never put myself in this position again, but it's like history repeating all over again."

"This is that guy you told me about before? The older man you were with when you were seventeen?"

"The older married man who insisted on keeping me his dirty little secret until his wife found out and broadcast a video of us fucking all over town? Yep, that's the one."

"I wish I could absorb your pain." She wraps her slim arms around me. "I wish you weren't hurting, but it won't always be like this. If Sawyer is too dumb to see what an amazing, wonderful, caring, smart, funny, unique guy you are, then it's his loss, not yours. One day, you'll find someone who truly appreciates you for the person you are. Until then, I am going to shower you with love and remind you every day that you are incredible and worthy of everything."

I hold her close, fighting tears. "I love you."

"I love you too."

Looking over her shoulder, I smirk at her husband. "I think

I should switch teams and you should dump the caveman, and we'll go live on an island in the Caribbean. Spend our days lying in the sun, getting drunk, eating, and fucking."

"I vote to bring Kai." Abby's nose twitches as she grins at her husband. "He can make our food and rub our feet."

"Do the laundry and clean the house," I add.

"We can take turns rimming his ass."

We crack up laughing, and just like that, my bestie has lifted my melancholy.

"You're hilarious," Kai drawls. "Seriously, you belong on stage." He flips us the bird, and more laughter rumbles from our chests.

"Ah, baby." Abby crawls into her husband's lap. "I'm sorry. We can take the ass rimming off the chores list if it upsets you that much."

I leave their house twenty minutes later, feeling much lighter than when I arrived.

CHAPTER SEVEN

Sydney

"Oh, Sydney, you look beautiful. Regal. Like a princess," Ava Hunt—my soon-to-be mother-in-law—says as I twirl in front of the mirror in the couture bridal boutique.

"It's stunning, Syd," my bestie Cayenne says. "And so very you. You made a good choice."

I came here with Ava a few days after our engagement party, and this was the first dress I tried on. I knew instantly it was the one. Made of Chantilly lace, it has a flowing skirt with a scooped neckline and spaghetti straps that crisscross over an open back. It is sexy but elegant, and it has a little boho vibe.

It's such a pity I'm wasting it on this farce of a wedding.

Ava smiles at Cayenne, but it's a feeble attempt. Sawyer's parents have been welcoming and warm, but they are super judgmental and total snobs. It's become abundantly clear status and wealth are the things they value most and the measure they use to assess others by.

I'm ashamed of the comment I made about Xavier that day in Sawyer's parents' penthouse. I was thrown off guard by the guy, and when Ava made her derogatory remark, I jumped in with mine without thinking it through. Sawyer said he was seeing someone, and I just assumed it was a woman. Which is ridiculous, because he doesn't hide his bisexuality. It was something he told me on our first date.

I wonder if my bestie's purple hair reminds Ava of Xavier. If that's why she took an immediate dislike to her. Perhaps it's her colorful clothes or loud personality. Or maybe it's the fact Cayenne is an aromatherapist and not a doctor or a lawyer or a banker. Ava has this in common with my father. Herman Shaw has never approved of my friendship with Cayenne because she encourages me to live my life the way I want to. Not that I have the guts to follow through, but maybe someday, her courage and her bravery will rub off on me.

"I think that's perfect now." The boutique owner scrutinizes the dress from all angles, checking it fits right.

"I agree. Thank you so much for rushing this through for me."

"You're welcome. We like to ensure all our clients are completely satisfied." After the extortionate sum of money my father has forked out for this dress, I would like to think so.

"What about a veil?" Ava asks, her face lighting up.

Seriously, what is with her and veils? I told her I didn't want one already. I plan to wear my hair loose and wavy with a delicate flower garland I saw in a magazine. I know it's not the done thing for New York society, but I'll be damned if I'm going to let Sawyer's mother dictate every aspect of the wedding. I have conceded to her wishes on everything else. How I look on the day will totally be my choice. "I'm not wearing a veil, and I believe I already explained my reasons why."

Cayenne coughs to disguise her snort of laughter.

After I get changed into my clothes, Ava collects the dress from behind the counter, and we leave the store. "I'll see this is delivered to your father's apartment," she says. "If you're sure you're not going straight home."

I loop my arm through Cay's. "I'm not. We have some catching up to do over dinner."

"Well, have a nice evening."

I lean down, kissing her cheeks. "Thanks for your help today and for everything." Ava might be a bit pushy, but I'm not complaining since she's doing all the legwork. I have very little interest in wedding planning when it's all one giant charade. I'm struggling to summon the requisite enthusiasm.

"It's my pleasure, Sydney." She beams at me, and I can tell it's genuine. "I know this must be hard for you without your mother around or any sisters. I'm glad I can be here for you." She squeezes my arm. "We're family now, or we will be in twelve days."

Don't remind me. I wave her off, and Cayenne and I head in the direction of the restaurant we have a reservation at. "She's a piece of work. Are you sure you want to marry into that family?"

"It's not like I have a choice."

"I still can't believe your dickhead dad is making you do this. I feel like I should report him to the authorities."

"I wish it were that simple."

"I should have reported him when you were in high school," she says, through gritted teeth, and a familiar red layer coats her eyes.

"I know," I whisper, clinging to her arm tighter. "But it's not like I can do anything about that now."

"I shouldn't have let you talk me out of it back then," she adds as we wait at the intersection for the lights to change.

"Reporting him wouldn't have mattered, Cay. Money talks, and he would've written a fat check and bought his way out of any charges they might have brought." The lights change, and we join the crowd walking across the street. "People like the Hunts and my father are above the law. Why do you think they're all so pretentious? They literally think they are gods. That they are above everyone and anything. That rules and laws and common decency don't apply to them."

"It's wrong. It represents everything that is wrong about society today," she says, pushing through the doors into the modern Greek restaurant.

After we are seated, we sip white wine while we mull over the menu without talking.

The instant the waitress is gone after taking our order, Cayenne props her elbows on the table and peers into my eyes. "I can't believe you are going through with this, babe. It's seriously nuts. He could be an ax murderer for all you know."

I giggle. "He's not a murderer, even if that scowl of his looks like it could kill anything stone dead."

"How are you going to live with him if he continues to be such a moody bastard?"

"It won't be forever," I say, gulping a large mouthful of the crisp Sancerre. "Just long enough for me to get a payout from the prenup, and then I'm getting the hell out of Dodge. I'm thinking Europe somewhere. I could find a cute little house by the sea and paint from sunup until sundown."

"Two years is a long time to live with a grumpy prick you don't like."

"I never said I don't like him. He's an acquired taste. Like anchovies on pizza. I used to hate those suckers, and now I can't order pizza without them."

Glancing around the busy restaurant, she lowers her voice and leans in closer. "How will it work if he has a guy on the scene? And what about when you need to get laid? It's not like you can just pick up a random hookup with that rock on your finger and Sawyer Hunt for a husband."

"I'll find a way, and I have a sneaking suspicion that guy might no longer be on the scene." It would definitely explain why Sawyer has been in such a foul mood every time I've seen him. Not that I've seen much of him. Apart from occasions where his parents force us to join them on a night out—because we need to be seen in public, apparently—Sawyer has pretty much ignored me.

"That might be a blessing in disguise," Cayenne says as the server slides plates of food in front of us. "The two years would be more bearable if you were at least fucking the guy."

"I don't think he'd be down for that," I say, cutting into my chicken souvlaki.

"Is the guy blind or something?" she asks, attacking her moussaka with gusto. "You're like a freaking supermodel. I give it one month of living together, tops, before he jumps your bones."

"I bark out a laugh. "You've changed your tune, and I doubt it. He's the most reserved, restrained guy I've ever met, and he gives nothing away. He has the art of cool indifference down pat."

"I figure if you're going through with this, you might as well make the best of it. He's hot, and it's clear he works out. If you're going to be forced to put up with his whiny ass, you deserve to at least get a few orgasms out of it."

"I wouldn't rule out fucking him, but I'm not holding my breath either," I admit, groaning as the succulent chicken and tantalizing flavors burst on my tongue. "I could be wrong about the guy. Maybe they are still together and the tension I picked up on is because of the wedding."

She sets her silverware down, eyeballing me earnestly. "My offer still stands. You can take my couch, and we can look for a bigger place."

"With what money, Cay?" I squeeze her hand, so grateful for her support. "I am currently unemployed, and you barely make ends meet as it is."

"Can't you take out a bunch of cash and hide it? Enough to keep you going until you find a new job?"

"I appreciate the suggestion, but I don't actually have a lot of cash." Heat creeps up my neck as I admit the embarrassing truth. "I only have my platinum card, but there is a block on it, which means I can't withdraw cash with it, and it's not like I can ask to do a large amount of cash back in a store or a restaurant."

"What about your bank card?"

"I don't have one," I sheepishly admit. "Daddy took it away from me after I overdosed," I whisper. "He doesn't trust me with money. If I need something, he has one of his assistants order it. My card has a small limit so I can't go crazy." Derision drips from my tone. "It's not like I know any dealers who take cards. I have told him, repeatedly, that I learned my lesson the hard way and I'm done with drugs, but he doesn't believe me. His way of handling it is to ensure he controls everything. Any measly salary I earn even goes directly into an account he manages, and he has instructions left with banks all over town to refuse me if I try to open an account or apply for a line of credit."

Her jaw hangs open. "That motherfucking bastard! He can't do that to you." Outrage splays across her pretty face.

"He can and he does." I put my silverware down, having lost my appetite. "I'm twenty-four years old, and I can barely breathe without my father approving it." It just serves to remind me what a pathetic bitch I am and how my disastrous life choices have led me to this point. Tears stab my eyes, but I force them back down. I'm done crying over the mistakes of my past and the pain of my present. At least, there is some sliver of hope for the future. "This wedding is my best chance at being free of that man. Sawyer has already agreed that he'll pay the settlement directly to me when it's time for us to divorce. Then I just need to find someone to get me a fake ID and I'm saying goodbye to Sydney Shaw and leaving my old life behind."

"Do I factor in this new life plan of yours?"

"Absolutely. If you want to come with, I would be overjoyed, but I'm prepared to do this alone."

"You are so brave."

I almost spit my wine all over the table. I stare at her with incredulous eyes. "I think you mean weak and cowardly."

"Nope." She glares at me. "You are not starting this shit again. After everything you've been through, the very last thing you are is weak or a coward." Her chest heaves, and my chest is heavy with pent-up emotion. Lifting my glass, I take a healthy glug of wine. "There is another option," she says. "You could go to him. You could go to Jared. Tell him what happened and ask for his help. He's loaded now. I'm sure he'd help you."

"Why would he?" I shrug. "It's been over eight years since I last saw him. In case you've forgotten, he left, and he never even attempted to contact me. It was as if all the years we spent together meant nothing. As if our friendship was fake. As if the things we shared those last few months before he moved overseas were inconsequential."

"They weren't to you."

"No, they weren't." My hand is shaking as I lift my glass to my lips. "He still means everything to me, Cayenne, even though I know he's forgotten all about me, and clearly moved on."

CHAPTER EIGHT

Sawyer

"Everyone is staring," Sydney whispers in my ear as we emerge from the beautifully decorated ballroom of the most expensive hotel in The Hamptons out onto the terrace.

"The crème de la crème of New York society is here. They know who we are and that our wedding is next week. What else did you think would happen?" I arch a brow, staring down at my fiancée as she slides sunglasses over her eyes.

Jackson and Van got a glorious day for their wedding. Sun beats down on my shoulders, and I silently curse Laurena Lauder for insisting on full formal attire. I'm accustomed to wearing suits, and I don't mind them when it's not unseasonably hot. It's okay for the ladies. They can look the part in expensive gowns while not sweating buckets under a suit.

Sydney is a case in point. She looks stunning in a gorgeous white, purple, and pink silk dress that crisscrosses around her neck and flows softly from her waist. The material swirls around her legs as a soft ocean breeze provides some minor relief from the oppressive heat.

"I expect that, but I'm not talking about the oldies," Sydney replies, brushing wayward strands of blonde hair back off her face. "I meant your friends." She nods to the left where my friends are seated at a long table on the terrace, chatting over glasses of champagne as they pretend like they're not staring at me and my date.

"They won't bite," I say, eyeballing her. "Much."

"That's reassuring." She clings more tightly to my hand as I lead her to the table. "This would've been easier if you'd introduced me to them before now."

I slam to a halt a few feet away from my friends. "Why would I have done that?"

"Because we're getting married," she grits out, looking annoyed. "And yes, I know it's not real," she whispers, "but you are stuck with me for two years, Sawyer. You can't leave me locked in your penthouse like Rapunzel in her tower. I'll have to attend events with you. You can't keep me away from your friends or isolated from your life."

Want to bet?

"I don't see how any of that is relevant to today. You're meeting them now. What difference does it make?"

She blows air out of her mouth. "I have a feeling I'm going to need a lot of alcohol today."

"Don't do anything to embarrass me," I warn, having uncovered a few startling truths about Sydney in the weeks since we became engaged. Tales of her rebellious streak were not exaggerated.

"You're such an asshole," she seethes, glaring up at me.

"He is," a woman with a familiar voice says, and I prepare myself for it. "At least you know what you're getting into. Trust me when I say your business arrangement is far preferable to a real relationship. Just ask Xavier. He's got the scars on his heart to show for it." Abby thrusts out her hand, smiling at Sydney. "I'm Abby, by the way."

Abby is lucky Sydney already knows about Xavier; otherwise, I would blast her for that admission. Recalling the unpleasant conversation I had with Sydney about my ex is not something I want to be reminded of either. "Abby loves stirring shit, and she's Xavier's best friend. I suggest you give her a wide berth,"

I say as the girls shake hands.

"If this wasn't Nessa and Jackson's special day, I would punch your dumb ass and knock you flat on your back," Abby retorts, waving her finger in my face.

"Control your wife," I tell Anderson as he materializes behind Abby, sliding his arms around her waist.

"How about you stop pissing her off?" Kai levels me with a dark look, but I'm immune to it. He forgets I've known him since I was ten, and those subtle threats won't work on me. Put me in a ring with him and that'd be a different matter.

"How about you find your balls?" I deadpan because he is such a pussy around his woman. Don't get me wrong. I love Abby. When she's not being a pain in my ass. She's perfect for Kaiden because she doesn't take any of his shit and she grounds him just by existing. But she has my best friend wrapped around her every finger, and the sap would do anything she tells him to do.

"How about you two quit that shit before I'm forced to throw both my best men out of my wedding?" Jackson says, tugging at the collar of his shirt. There is a small ceremony taking place on the beach, before the wedding brunch and party, and I can tell Jackson is already itching to ditch his suit. "You must be Sydney," he says, smiling at the woman squeezing my hand to the point of pain. "It's good to finally meet you."

"Thanks for inviting me, and congratulations."

"Let's sit down," Abby says. "My feet are already killing me in these heels, and I want to finish my champagne before we head back to Nessa."

We walk to the table where the rest of my friends are seated. I get the necessary introductions out of the way first, introducing Sydney to Charlie and his fiancée Demi, Anderson's mother-in-law Olivia and her plus one—her friend Sylvia Montgomery—and Drew and Shandra. They either came alone or as each other's date. I never know with those two. They are worse than Xavier and I were. Speaking of the devil. Where is he? I cast a sneaky glance around as I pull out Sydney's chair for her, but I don't see him.

It would be easier if he wasn't here, but I know I won't be that lucky.

I've been on edge all morning as we drove from the city, wondering if he's going to come alone or bring a date. This past month, I've had to stomach the nonstop flirting between Xavier and Jamison, and I'm this close to losing my shit with that scrawny punk. I don't care he's hit the gym and bulked up. He's still a scrawny punk, and he's in no way worthy of a guy like Xavier.

"Jackson, come sit," Abby says, patting the empty chair beside her. "Stop looking worried. She's fine."

"I don't want Nessa upset today. She didn't want Ruth here for a reason."

"Your mom is with her. She won't let Nessa's mom do or say anything to upset her," Abby replies, and I wonder what drama I've missed.

"She seemed sincere," Shandra adds, sipping her champagne.

Jackson leans his hands on the table. "Was she drunk?" he asks in a low tone.

Abby and Shandra both shake their heads. Abby knocks back her drink and stands. "We'll go back and check on her, but I'm sure she's fine." She stretches up, kissing him on his cheek. "Sit down and relax. If there is anything wrong, I promise Shandra and I will come and get you."

Air whooshes out of his mouth in grateful relief. "Thanks."

The girls disappear, looking like two peas in a pod in their matching knee-length dresses.

"I'm Kaiden," Kai says, looking at Sydney from across the table. "Hunt left me off the introductory list for some reason."

"Oversight, caveman. Settle down." I toss him a wry smile, and he flips me the bird.

"Nice to meet you," Sydney says, gulping back her champagne.

"Take it easy. It's still early," I remind her.

She's wearing sunglasses, but I feel her shooting daggers at me. "You're not my dad, and you're not my husband yet, so quit with the lecture. If you want to get technical, you shouldn't be drinking alcohol as you're underage. I'm twenty-four and perfectly entitled to drink whatever I want."

"An older woman. I should've guessed. You have a bit of a thing for older partners, don't ya, Hunt?" Xavier says from behind me, pretending like he didn't google everything to do with Sydney Shaw the minute he found out about her. My shoulders stiffen, and a muscle clenches in my jaw, but I don't turn around. I don't want to confirm what I already suspect.

"Xavier." Sydney stands, removing her glasses and turning to face him. "I owe you an apology. I was a little rude the last time we met. I was caught off guard, but I didn't mean to take it out on you."

"You weren't rude, and no apology is necessary, but I appreciate it." Out of the corner of my eye, I see him taking her hand, and I wonder what game he's playing. "It seems I wasn't the only one kept in the dark." He kisses the back of her hand before releasing her. "Aren't you going to say hi, Hunt?"

He throws down the gauntlet, and I have no choice but to respond. I stand and turn around, bracing myself for it.

"Hunt." Jackson's tone carries considerable warning, and I heed it. I won't cause a scene at their wedding.

Xavier is wearing a lightweight vivid blue suit, with a black shirt and a purple tie to match his hair. The suit fits his toned body perfectly, and a pang of longing jumps up and bites me. If I'm not mistaken, he's bulked up a little more, and he looks damn good. He is holding hands with Jamison who is more traditionally attired in a black suit with a white shirt and a replica purple tie.

"Matching ties. How very cliché."

"You're wearing a purple tie to match your fiancée's dress, which is no different. Or do you like to pretend you're not a hypocritical ass?" Xavier retorts.

Ignoring him, I focus on the main point of my rage. "Jamison. I'd like to say this is a surprise, but it really isn't. You two have been drooling over one another like dogs in heat."

"Jealous, Hunt?" Xavier flashes me a grin. "Don't mind him, baby." He rubs Jamison's arm, beaming at him like the Cheshire Cat while I grind my teeth. "I warned you he would be like this."

"What. The. Ever-loving. Fuck?!" Lauder gets up from his chair and walks to my side. His eyes pop wide as he gives Jamison a quick once-over. "Dude! Look at you! Have you been overdosing on steroid cocktails, or are my eyes playing tricks on me? Wow. You look amazing, man."

I narrow my eyes at my so-called best friend. "Really?"

Lauder slings his arm around my shoulders. "Don't get your panties in a bunch, Hunt. I'd still do you, if I swung that way."

"Jackson." Travis Lauder approaches, and it's a timely intervention. "It's time." Looking beyond him, I spot guests leaving the ballroom and making their way down to the rows of seats set up on the beach. "Vanessa is on her way."

"Come on." I hold my hand out for Sydney. "I'll walk you to your seat."

After getting Sydney settled with my parents, I wait with Lauder and Anderson to one side of the raised terrace area where the celebrant waits to conduct the civil ceremony while the guests quickly fill up the seats.

"This will be you next," Anderson says, glancing over his shoulder, looking for a glimpse of his wife.

"Don't remind me," I murmur.

"At least she's hot," Lauder says.

"What the hell has that got to do with anything?"

"If you're going to be waking up beside her every morning for two years, it helps if the view is pretty."

"Does Van know how shallow you are, and who the fuck said anything about waking up beside her? She won't be in my bed."

Lauder smirks. "You planning on staying celibate? Casual hooking up will be too risky, and Xavier—"

"Has moved on." I cut across him because I don't want to hear what he was about to say, and I don't want to argue with him at his wedding. "Let's agree to just focus on you and Van. This is your day, and I'm sure no one wants to hear about my shit."

"That's the smartest thing you've said in weeks," Anderson drawls, and I barely resist wrapping my hands around his throat.

"It's not too late to pull out," Lauder says, his expression turning serious. "I spoke with my dad. He said he'll invest. He's planning to talk to your dad later."

"Travis said that? He's really willing to invest?"

"Why are you surprised? You know our fathers have been best friends since they were seven. And if what you suspect about the elite is true, we're all in this together."

"I know my dad will appreciate it, but there's no way he'll let your father get involved. It's not just about the money either."

"Can't you delay the wedding a bit longer? If we have more time, I know we'll find who's responsible."

"I would if I could, but I'm not sure a few more weeks will make much of a difference. Even with Xavier on the team and all of us working around the clock, we haven't been able to confirm anything. Every lead is a dead end, and we haven't found any trace back to the elite."

"We'll come up with another plan tomorrow," Anderson says, and I nod. We're meeting at my parents' house in the morning to discuss the situation. "The person couldn't be this good. There has to be something there. It just hasn't been discovered yet."

"I want to know what's going on," Lauder says as music starts up. "Keep me updated daily while I'm away."

"Absolutely not," Anderson says. "You'll be on your honeymoon, and you need to devote every second to your wife. This shit will still be here when you return from Italy."

"I agree. We can handle things until you return."

We straighten up and turn around, watching as Nessa's young brother and sister walk up the makeshift aisle toward us. Hunter is carrying the ring cushion while Kayleigh is throwing rose petals on the ground. Both are smiling and clearly enjoying themselves. Lauder high-fives Hunter and swings Kayleigh around, before helping them into their seats beside Laurena. There is no sign of Ruth Breen, so she must have said her piece and left. I'm glad. Vanessa doesn't need that shit today.

Abby and Shandra appear next, walking gracefully up the aisle. Predictably, Abby's eyes are locked on Kai, and I'm sure they are probably remembering their beach wedding. Drew is staring straight ahead, purposely not looking at Shandra, and there is a strange look on his face. He's a hard one to figure out. I don't know if he confides in Anderson, because they are close, but if he does, Kai never says.

Lauder's sharp intake of breath snaps me out of my head, and I lift my chin, a genuine smile coasting over my face when I spot Travis walking a clearly emotional Vanessa up the aisle. Lauder's eyes turn suspiciously glassy, and I clamp a hand on his shoulder for moral support. His Adam's apple jumps in his throat as his eyes remain fixated on his beautiful bride.

Van looks stunning in a princess-style ivory dress. Her blonde hair is pulled into a bun, and she's wearing a tiara with a lace veil flowing down her back. Tears are pouring down her face, and the look of love in her eyes as she stares at Jackson is unmistakable.

"I'm happy for you, man," I tell him, feeling a little choked up. "She looks beautiful, and she's a wonderful woman. She's good for you."

"You're good for each other," Anderson adds.

"She is the best thing to ever happen to me," Lauder agrees, unable to tear his gaze from her.

"No one should be forced into marrying someone they don't want to," Anderson says, in a hushed tone, his mouth pressed up against my ear. "It's not fair to you or Sydney."

"Life isn't fair," I reply, swallowing thickly as my eyes meet Xavier's. He's seated beside Jamison. Their hands are clasped together on his thigh, and a lump forms in my throat.

We should be here together.

That should be me holding his hand, not that scrawny punk who doesn't deserve him.

I step back a little as Jackson reaches for Van, eyeballing Anderson. "Not everyone gets their heart's desire."

CHAPTER NINE

Sawyer

"I'VE BEEN LOOKING for you all day," Abby says, coming up alongside me. I've been hiding out on the terrace the past twenty minutes, tucked into a corner out of view of the main room. Sydney is sitting with my parents, and I just needed a breather. She rests her elbows on the rail and we stare in silence at the placid ocean, bathed in a silvery glow from the moon, as gentle waves lap at the shore.

Behind us, the party is in full swing. It's a miracle I survived the day, and I'm glad it's almost over.

"I've been avoiding you," I truthfully admit after a few beats of silence.

"I don't understand it, Sawyer." She glances sideways at me, and I meet her gaze. "You are the one person who has always danced to his own tune, so how is this happening? Does Xavier really mean so little to you that you'd throw what you have away?"

"Xavier doesn't have anything to do with this decision, Abby."

"And that's my fucking problem," she hisses, grabbing my elbow. "Why not? Why isn't he at the forefront of everything? Don't try to pretend you don't care. I know that's bullshit."

"What do you want me to say, Abby? You want me to tell my dad to take a hike? To watch him and thousands of his employees lose the shirts off their backs? To stand back and let the elite win this round, because proof or not, I fucking know they are involved. If they succeed in taking my dad down, it will encourage them to keep going. Who is their next target?" I drill her with a look because we both know they'll come after the Andersons next. "I'm sick of everyone giving me shit when I'm trying to do the right thing. I'm the one who is paying the price, yet I'm the one getting yelled at." My chest heaves as everything I've been keeping bottled up inside me today erupts. "You think it's easy for me to be here watching the guy I want with someone else? Having to pretend I'm all loved up with a woman I barely know and have little desire to?" I throw my hands in the air. "Tell me again how little he means to me! How little you all mean to me," I snap.

"We'll find another way. You don't have to do this." Tentatively, she touches my arm.

"There is no other way." I shuck her hand off, staring into the distance as two shapes come into view.

"You're going to lose him," she says in a soft tone. "You've pushed him away one too many times."

"I tried not to catch feelings for him," I admit. "I tried to stay away, but he got under my skin." Propping my hip against the railing, I turn and face her. "I didn't get it. On paper, we don't work. We are complete opposites in so many ways. We drive each other insane half the time, but in every other way, it's perfect. He gets me, even if he doesn't always understand the way I am. He knows when to push and when to pull back. He lets me take the lead even though we both know he's the one in charge. The bigger man. The better person."

She glances over my shoulder, urging me to continue with her eyes.

"I love how he knows all these random facts. No matter how obscure or bizarre my question is, he always knows the answer. Or how he's always spouting movie quotes, and he has an entire drawer full of superhero underwear. I love that he conquered his fear of motorcycles and now he has two. I even love how ridiculous he is in those Batman leathers. I love how fucking smart he is. Honestly, watching him work gives me the biggest hard-on. I love his smart mouth and his witty comebacks. I love the ridiculousness of his humor and how he has no filter. I love how loyal he is and how he'd do anything for his friends. I love that he has the biggest heart and how he was willing to make himself vulnerable for me even when I couldn't give him the same in return."

"Why have you never said any of those things to me?"

I squeeze my eyes shut, torn between chewing Abby out for goading me into my admission, turning around to face Xavier, or running off and pretending like he didn't hear me saying all that shit.

"Answer me." Xavier tugs on my arm, and the air swirls as he moves to stand in front of me, obliterating my choices.

Slowly, I peel my eyes open, noticing the creases in his suit and the sand stuck to one side of his neck. Jamison stands awkwardly to the side, his clothing in similar disarray, and I don't need an overactive imagination to know what they were doing. Bile crawls up my throat, and pain quickly turns to anger as liquid rage floods my veins.

"This was a private conversation, and you know what they say about people who eavesdrop." I shove his hand away. "Go back to your fuck buddy."

"We're more than that," Jamison, bravely or stupidly, says. "You didn't want him, but I do."

"Shut your face, or I'll shut it for you." I glare at him. "This has nothing to do with me not wanting him, and you know nothing."

"Jon Snow," Xavier says, and I whip my head around to him, only half surprised he'd make a joke right now. My lips twitch, and he shrugs. "I couldn't help it. You handed it to me on a platter."

God. I have missed this. Missed him.

"What?" Jamison asks, looking confused.

"He hasn't watched *Game of Thrones*. That's a dumping offense if ever I heard one." I step closer, all my anger fading. "Can we talk? Alone. Please."

He stares at me, and a whole host of emotions washes over his face. His hair is down again, and I'm itching to run my fingers through it. He seems to have ditched the Mohawk in favor of this lazy, messy style, but I love it. Unable to resist and uncaring we have an audience of two, I reach out, toying with his hair. "I miss you. I miss you so much." I move my hand, cupping one side of his handsome face. "Today has been agony."

Xavier moves his arm, lifting it toward my face as his eyes glisten with need. We move at the same time, our chests brushing as he cups my cheek, and our faces move closer, our mouths lining up at the perfect angle. His warm breath dances over my lips, and I need to taste him so badly it feels like I'll die if I can't kiss him right now. My heart is pounding behind my rib cage as I close my eyes, brushing my mouth against his, wishing we were alone, with a bed, so I could show him how much he means to me.

"Get off him." Jamison storms over, yanking my arm away and ruining the moment.

"Fuck off. You're fired." I jab my finger in his face. "If you ever lay a hand on me again, I'll flatten your ass into next week."

"You can't fire me," he blurts. "I haven't done anything wrong!"

"I'm your superior, and you just pushed me."

"You were hitting on my boyfriend!"

"He's not yours," I growl, ready to toss the asshole over the railing any second now.

"You can't fire me because I'm dating your ex!"

"I fucking can, and I just have. Now get lost."

"Unbelievable." Xavier steps back, shaking his head. "You almost pulled me under again." He links his fingers with Jamison's, and a tight pain rips across my chest. He stabs me with a determined look. "If he goes, so do I."

I bark out an incredulous laugh. "You'd sacrifice your career for him? Are you insane?"

"He must be some lay," Abby, unhelpfully, adds. She's been uncharacteristically quiet.

Xavier smirks. "Best lay I've ever had."

I know he's trying to hurt me, and I know it's not true, but his words are like knives slicing across my exposed flesh. Before he can see my pain, I force every sliver of emotion back into a box, shoving it down deep inside me. I plant my usual mask on and smile. "I'm having the best sex of my life too," I lie, "so I guess it's a good thing we broke up since we were clearly so incompatible." I stretch out my hand toward Jamison. "I apologize, and I retract my statement. You two are good together. Look after him." The words feel like poison leaving my mouth, but I say what I need to before turning to Xavier. "Be happy, man. That's all I want for you."

I walk off in the direction of the beach, needing to lick my wounds before I return to my fiancée.

"Wait up." Abby runs after me.

I slam to a halt, looking over my shoulder, spotting Jamison and Xavier walking back to the ballroom, hand in hand. "I'm not in the mood for company, Abigail."

"I don't like him," she blurts. "He's all wrong for him, and Xavier may think you're a lost cause, but I know you're not." Silence engulfs us as she comes around in front of me.

"If you're waiting for me to say thanks, you'll be waiting awhile."

"I know you meant what you said before they arrived. I know you meant every word." She plants her hand on my chest, lifting her head to stare me in the eyes. "You know how I know?" She pauses, and I roll my eyes.

"Just say it. I know better than to try to walk away before you've said your piece."

"Your entire face came to life, Sawyer. You were so animated when you spoke about him—in a way I have rarely seen." Her beautiful features soften. "You love him. You don't even realize it, but you do."

"You want everyone to be in love because you are, but that's not the way the world works. It's not the way *my* world works."

"I don't want this for you. I know what it's like to be trapped."

"Sydney is no Trent. This might not be my choice, but it's not the same. She's not forcing me to do anything. We are on the same page, and that's how I know I can do this for however long it takes to prove the elite are behind this and take back the reins."

"I want in." Steely determination glints in her eyes as I spy Kai advancing on us. I wondered how long it would take for him to show up.

"Of course, you do, and I'd never refuse your help. Only an idiot would."

"I'm still pissed at you for hurting my bestie, but I understand it better now."

"What's up?" Kai asks, winding his arms around Abby's waist from behind. "Xavier came back inside with a face like thunder."

I need to walk. "I'm going to the beach. Keep an eye on Sydney for me?"

"She's at our table, and she's fine. She's talking weddings with Demi," he confirms.

That's a hard pass for me. "I'll catch you guys later," I say, walking off with my hands shoved in the pockets of my black pants.

Abby's words linger in my mind as I walk barefoot in the sand. Do I love him? Is that what all these whirling emotions churning inside me mean? And what does it matter whether I acknowledge it or not?

I have lost Xavier.

I see that now.

Even if I could do anything, there is nothing left to salvage anymore.

CHAPTER TEN

Sawyer

"Can you call him, please?" I ask Abby the following morning when we are gathered at my parents' place for our meeting. Everyone is here except my ex, and he's delaying things.

Mom has taken Sydney shopping while Dad is playing golf with Travis, but I don't know how long they'll be. I'm eager to have this conversation and come up with a plan.

"Tell him not to bring his boyfriend," Anderson says, and I work hard to show no emotion.

"That's a given," Shandra says, shooting me a pitiful look I hate.

Initially, I had only taken Lauder and Anderson into my confidence, but given our lack of progress and my mounting concerns, we chose to bring the whole gang in. There is strength in numbers.

"Not entirely," Charlie says, crossing his feet at the ankles. "Jamison is on the official case at Techxet, so Xavier might ask him to tag along."

Charlie didn't bring Demi. She's having brunch at a local restaurant with his mom and sister. Charlie likes to keep Demi out of elite business, even though she is fully aware of everything.

Which defeats the purpose, if you ask me. But I understand it. His dad kept his mom sheltered from that life, and he's determined to protect his fiancée and keep her safe from the vultures who would set their sights on her the second they are married.

"No outsiders," Drew says from his position in front of the large windows. He's been staring out at the ocean since he arrived. He and Shandra can scarcely look at one another this morning, which could mean they fucked or they didn't fuck.

The only positive to come from my situation is I don't have to deal with relationship drama anymore.

"Agreed. We can't trust anyone we don't know with this," I say.

Abby lifts her head from her cell and stands. "He's here now. I'll let him in."

Drew turns around, walking to stand behind the couch. Shandra looks up at him, and there's no disguising the hurt in her eyes. I drop down on the seat beside her, squeezing her hand. "Are you okay?"

Her chest heaves. "Not really," she murmurs, turning her head into me. "Am I that obvious?"

"Maybe heartbreak recognizes heartbreak in others," I say in a moment of stark honesty.

"I'm sorry." She leans into my side, looking up at me. "At least Sydney is nice and she seems to understand."

I shrug. "She has her own reasons for doing this."

"Sorry I'm late." Xavier bursts into the room looking like he crawled out of bed mere seconds ago. His messy hair falls over his brow and into his eyes. His T-shirt is wrinkled, and he's wearing jean shorts with Nike slides, in a look that's unusual for him. "I overslept."

Ignoring the nausea swimming in my gut, I plant my usual façade on. "I don't know how long we have before Mom and Sydney return. Let's get started."

Everyone takes seats, and Xavier and I spend time updating them on what we've been doing to date. No one interrupts. Everyone gives us their undivided attention.

"You've gone through all the personnel files and no one stood out?" Abby asks when I finish explaining how I've been focusing on staff members, especially those who work in IT roles, delving into backgrounds and looking for anything that doesn't stack up or any potential links to the elite.

"I had a short list of suspect employees, but all of them checked out."

"How do we know it's someone in the New York office?" Shandra asks. "It could be someone from another Techxet office."

"It's possible," I admit as Anderson doles out coffees. "But we have thousands of technical staff in hundreds of offices globally. It would take forever to go through every staff file."

"We could do it if we split them up between us," Charlie suggests.

"My gut tells me this person is in New York," Xavier says, blowing on the steam rising from his mug.

"So does mine," I agree. "Whoever is doing this is very smart, and there's an air of—"

"Arrogance about it," Xavier finishes for me.

"Thank you." I purse my lips and narrow my eyes at him. "I'm capable of finishing my own sentences."

"In what way?" Abby asks, jumping in before things escalate.

"Someone who has the balls to come into one of the world's best technical firms and essentially hold them to ransom is arrogant as fuck. They've got to be to pull off something like this with so much audacity."

"Hunt is right," Xavier says. "I cannot understand how we can't find any trace. If this was a normal company with standard systems, I could fathom it. But not us. Not Techxet. We have systems in place to protect against this, so how the fuck can someone leave no trace? Every time I think I'm finding a footprint, it leads nowhere. It's driving me insane trying to work out how this person or persons did this."

"And they haven't stolen any more cash since the last time?" Drew asks, leaning forward on his elbows.

"Nope. Our finance guy has eyes on all the bank accounts

twenty-four-seven. They're continuously moving funds around and opening new accounts in far-flung places in an attempt to make it harder for anyone who may be inside our systems watching."

"That's got to be it." Anderson slings his arm around Abby's shoulders. "There must be someone inside watching what's going on."

I throw up my hands in frustration. "We have looked at every single employee at headquarters. We have had additional cameras installed. We have eyes on everyone."

"This doesn't make sense." Charlie frowns.

"No shit, Sherlock. What have we been telling you for the past hour?" Xavier levels a look at Charlie.

"I'd like to look at the bank statements six months before and after the occasions where the funds were stolen. I am guessing these guys did a trial run first," Charlie says.

"Our finance people have trawled through all the statements and found nothing," I confirm.

"Maybe you still have a mole on the finance side," Charlie adds. "Didn't you say it was your finance and IT guys working together the first time?"

I nod. "I can get you the statements. It can't hurt to have fresh objective eyes look at it." Charlie holds a senior position at his family's banking and investment firm, and he's worked there, in some capacity, for years. He knows his stuff, and I know he's keen to prove to all of us he's completely on our side, having fucked up spectacularly our senior year of high school.

"What about talking to that guy in prison?" Anderson says. "Did you ask your father about it?"

"Yes, and he said the same thing again. To leave it. He won't cooperate, and he knows nothing."

"I'm calling bullshit on that," Drew says.

"So am I, but it's not like I can just walk up to the correctional facility and demand to see a prisoner," I say.

Drew flashes me a dark look. "Leave that one up to me. Message me his full name, and I'll get you in to see him."

"Both of us," Xavier says, looking me squarely in the face. "You need backup."

"I can go with Hunt," Anderson offers, and I appreciate what he's trying to do.

"We're professionals." Xavier lifts his shoulders, pinning Kai with a smug look. "I know that's difficult for you to understand, caveman, but we can work together and keep things strictly business."

"Like you're doing with Jamison?" I blurt, unable to help myself.

Xavier stares at me like he wants to rip my head off my shoulders. "You're going there? Really?"

I clear my throat, annoyed at my lapse in control, choosing to ignore his question. "So, we are agreed on those things. We need to talk about the elite. Who do you think is doing this?"

"It's got to be Hamilton," Drew says. "He has it in for us, and we knew he'd come for us sometime."

"But this was set in motion before anything had happened with us or before Hamilton was president," I remind them.

"What if it was whoever was helping Atticus?" Anderson pipes up, and an eerie hush descends over the room. "We never discovered who it was."

"Wasn't it your dad?" Abby softly asks Charlie.

Charlie sits up straighter, wetting his lips. "There was someone else. Someone who brokered the connection between Atticus, Wes, and my dad. I don't know who it was. Dad would never tell me."

"Could that be the link?" Anderson asks.

"Would Wes know?" Abby asks, and Anderson shakes his head.

"He knew very little. Dad purposely kept him in the dark, only pulling him in when he needed to use his money or his resources or his contacts."

"It could've been Hamilton," Shandra says. "He could've been involved from the start."

"We have looked into his background, and we can't find

anything which ties him to this, but that could be because he's hiding his tracks," I say.

"This seems to be tied to the past, right?" Xavier says, and I recognize that look on his face. He's spinning an idea in his head.

"It appears that way."

"So, what if this is the same retaliation that drove those bastards to kidnap Dani and threaten Lauder's family."

"That was Montgomery."

"And he's rotting at the bottom of the ocean," Anderson supplies, as if we don't know.

"What if it was Mathers?" Charlie says. "And yes, I know he's dead too, but these guys never worked alone. What if it's the same team who was working for Montgomery and Mathers who are behind this?"

"Why would they continue to pursue dead men's agendas?" Abby says. "It makes no sense."

"Or it makes total sense." Xavier's eyes pop wide as he stares at me. "Lauder's father told him your father unearthed something on Montgomery and the elite that was scary enough for them to back out of the deal. What if they are looking to retrieve that intel? And the stealing is a smokescreen to mask their true agenda."

"You could be onto something," Anderson says as I nod, adrenaline coursing through my veins.

"If the evidence is that damning, why is your father still sitting on it?" Drew asks. "There is something fishy about all this."

I bob my head, thinking the exact same thing. If I wasn't licking my wounds over losing my lover, I might not have been so agreeable to meet my father's demands. How the fuck can he ask me to make such a big sacrifice while keeping me in the dark on certain things? I'm an idiot for not demanding more answers, and it's time to fix that. I stand and grab my car keys. "I need to speak to my father, and it can't wait."

CHAPTER ELEVEN

Sawyer

"HE'LL FREAK IF we interrupt him in the middle of his game," Anderson says as we climb out of my SUV at the golf club where Dad and Travis Lauder are playing a round.

I check the time on my Tag Heuer watch as I lock the car with the fob. "They should be almost finished. We'll wait for them at the eighteenth."

"What kind of information do you think your dad discovered?" Kai asks as we walk along the path that will take us to the eighteenth hole.

"I'd rather not speculate." I shove my hands in the pockets of my shorts as I contemplate all the ways this could go down.

"I hope to fuck he has something we can use."

"I wouldn't hold my breath. If he has intel and he held on to it, even after Dani was kidnapped, then it means it's either not viable or too risky to reveal it. Neither scenario will help us."

"I'm getting desperate, man." He rubs his temples. "Hamilton went apeshit on me and Rick for not handing Joaquin and Harley over for the last initiation program. There's another one planned for the fall, and if they're not there, I know he's going to make some official elite move against us."

"That shady fucker has his fingers all over this situation with

Techxet. I just know it. We'll find evidence to nail his ass to the wall. He won't be around to force your brothers into initiation."

"I hope you're right."

"Have you done anything more about Spencer and Rogan?" I inquire. Kai's two younger brothers were put up for adoption by their prick of a father when they were only one and two, respectively. During senior year, Kai and Rick worked with their uncle Wes to try to find information on where their brothers could be, but they hit a shit-ton of red tape and didn't get anywhere. I know he wants to find them. That he won't feel complete without them.

Most assume Anderson is incapable of feeling deeply, but that's a gross misconception. Kaiden feels things intensely, and family means everything to him. Being with Abby has only further highlighted that part of his personality.

His heavy sigh speaks volumes. "I want to search for them so fucking bad, but the timing is shit." We round the bend and stop at the marker with the large numeral eighteen on it. "I can't look for them with all this elite crap hanging in the air. I'm struggling to protect Joaquin and Harley as it is. As much as it kills me, I have to drop the search until I know it's safe to bring them into our world."

"How the fuck did our lives get so damn complicated?" I murmur as I see my dad and Travis Lauder walking toward the green with their two caddies in tow.

"I used to think it was the day we stepped foot in Rydeville after agreeing to my dad's insane plan, but we were involved way before that, whether we knew it or liked it."

"That's abundantly clear," I agree, watching the frown appearing on my father's face. We are quiet as we wait for both men to putt their ball and end the game. Dad and Travis shake hands, handing their clubs and golf bags to the caddies before walking our way.

"What is going on?" Dad's gaze bounces between me and Anderson as he removes his golf glove.

"We need to talk, and it needs to happen now." I level him

with a stern look. He's not going to brush me aside anymore. Travis nods as if he knows where this is leading. He clamps a hand on my dad's shoulder. "It's time, Ethan."

Dad shakes his head. "I told you I—"

"No, Dad." I cut across him. "I stupidly agreed to this sham of a wedding without demanding answers. Well, now I am demanding them, and I won't take no for an answer. If you want me to make this sacrifice, I will only do it with the full knowledge I deserve."

Dad stares at me for an indeterminable amount of time, and I hold his stare, refusing to back down.

"Very well." He admits defeat, his shoulders slumping. "But not here. We need someplace private."

"We can talk at my house," Travis says. "Jackson and Vanessa left in the early hours for Italy, and Laurena is out with Elizabeth and Demi. We will have privacy."

We leave in separate cars to drive to the Lauders' beachfront Hamptons house, which is only a couple of houses away from my parents' vacation place.

Once inside, we take seats at the long dining table while Travis procures some cans of soda and bottles of water from the refrigerator.

"Okay," Dad says, uncapping a bottle of water. "What do you want to know?"

"What information do you have on the elite that caused you to pull out of the robotics deal with Montgomery back in the day?" I ask, pulling no punches.

"You're like a dog with a bone, son." There's a hint of pride in his otherwise tight smile. "I told you the elite weren't involved in the embezzlement and the security breach, but you just won't leave it alone."

I lean forward. "For a reason, Dad. We know Hamilton wants to make us pay, and that's before we consider all the other loose ends. Like whatever evidence they know you have. You can bury your head in the sand if you want, but I know they're involved. I feel it in my gut."

"Mine too," Anderson says, sipping from a can of soda. "And Jackson agrees. We all do. It can't be a coincidence. Maybe the first time, you can pin it on your finance guy and the IT guy who died, but the subsequent breaches confirm they were just pawns in a game they didn't realize they were playing."

"For what it's worth." Travis speaks up. "I'm with the boys. I know what you think, Ethan, but I think you're mistaken."

A shuddering breath leaves Dad's lips before he speaks. "I felt sure they were behind the first embezzlement too, and I was tempted to reveal the information, but it involves a large sex ring, a group of powerful, important men, and the murder of innocent women and children."

I rest my elbows on the table. "You have proof the elite were involved in that?"

He nods.

"Which elite?" Kai asks.

"All of them. Montgomery. Hearst. Mathers. Hamilton and some others you most likely don't know."

"Why have you sat on this? Why haven't you used this any of the times we needed it?" Exasperation bleeds into my tone.

"I wanted to, but I couldn't."

"Revealing that information would have sealed all our deaths," Travis adds.

"Why? What aren't you saying?" Anderson asks, his gaze bouncing between both men.

"This goes all the way to the White House," Travis replies.

"And it involves several senior politicians and heads of government from key foreign nations," Dad adds. "There is no way we could release the information and keep our families safe. This intel has the power to take down our president and other governments around the world. We would be bringing a lot of very influential people down on us."

"People who shoot first and ask questions later," Travis says, twirling his bottle cap on the table. "It would make what happened to my daughter look like child's play in comparison."

"We couldn't use it directly, and we knew they would come

after us, so it's one of the main reasons we both got behind Atticus and his plan. I was happy to bankroll it from the shadows," Dad explains.

"We couldn't have our involvement public knowledge, so we did everything we could behind the scenes," Travis supplies, and it's making more sense now.

"Because if my dad succeeded, if *we* succeeded, we would bring the elite down, and the evidence would no longer matter. They wouldn't be coming after you if they were dead or locked up," Anderson surmises.

"Exactly, except it didn't go as planned." Dad wets his lips as he stares at me. "They made threats on your life and your mom's. It wasn't just Travis who was protecting his family. They were gunning for us too."

"Yet you chose not to share that with me." Derision drips from my tone. "How the hell is that protecting me?!" I am having a hard time holding on to my usual calm manner in the face of such outrageous naivety.

"You were playing your part, and it was your senior year of high school. You were Rydeville High's QB. Sue me if I wanted you to have some kind of normal life," he hisses.

I smother a laugh. Is he for real? There was nothing normal about my life senior year. There hasn't been since we got involved in all this elite shit.

"I ensured you were safe," he continues. "I used the same company Travis did, and you and your mom have had a security detail twenty-four-seven for years. Our men have thwarted several attempts on your life." Reaching across the table, he grabs my hand. "You are safe, son. If I thought you weren't, I would have told you." He exhales as if he's carrying the weight of the world on his shoulders.

"But they know you have this information, so how are any of us safe?" I frown, because this part doesn't add up. "Why aren't they coming after us? Surely, that's what this breach is about. They are looking for that evidence, and the stealing is a front to put us off the right track."

"We thought it was over after the Parkhurst arrests," Travis says.

"Until Mathers paid me a visit," Dad says.

Anderson and I exchange wary looks. I cannot believe we are only hearing this now. Jackson is going to be so pissed when he finds out his dad was holding this stuff back from him too.

"He had video footage showing you two and Jackson killing Montgomery," Dad confirms. "He made me a deal I couldn't turn down."

I hop up, connecting the dots. Horror washes over me. "No, Dad. Please tell me you did not trade evidence with that conniving bastard?"

"I had no choice, Sawyer!" Dad climbs to his feet. "You would've gone to jail!" He casts a brief glance at Anderson. "All of you would've gone down for it. I was damned if I did and damned if I didn't. Revealing the intel would have signed all our death warrants. Refusing to deal with Mathers would have sent you boys to prison. I didn't have a choice."

"So, what? You gave him your recording and he gave you his, and we're supposed to believe that's the only copy he has?" Anderson's jaw ticks with agitation.

"I'm not an idiot, Kaiden," Dad says, in a clipped tone. "I know who we are dealing with. Of course, I kept a copy, just like I know he did."

I pace the room, struggling to hold on to my self-control. "Dad, if that video surfaces, we will be lucky if we get life in prison."

"After the way Jackson butchered Montgomery, we'll all get the death penalty," Anderson says.

"Both of you, stop with the dramatics," Dad says. "There is no capital punishment in Massachusetts, New York, or Spain, which holds legal jurisdiction over the Canary Islands."

"So, life imprisonment without parole. Awesome." Sarcasm seeps from Kai's pores.

"It won't come to that because I dealt with it."

"You haven't dealt with it!" I snap. "Mathers may be dead,

but that evidence is out there somewhere. And if they kept a copy, they know you did too. Open your eyes, Dad! That is why they are sniffing around Techxet."

"We have to use it. It's the only way," Anderson says.

"No." Travis and my dad speak at the same time. "It's out of the question."

"As long as we have this evidence, they won't make a move on me. On us," Dad says. "They won't risk it."

"Like we can't risk making any moves on them," Travis says. "This agreement works because both parties have something significant to lose. We don't like this any more than you do, but it's the only way it has to be."

"Except they are breaking their end of the agreement," Anderson seethes, thumping his fist on the table. "How can this not be connected? This has got to be the elite trying to find your evidence. If they have that, then they hold all the cards."

"There is nothing to stop them turning us over to the authorities then," I say.

"Perhaps you are right. Maybe they are behind this, but they won't find that evidence within Techxet. We have covered all of our bases, and we have made contingency plans. We have several copies in secure locations with procedures in place that will be automatically enacted if anyone tries to retrieve it. These people are smart enough to know I wouldn't keep it within my company."

"I agree with that," I say, sinking into the seat beside my friend. "But that doesn't mean they aren't trying to bankrupt you and ruin you to serve the same end goal. That they won't try to do the same to all of us until we are forced into selling it to them."

"They have a point," Travis says to my dad. "It's not like we haven't considered this."

"And we discounted it because it was too risky." Dad swings his sober eyes on me. "We can't go after the elite, son. We stick to our original plan. If we keep investigating, we will find something. I know we will."

"And if we don't?" I ask.

"Then Techxet goes under." He clasps his hands together on the table.

"You are remarkably calm when discussing losing the company you have invested blood, sweat, and tears in."

"I am because this whole elite situation has taught me one valuable lesson. Nothing is more important than keeping my family safe. You and your mother are what matter."

"That's bullshit," Kai snaps. "Look at what you're forcing your son to do?! If you truly cared, you would find another way."

I say nothing because Anderson is right. How can he claim I'm so important, yet he has asked me to do this?

"It doesn't have to be forever," Dad says, looking a little sheepish as he peers into my eyes. "I know you understand why this needs to happen. I hate that I had to involve you, but desperate times call for desperate measures. We won't go down without a fight, but if it comes to it, we'll survive. As long as we have each other."

CHAPTER TWELVE

Sawyer

"Did you think your dad meant it?" Anderson asks six nights later as we wait in a trendy bar in New York for Charlie, Drew, and Rick to arrive. I'm getting married tomorrow, and the guys insisted we go out for drinks. Not to celebrate—to commiserate. The need for distraction is the only thing that made me agree.

"Which part?" I ask, knowing he's referencing the shocking conversation we had with the two dads last weekend.

"Where he said nothing matters but keeping you and your mom safe."

I shrug. "Your guess is as good as mine. Actions speak louder than words, and the years of neglect speak volumes." Anderson arches a brow. "What?" I ask.

"You rarely criticize your parents. Even when we were younger, you never bitched about them like Lauder and me did."

I shrug again. "I'm older and wiser now. And if it sounds like bullshit, it usually is." I swallow a healthy mouthful of beer, grateful for fake IDs and my name.

"I think the oldies are scared shitless. Do you think they told us the truth about the evidence they have?"

"Honestly? I don't know what the fuck to think anymore." I pick at the label on my beer bottle.

"Sup, assholes," Rick says, sliding onto the stool across from Kai and me.

"You're late. Again," Kai drawls before reaching across the table to hug his older brother. "It's good to see you, man."

"You look way too sober." Rick whistles to gain the attention of a passing waitress. He orders another round, adding two more beers as Charlie and Drew saunter over.

"This looks more like a funeral than a bachelor party," Charlie says, sliding onto a stool beside me.

"Being forced into marriage is hardly something to celebrate," I say before draining the last of my beer.

"I'm glad I dodged that bullet," Drew says as the waitress arrives with our order. We don't speak as she sets our drinks down, shooting fuck-me eyes at Kai.

"He's married, sweetheart, and hopelessly devoted to his wife," I say. "You're wasting your time."

Her gaze roams over me, and I almost laugh. "I'm getting married tomorrow, he's also engaged"—I point at Charlie—"but those two are single-ish," I add because I'm not one hundred percent sure.

"I'm not," Rick says, taking himself out of the running. "It's kind of back on with Rebecca. She's coming with me tomorrow."

The waitress grins flirtatiously at Drew as she pockets the hundred-dollar bill Rick just gave her.

"I'm not interested." Drew drills her with a look that warns her to try her luck elsewhere.

"The hot ones are always taken," she mutters under her breath, finally walking off. What a tool.

"What's up with you and Shandra?" I ask, swiping a fresh beer.

"Nothing is up with us."

"You sure about that?" Kai smirks. "I'd say there was definitely something up last weekend unless you were stuffing socks down your pants."

Drew flips him off. "I'm not discussing Shandra."

"What about Jane?" Charlie asks. "Have you heard from

her?"

Drew slams his bottle down on the table, glaring at Charlie. "I'm not discussing Jane either." He drains half his beer, looking like he's ready to punch something or someone.

I take pity on him because I can relate now. "Any update on the prison visit?"

"I'm working on it. By the time you return from your honeymoon, I'll have it lined up."

"I'm not going on a honeymoon, and I'm really hoping you can set up the meet for next week."

"I'm calling in a few favors, so it's not directly within my control. But I'll see if I can speed things up."

"Where's Sydney tonight?" Rick asks.

"I don't know. At her father's place, I guess."

Rick stares at me. "Do you not speak to her at all?"

"I speak to her if there is something we need to discuss. It's not like we're even friends."

"I'm starting to feel sorry for Sydney," Charlie says.

"Don't. She's in it for the money."

"Fuck, I think you're even colder than me." Drew's lips twitch. "I'd love to be a fly on the wall at your penthouse next week. Talk about Awkward City."

"Remind me why I invited you again?"

He flashes me a full-on grin. "Just keeping it real, dude. You might want to make a little bit more of an effort. She doesn't seem like a horrible person, and she's easy on the eyes. It could be a lot worse. You could've been saddled with someone like Alessandra Mathers. Man, she was a fucking bitch."

"She was a cunt," Anderson agrees. "All those Mathers women were."

"They still haven't declared Denton a missing person," Charlie says. "I wonder why that is."

"Obviously, it suits them for some reason," Rick guesses.

"Could they be involved?" I ponder out loud as the thought pops into my head.

"Honestly, I wouldn't rule anyone or anything out," Drew

says, and we all nod.

Silence descends for a few beats.

"It's quiet without Jackson," Anderson says. "He should be here."

"He was going to come back early, but I told him not to bother. It's not like this wedding is the real deal." My friends are all attending tomorrow, with the exception of Van and Jackson, but it's only for moral support.

"It's quiet without Daniels too," Drew adds because he likes to stir shit on occasion.

To think I just took pity on him. I feel an urge to punch him in the face. "Because inviting my ex—my very loved-up ex—would've been the cherry on top," I drawl, deciding I want to do shots. Curling my fingers at a passing waitress, I reel her in and order a round of tequila shots.

"He's not loved up," Anderson corrects after the waitress has left. "You know that's for your benefit."

Memories of Xavier with his tongue down Jamison's throat resurrect in my mind, and a sour taste floods my mouth. It's like he's been on a mission this week to ram his relationship in my face. I guess threatening to fire his lover really got him wound up. "You haven't seen them this week. They are all over one another. Xavier's not that good of an actor. Anyway, it doesn't matter. We're done. I'm over him."

Four pairs of eyeballs stare at me. "I am!" I growl, snatching a shot off the tray before the waitress has even had time to set it down.

OKAY, MAYBE I'M not, I think as I take the stairs to Xavier's apartment, two steps at a time. This seemed like a good idea when I was leaving the bar, but I'm more drunk than I realized, and this might not be the best plan. Oh well. I'm here now. Might as well say hi.

I almost stumble, clutching the banisters to stop myself from falling. Perhaps I should have waited for the elevator. Sydney and Mom would string me up if I showed up tomorrow with a broken limb. I imagine me rocking up in a wheelchair or on crutches, and I snort out a laugh as I make my way along the hallway.

It's late, but Xavier is a night owl, and he's usually up working or watching reality TV. I rap on his door, holding on to the door frame as the world spins a little. Woah. I'm definitely more drunk than I thought. No one answers, and I frown. Light spills out from under the door, so I know he's still up. I bang on the door. "Xavier. It's me. Open up!"

My cell vibrates in my pocket, and I pull it out, cursing when I drop it on the floor. I'm bending down to retrieve it with one hand on the door to steady myself when it swings open, and I topple sideways into the apartment. "Shit." I grab at my phone, seeing Sydney's blurry face swim before my eyes on the screen. Rejecting the call, I slide my phone back in my pocket and scramble awkwardly to my feet.

"You shouldn't be here," Xavier says, folding his arms across his naked chest.

My gaze is laser-focused as my eyes travel the length of his body. Rivulets of water roll down his impressive chest and abs, sneaking under the towel he has wrapped around his waist. Xavier runs his hands through his wet hair, pushing it back off his face.

"You should wear your hair like that more often. You look hot. Sexy." I have a feeling I'm slurring my words and swaying a little on my feet.

Xavier scrutinizes my face. "Fuck. You're smashed." Concern mixes with uncertainty on his face before he sighs. Taking a hold of my arm, he leads me into the apartment, shutting the door after me. "Sit." He pushes me down on the couch. "I'm going to get you some water and coffee, and then I'll call an Uber to take you home."

"I don't want to go home." Reaching out, I grab his hand. Familiar tingles shoot up my arm the instant our skin makes contact, reminding me our connection is still very much alive. "It's lonely there. I want to stay with you."

"Sawyer, you don't get to do this anymore. We're not together."

"I miss you, and I'm getting married tomorrow to someone who isn't you, and I just need to hold you one more time. Please, Xavier. I promise I won't touch your dick. Just let me sleep beside you one last time." I know I'm a rambling mess, but I'm too fucked up to care.

"You are fucking pathetic," Jamison says, coming up behind Xavier. He's also wearing a towel and dripping wet. His hands land on Xavier's waist, and I have never hated a person more than I hate that asshole in this moment. "To think I used to respect you."

I want to tell him he's a dick, but my vocal cords won't cooperate.

"Jamie, don't." Xavier turns around until they are chest to chest. "He's drunk. Just let me help to sober him up, and then I'll get him an Uber."

"He's not your responsibility anymore, baby." Jamison grabs Xavier's ass, pulling him in flush against his body as he grinds his hips against his. "And we were in the middle of something good."

"It can wait." Xavier pushes him away. "Please. Just go back in the bedroom, and stay there."

Jamison's nostrils flare as he glares at me. His features soften as he cups Xavier's cheek. "You're too forgiving, X. It's not always a good thing." Jamison eyeballs me before he lowers his mouth to Xavier's, claiming his lips.

Pain lashes me from all sides, and I think I might puke. What the hell was I thinking coming here? I know they are hot and heavy. I should've known his boyfriend would be here. So much for Anderson and "he's not all loved up."

Xavier doesn't prolong the kiss, much to Jamison's obvious disgust, but I know when I'm not wanted. "'Sokay. I'm leaving." I struggle to my feet, wishing I could click my fingers and be zapped out of here.

"Sawyer. Stay put. You need to sober up a little," Xavier says, concern reappearing on his gorgeous face as he moves in front of me.

"You're right," I say, barely able to look at him. "I shouldn't have come here. It won't happen again." Shoving past him, I rush out of his apartment, cursing my own stupidity and vowing to evict Xavier Daniels from my head once and for all.

CHAPTER THIRTEEN

Sawyer

I STARE OUT the window of the limousine as I twiddle the silver platinum band on my ring finger. It still feels surreal. All day, it felt like I was undergoing an out-of-body experience. But it is real. I'm married. Bound to the woman in the gorgeous white dress sitting at the opposite end of the seat, staring out her window as New York City flashes by en route to my penthouse.

Sydney's things were moved over earlier while we were giving the performance of our lives in the grand ballroom of the New York Majestic Hotel.

"What?" Sydney asks, and I snap out of my head. I didn't realize my gaze had shifted and I was staring at her.

"Nothing." Looking away, I return to staring out my window as her long sigh echoes in the space between us.

"Are you still hungover as fuck?"

I shake my head, grateful the incessant pounding in my skull and my constant dry mouth has finally passed. "I didn't realize I was that obvious." After Xavier dragged me back into his apartment last night, he practically threw coffee down my throat before forcing me to take a couple of pain pills. I guess I should thank him that I was actually able to get out of bed this morning.

"Don't worry, you pulled it off," Sydney says. "No one

looking at you could tell. It was your tequila breath that gave the game away."

We have been kissing up a storm all day, and I feel a little guilty. "You should've told me. I would've grabbed some mints or guzzled a few gallons of mouthwash."

"It's fine. It's all part of the role-playing, right?" Her features harden, and her hands clench at her sides. "It's not like my comfort, or anything to do with me, is anywhere near your priority list. I'm the dirt at the bottom of your shoe. You've made that abundantly clear."

"Wow. You're really entering into the spirit of it now. You've definitely got the nagging wife part down pat."

"Fuck you, Sawyer," she snaps before pressing her face to the window and ignoring me. The rest of the journey is filled with tense silence, and I wonder how on earth I'm going to handle two years of this. I pray we get a breakthrough soon. The quicker I can file for divorce, the better.

I step aside when the elevator opens, at the hallway of my penthouse apartment, to let my bride exit first. Sydney storms past me, her heels clicking on the porcelain floor as she strides toward the main living area. Removing my tie, I unbutton the top three buttons of my shirt, breathing more easily than I have all day.

Sydney is standing in the middle of my living room, drinking everything in. She still has the pretty flower garland in her hair, and I wonder what it was sprayed with to make it look so fresh.

"Can I get you anything to eat or drink?" I ask, shucking out of my suit jacket. I place it on the back of one of the kitchen stools as I walk toward the refrigerator.

"No, thank you," she clips out, and I can tell she's still in a pissy mood.

This doesn't bode well for our married life, no matter how short-lived it turns out to be.

I open the refrigerator and retrieve a bottle of water and a small bowl of salad Florentina must have left behind today. I arranged for my cleaner to show up after the movers had moved

Sydney in, because I wanted the place to be perfectly clean and tidy for my new wife.

Fuck. Those words sound so wrong coming from my mouth.

"You haven't even told me I look nice," Sydney says, spinning around and piercing me with her emerald-green eyes.

"What are you talking about?" I regard her coolly as I uncap the bottle. "I've been saying you look beautiful all day."

"To other people!" She throws her hands in the air. "You haven't said one genuine thing to me today."

"What the hell is this, Sydney? We get married and you turn into a nagging shrew? We had a deal. We both know where we stand."

"That has nothing to do with this and everything to do with being a decent human being!" She stalks toward me, her long wavy blonde hair bouncing on her shoulders with the movement. "I know what this is, Sawyer, but there is a certain level of common decency I expect. Would it have really killed you to tell me I looked nice?"

"You know you are completely overreacting, right?" I stare her down as I lift the bottle to my lips, drinking slowly as the ice-cold liquid glides down my parched throat.

"You know you are a complete prick, right?" Tears glisten in her eyes before she forces them away. "We are stuck with one another whether you like it or not. Treating me like I'm a pariah will not make this pleasant for either one of us."

"Quit with the fucking nagging, Sydney. I am not in the mood for this after one of the shittiest days of my life, so shut your mouth unless you've got something positive to say."

I don't see the slap coming until my cheek is stinging, and I drop the open bottle of water on the floor.

"I hate you." She rips the garland off her head, crushing the flowers between her fingers. Petals scatter on the floor. "I'm going to bed. Alone."

"Don't worry, sweetheart." I smirk. "The last place you'll ever find me is in your bed."

She stomps off in the direction of the only other hallway,

assuming correctly it's where the bedrooms are located.

"You're in the middle room on the right," I call out after her, working hard to keep the annoyance from my tone. Grabbing some paper towels from the kitchen, I clean up the mess on the floor. I snatch another bottle of water before turning off the lights. Taking my tie and jacket, I head to my bedroom, ready to bid this day adieu.

After a bristling hot shower, I change into light sleep pants and sit out on the balcony off my bedroom, guzzling water as I watch New York buzz and hum all around me. It's after midnight, but the city is still full of life. Unlike me. My heart is heavy as I contemplate what the future might bring.

A couple of hours later, I'm still awake, much to my consternation. I think I'm overtired and that's why my brain won't stop rehashing every mistake I've ever made with Xavier. I should have done everything differently. I should have made him a priority instead of hiding him, afraid what my parents would say.

After more tossing and turning in bed, I get up, heading into the kitchen to grab more water when the sound of crying tickles my eardrums. I slam to a halt outside Sydney's bedroom, listening to her sobbing with a lump in my throat.

Realization slaps me in the face with every fresh cry, and I feel like the world's biggest ass. I gave Anderson and Lauder shit for their cruel treatment of Abby and Vanessa at the start, and I'm acting no different. It doesn't matter they were falling for their women and that's the last thing that will happen to me. I'm not into Sydney, and there isn't any happily ever after in our future. But this isn't about that. It's about respect. About common decency, like she pointed out earlier.

I have taken all my anger and frustration and channeled it in Sydney's direction. Which is brutally unfair because it's not her fault. She has been trying to make the best of it, and I have been a complete prick. A shitty human. My friends would call me out on my behavior if they saw how I have treated my bride today.

I gently rap on the door. "Sydney. May I come in?"

SAWYER

The sobbing stops. "Go away, Sawyer."

"Please. Let me come in." When I get no reply, I take that as permission. Opening the door, I enter the dark room. The window is open, and the gossamer curtains are swaying in the light breeze. I hired an interior designer to remodel this room for Sydney. Something I didn't even tell her.

Boxes of her possessions are stacked up against the wall, and I maneuver my way past them. She is lying in the bed with her face buried in her pillow. The sheets are bunched at her waist, showcasing her slim form in a soft pink silk nightdress. Her hair hangs in tangled strands over her face, and I wonder if that's by design. If she's trying to hide her emotions from me. I wouldn't blame her if she was.

Without stopping to second-guess myself, I crawl onto the bed behind her, lying down on top of the sheets and wrapping my arm around her. She stiffens against me as I pull her closer.

"What are you doing?" She sniffles, lifting her head a little.

"Apologizing and comforting you."

Her body doesn't relax against me, but she says, "Go on. I'm listening."

"You are right. I'm being a horrible prick and a shitty human. I'm sorry." It takes a lot for me to say those words, but I know I'm in the wrong and there is no point in attempting a half-assed apology. "I've been taking all my frustration out on you when it's really directed at my parents and your father for forcing us to do this."

Her muscles loosen, and she turns around in my arms until she's on her back, looking up at me.

I brush knotty hair back off her face, ashamed to discover her red-rimmed eyes and splotchy cheeks. "I hurt you, and that is unforgivable. I'm sorry." I peer into her eyes hoping she can see how genuine I am. "For the record, you were stunning today, and I should have told you that the second your hand was placed in mine at the ceremony."

"Do you really mean that?" she asks, twisting on her side.

"I never say things I don't mean."

"I'd like us to be friends, Sawyer. I'm sharing your life whether you like it or not."

"I know, and I'd like to be friends too. I know this is as hard for you as it is for me. Actually, it's worse for you because you've been uprooted from your home." Even if it is more than time she left home. I can't think of anyone else I know, within wealthy circles, still living under Daddy's roof at twenty-four.

She shakes her head, inching a little closer to me. "I'm glad to be out of that prison. Living here is not unwelcome."

I arch a brow, opening my mouth to ask her exactly what she means, when she places her slim fingers against my lips. "I don't want to talk about my father right now." She bites down on her lower lip, and it's sexy. Her eyes lower to my chest, and I watch as her pupils dilate. Her chest heaves, drawing my gaze, and blood rushes to my cock when I notice her hard nipples poking through the flimsy silk material of her nightie. "I don't want to talk at all," she says in a breathy tone I feel all the way to my toes.

My dick hardens. From neglect or having her pressed so close to me, her arousal obvious in the extreme, I'm not sure. Maybe it's a combination of those things. "This could be a very bad idea," I say, nipping at her fingers as she attempts to withdraw them from my lips.

"Or a really good one." Her fingers are on the move, trailing along the smooth lines of my jaw and down the side of my neck. "You at least owe me a kiss. It might have been fake, but it was still my wedding day. I deserve one genuine kiss."

I think she deserves a lot more than that, but I have no clue what I'm doing, and I'm making no promises. All I know is she's turned on, I'm turned on, and I'm tired of feeling lonely and frustrated.

Xavier has moved on with his life. It's time I did too.

"Are you sure?" I ask, moving my hand around and up her body.

"I will take anything you're offering, Sawyer." She sucks in a gasp as my fingers brush the underside of her breast through her nightgown.

I thrust my erection at her as my fingers knead her breast through the silk. "It's just sex," I tell her because I can't offer her anything else. "Nothing more."

"I'm good with that," she says, palming my hard-on through my pants.

I hiss through my teeth, enjoying the feel of her small hand on my straining cock.

"Kiss me, Sawyer. Kiss me now, please."

"As you wish." Clasping the back of her head, I lower my mouth and claim her lips.

CHAPTER FOURTEEN

Sydney

"Someone looks happy," Cayenne says as I slip into the booth across from her in the little Italian place around the corner from my new home. "Did you find a new job?"

I shake my head, smiling as the waiter sets a menu and a glass of water down in front of me. "I've attended a few interviews, but so far, I've had no offers."

"You haven't been looking that long. Don't worry. I'm sure something will turn up soon." Removing the bottle of wine from the chilled bucket, she pours me a glass. "Do you even need to work now you have a rich husband?"

I haven't told her what Sawyer confided in me about the precarious position Techxet is in; if the stock market got wind of their financial difficulties, their share price would plummet, and the value of my father's investment would dwindle overnight. I'm not sure how wealthy Sawyer is in his own right, but he doesn't seem too concerned about his personal financial situation. The conversations we've had in the week since we got married have largely been focused on getting to know one another without prying too deeply.

"You know it won't last forever, and I want my independence," I explain. "Besides, what the hell would I do all day if I didn't work? Sawyer has a nice lady named Florentina who comes in twice a week to clean and do the ironing, so I've been twiddling my thumbs when I'm not job hunting. I would go fucking insane without something to distract me, even if it is a shitty low-paying admin job."

"I think you should change things up. You said yourself this is the perfect opportunity. I think you should ditch the admin work you hate and look for something you would actually enjoy. And you know what you would do all day if you didn't work." She drills me with a knowing look. "Don't tell me your new husband doesn't have room for a studio? I'm sure there is some idle space in that luxury penthouse apartment I haven't yet seen for an artist's studio."

"I haven't spoken to him about my art because what's the point? It's not like I can get anywhere in the art world with an NYU degree in languages."

"You won't know if you don't try."

It's not a bad suggestion, but I have long since given up on my dream, and I'm not sure I'm ready to open that box again. "I'll think about it." I reach over the table, squeezing her hand. "You're a great friend, Cay. I'll have you over one night for dinner. I promise. I'm just getting to know Sawyer now. I don't want to spring my friends on him this early into our marriage." Though, I am around a lot on my own at night as Sawyer works super hard and regularly works late nights.

"So, is Sawyer responsible for that smile on your face?" she inquires, waggling her brows.

The waiter returns then to take our orders, and I refrain from answering, quickly perusing the menu while Cayenne makes her choice.

After we have ordered, she pins me with one of her demanding looks. I can't keep the smile off my face. It's amazing how some good sex can completely alter my mood. "He is," I admit before sipping my wine.

"Oh my God. You did the deed." She squeals, and I almost choke on my wine.

SAWYER

"Say it a little louder for the people in the back." Sarcasm drips from my tone.

"Tell me everything! How was it? How big is his cock? How many orgasms did he give you?"

I bury my head in my hands because my bestie is so. Freaking. Loud. Cayenne giggles. "It's not funny," I tell her. "Keep your voice down. It's only a casual arrangement, and if someone records you mouthing off and puts it on social media, I can wave bye-bye to my orgasms."

"Sorry," she says, sounding in no way apologetic. "I'll be quieter. Just give me the goods."

"It was the night of our wedding," I admit. "And it was fucking incredible. His cock is huge, and he sure knows how to use it. He's a damn beast in the bedroom."

A throat clearing has me jerking my head up, and my cheeks heat as the waiter stands there, holding two plates, with an amused grin on his face.

"Newlyweds," Cayenne explains as I die of mortification.

"That's your fault," I hiss when he has left our food and departed. "I'm not discussing my sex life in public again."

"At least you have one now. This is great. I'm happy for you."

"Don't get carried away. He made it very clear that night and the following morning that it was a friends-with-benefits thing and nothing more."

"Who cares as long as you're getting all the O's."

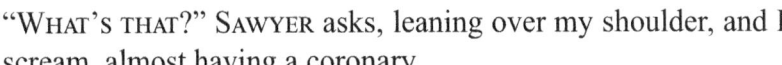

"What's that?" Sawyer asks, leaning over my shoulder, and I scream, almost having a coronary.

"How the hell did you come in without me hearing you?" I tilt my head back, looking at him.

"I'm stealthy." He smirks as he loosens his tie.

"I wasn't sure if you had dinner, so I brought some takeout home from the restaurant for you. It's on a plate in the microwave if you want to heat it up."

"Thanks, Syd. That was thoughtful."

I smile. "No problem." Things have been so much better since we cleared the air. I thought it might get awkward after we had sex, but it hasn't been. We are both on the same page, and while we haven't had sex since our wedding night, I'm hopeful it will happen again.

"You didn't answer my question." He points at my tablet. "What's up?"

"Oh, that. Nothing." I downplay it, placing my tablet down on the coffee table. "It's just me being silly."

"Uh-huh." He drills me with one of those intense looks of his. I stare back at him, squirming on the couch. "I'm going to get changed while you heat my dinner, and then we're talking about it."

"You are so goddamned bossy." I pout, unfurling my legs and standing.

"Never pretended otherwise." He flashes me a quick grin before walking toward his bedroom.

I set a place at the island unit for him while his food is reheating. He reappears a few minutes later in a plain white tee and gray sweatpants, just as the microwave pings. Sawyer Hunt can make anything look good, and I drool every morning when he's dressed in a suit, ready for work. But there is something downright sexy about casual Sawyer that really gets my juices flowing.

"You're ogling me like I'm man candy," he says, leaning over me to take the steaming plate from the microwave.

"You're a good-looking guy, and I'm a red-blooded woman. Can't blame me for looking."

"Thanks? I think," he says, placing the plate on the counter and sitting down.

"Want a glass of wine or a beer?" I ask as I remove the chilled Sancerre from the refrigerator.

"I'll take wine. Thanks."

I top up my own glass and fill a fresh one for him. I climb onto the stool beside him, watching him wolf down the pasta in record time. The silence isn't uncomfortable though.

"I'm starving," he says in between mouthfuls. "I haven't eaten anything since lunch."

"You work too hard." I take a sip of my wine.

"Why were you looking up art galleries?"

I shrug.

"Sydney." He eyeballs me. "I thought we agreed to be more open. Tell me what's going on?"

"It's something Cayenne said over dinner. She thinks I should pursue my art dream instead of looking for more admin work that I'm sure to hate and bound to get fired from."

"What art dream?" he asks before shoveling food in his mouth.

"I wanted to study art at NYU, but Daddy refused. He has never understood my love of painting, and he only indulged me growing up because I spent hours painting in our home studio and it kept me out of trouble." To a point.

"Let's park that for a second." He finishes his meal and wipes the corner of his mouth with a napkin. "I know you were kicked out of West Lorian High and you had to go to public school. And I know you got arrested for shoplifting a couple of times. What was up with that?"

A red layer flits over my eyes as rage and embarrassment do a number on me. "You dug into my background?" I yell, jumping up. "How could you do that?"

"You honestly have to ask?" He quirks a brow before softening his expression and his tone. "I wanted to know who I was marrying."

"And you couldn't have just asked me?" God, this man. He's insufferable. Just when I was starting to like him.

"Be truthful. Would you have told me if I had asked?"

"No." I don't hesitate to reply. "Of course, I wouldn't. I didn't want you to think badly of me."

"I don't think badly of you." He stands, taking his wine in one hand and my hand in the other. "Let's talk on the couch."

I let him lead me over to the couch and pull me down beside

him. He puts both our glasses down on the coffee table. "Look at me." He takes my chin when I don't obey. "Syd. I don't think badly of you. Everyone goes through shit when they're growing up. I was just curious, but you don't have to tell me. It's cool."

"I went through a bad time when my best friend moved overseas."

"You must have been very close. Are you still in contact with her?"

"We were. It was a he. And that would be a big fat nope. He ghosted me, and it hurt. I acted out. Got in trouble enough times at school they kicked me out. I think you can guess the rest." That's as much as I'm prepared to reveal. I don't like talking about that part of my past because it usually involves a mini breakdown of sorts. I have worked hard the past few years to blank it from my mind before I drove myself insane. Or murdered my father or Jared.

"I got kicked out of WLH for banging one of the teachers and her friend with Anderson and Lauder. My parents went apeshit," he explains, and my eyes pop wide.

"No fucking way? Which teacher?"

"You wouldn't know her. She was young, and it was only her first year teaching. I'm pretty sure we ruined her career. It was a shitty way to repay her for a fucking awesome night." He flashes me a wicked grin, and I test myself for jealousy, but there is none.

"Do Vanessa and Abby know that?"

"They do. My friends don't keep secrets from their wives. But back to the art dream," he says, bluntly switching the subject. "Tell me what you want."

He picks up our glasses, handing mine to me. I curl one knee up underneath me as I twist around so I'm facing him. "I would love to do something connected with art, but my options are limited without an art degree. I saw an opening for a receptionist at a small art gallery a few blocks from here, and I was considering applying."

"What's stopping you?"

"Fear and money, mainly."

"Money?"

I nod. "The pay is really low."

He curses under his breath. "Sydney, if you need money, I'll give you money. I didn't stop to think. Just message me your bank details, and I'll wire you some funds."

"I don't have a bank account."

He frowns. "What do you mean you don't have a bank account?"

I explain how my father keeps me on a tight leash, watching the skin on his face turn redder and redder the more I speak.

"He's a motherfucking asshole. I don't care what you did or didn't do. He has no right to treat you like that."

"I was pretty messed up on drugs for a while though I'm sure you already know that if you looked at my background." He nods. "I'm clean now. Have been for four years, but he doesn't trust me."

"That's some straight up controlling bullshit, and I'll fix that tomorrow. I'll call my friend Charlie Barron. He'll have an account and a bank card to you by the end of the day. And I'll transfer money to you. How much do you need?"

I'm assuming Charlie is the Barron in Barron Banking and Financial Investment Services. "I don't need any money. My father is still lodging my monthly allowance. I'm fine."

"How much, Sydney?" he growls, looking angry now for a different reason.

"I don't expect you to give me money, Sawyer."

"You're my wife, and I won't have you going without."

"In name only, and I don't want to be a burden. I know your family's financial situation isn't the greatest right now."

He chuckles before taking a healthy gulp of his wine. "Things aren't that dire. If you don't think my father has money stashed in secret personal offshore accounts, you're more naïve than I thought. As for me, my parents threw money at me instead of giving me their time. I've been investing in the stock market and trading on the foreign currency market since I was fifteen.

I'm independently wealthy. I own this place outright, and I have plenty of money in the bank. If Techxet goes under, I'll be fine."

"Why do this then? If your parents and you will be okay personally, why did you marry me?"

He sits up straighter. "My parents won't go broke, but they would lose a lot of the lifestyle they've grown accustomed to. They are more concerned with perception and appearance. The main reason they want to save the business is both of them are married to it. My dad built that company from the ground up, and he sacrificed a lot to do it. A normal marriage. A proper relationship with his son. Techxet is how my parents met."

"I didn't know that."

"Mom was Dad's secretary, and she was studying marketing at night. I'm not sure how they got together, but when they did, Dad promoted her to the marketing team and he covered her college fees and student loans. A year later, they were married and Mom was the VP of marketing. Now she runs the whole department."

"She must be good at her job."

"She is. They both are great at their jobs. Parenthood, not so much." He shrugs, and I want to ask him more, but he doesn't give me the opportunity. "Anyway, they love that company. Seeing it go under would kill them. As for me, I'm doing this because I'm an idiot who can't say no to his father and I feel a sense of responsibility for the employees. If Techxet goes under, thousands of people in hundreds of countries around the world will lose their jobs and suffer. If I can stop that from happening, then I owe it to those people to try."

"You're a good person, Sawyer."

His brow puckers. "I'm not so sure you'd say that if you knew some of the things I've done. Trust me when I say the jury is definitely out on that one."

CHAPTER FIFTEEN

Xavier

I STARE AT the pictures with my heart wedged at the back of my throat and acid churning in my gut. It doesn't matter that I know Sawyer is miserable behind the wide smile he's wearing. It still hurts seeing him posing with his bride on their wedding day. It's the main feature on the celebrity site today, and I swore I wasn't going to look, but I must be a glutton for punishment.

Tossing my tablet aside, I lean back on my couch, twisting my head so my face is pressed against the cushion. The scent is faint now, but I can still smell it. Still smell him as his spicy cologne lingers where he sat.

It hurt me to see him in that state. Sawyer is usually so in control. Getting drunk is not his thing. In our relationship, he was normally the one taking care of my drunk ass, not the other way around.

Forcing my feet to move, I head to my bedroom and pack an overnight bag. I'm glad I chose to head to Rydeville tonight, ahead of the meeting with my boss in the Boston office tomorrow.

I need me some Abby time.

I blast the music in my car as I set out on the three-and-a-half-hour journey, emptying my mind of all thoughts of Sawyer Hunt and his new wife, focusing instead on our lack of progress with the Techxet breach. Something is very wrong, and I have a feeling it's right under my nose and I'm missing it. I pride myself on being one of the best hackers of my generation, and the fact I haven't been able to find even the tiniest trace of this person makes me feel like a complete failure at a time when I'm already feeling low.

I need to find this person. Not just to sate my ego. I want to put an end to this person so I can quit my job and start properly putting Hunt behind me. As long as I'm working for his father's company, I will never be able to fully move on. As long as I'm forced to work closely by Sawyer's side, I will never be able to forget the devastating hole in my heart, and my life, caused by his absence. I know he goes back to school in five weeks, but it's five weeks too long for me. Every day shaves another layer off my fragile sanity. Jamison helps to distract me. But that's all he is right now, and I doubt he'll ever be anything more.

I pull up in front of the ballet studio a little early. Locking my car, I head into the building, hoping to catch the end of Abby's rehearsal. I know she's been busy practicing like crazy ahead of the two-week performance run, which commences next week. Finding Anderson in the back row, I slip in beside him, plonking my sorry ass down on the chair next to him.

"You're early," he says, talking in a low voice, his eyes glued to his wife on the stage.

"I know. Shocker."

He rolls his eyes.

"Who's the guy?" I ask, watching some tall lanky dude in spandex lifting Abby into the air.

"Some dweeb who goes to our school. He's a senior. Has a steady girlfriend. No arrests or priors."

I gawk at him. "Dude, you have serious problems. Even more serious than I realized."

He flips me the bird. "You think I'm going to let some degenerate put his hands on my wife without checking him out? Come on, man. You know what the elite are capable of. No one is getting near my woman without a rigorous background check."

"Dude. Look at the guy." I wave my finger in the air. "He's wearing spandex for fuck's sake. One look and I know he's harmless."

"I've seen you wear spandex, and other questionable attire, and you're far from harmless."

"I can't work out if you've just insulted me or complimented me."

Anderson grins, raising his clenched fist for a knuckle touch. "It's good to see you, Daniels. We've missed you. Abby was grinning like a loon after you called her to say you were visiting."

"I still say we should have tried the three thing."

"What three thing?" He frowns.

"You, me, and darling Abigail. It could've worked."

He sits up straighter, glaring at me. "Dude, I don't even have words for that." He shakes his head, looking a little pale in the face. "You need to start fucking Hunt again."

I bark out a laugh. "Hunt is married, in case you missed that memo."

"I was there. I am well aware, but it means jack shit to him. You know that."

"I know he had a whopper hickey on his neck last Monday morning. Unless he went trawling for pussy or dick just after getting hitched, he's banging his pretty blonde wife. Which definitely means something to him."

Shock splays across Anderson's face. "No way? Are you for real now?"

"You think I'd make up shit about Hunt with a hickey? Have you any idea how traumatized and heartbroken I've been all week?"

"Why?" Abby says, materializing at the end of the row, as if she's just magically poofed herself there. "What's happened?"

"Hey, baby girl. Come and give Daddy a hug." I open my arms and smile at my bestie.

"You are so fucking weird," Anderson says, as if I haven't heard that before.

I grab his wife into my arms before he turns all caveman

on me. "Missed you," Abby says, squeezing me tight. "Let me get changed, and I'll meet you guys out front." She eases out of my embrace, looking over my shoulder. "Did you make a reservation?"

"I did." Anderson shoves me out of the way to get to his wife. "I booked that seafood place you like." He rubs himself up against her. "Why have you never worn this in the bedroom?" he murmurs, grabbing her ass. "It gets me so hot."

"Hello! I'm standing right here, and I can hear you."

"Ignore him. He's annoying," Anderson says, leaning down to kiss his wife.

"You're both annoying," she says, pushing him back and withholding her kiss. "But I love you. Go wait outside before you scandalize Madam."

We do as we're told, shuffling outside like scolded little boys.

"OKAY. I WANT all the deets," Abby says after we have ordered in the gorgeous oceanside restaurant that's Abby's favorite.

"Deets on what?"

"What you two were talking about at the studio."

"Apparently, Hunt's screwing Sydney," Anderson says, and I wince.

"A little discretion, please, or did you forget the part where I'm traumatized and heartbroken."

Anderson looks pensive as he chews on a breadstick. "Are you really though? I don't see you pining. You're with Jamison now, and according to Hunt, you've been shoving his face in it any chance you get."

"He said that?"

Anderson nods.

"Good." Sue me if I'm feeling spiteful and glad my new relationship is getting to him as much as his is to me.

"Level with me," Abby says, sipping from her soda. "What is the deal with you and Jamison? Are you just using him to get back at Hunt or do you genuinely like the guy?"

I take a mouthful of beer to calm myself before I reply. "Darling," I say, looking her directly in the eye. "Do you know me at all?"

"I'm worried," she says. "I know you're hurting, and I know you'd never intentionally use someone. I know that's not your MO."

"But it doesn't mean that's not what you're doing," Anderson says, arching a brow as he drinks from his beer.

"I like Jamison," I protest. "He's sweet and sexy, and he goes with the flow. He is drama-free, and there are no complications. I know where I stand with him, and he's not trying to hide me away and pretend like he doesn't have feelings for me."

"That right there." Abby pokes her breadstick in my direction. "That's what I'm talking about. You're still hurting, and you haven't gotten Sawyer out of your system."

"You don't get over someone you love just like that." I click my fingers. "But I'm trying to move on. To put him behind me."

"Are you sure that's the right thing to do?" Concern is etched upon her pretty face. "I love you guys, and you're both in pain. I hate seeing that."

"He never prioritized me, Abby. We have talked about this, and I really don't want to talk about it again."

"I'm concerned you're settling."

"I'm not settling. I'm back in the dating game after having my heart broken. So what if Jamison isn't the love of my life? He makes me feel good about myself, and I need that right now."

Abby opens and closes her mouth.

"What? Don't hold back now, darling." There's a hint of snideness in my tone because I didn't come here expecting this shit.

She gets up, coming over to my side, draping her arms around me. "Let me make one thing clear, Xavier. I'm Team Xavier for life." She squeezes me tight, kissing the top of my head. "I love you, and I want you to be happy."

Anderson makes a grunting sound. "Where's my hug?" He

pouts, and he looks ridiculous. He is so possessive of her, but I can't ever find it in me to criticize the guy because the way he loves my bestie is a thing of beauty. I am under no doubt Kaiden would take a bullet for his wife. There is nothing he wouldn't do to protect her, and there is nothing hotter or more adorable.

Abby gives me one final hug before reclaiming her seat. She rolls her eyes at her husband before kissing him quickly on the lips. "You're extra needy tonight."

"I'm always needy when it comes to you." His gaze is worshipful as he stares at her, and they share a long, lingering look, like they so often do, and a pang of envy blooms in my chest. Which I hate. Because I'm happy for them. I truly am. But it reminds me of how Sawyer made me feel, and his loss is as raw as the day it happened.

"Ahem." I clear my throat to remind them I'm here. "I'm still here. In case you thought the Tardis appeared to whisk me away."

"We should be so lucky," Anderson mumbles, reluctantly breaking his eye-lock with his wife.

I flip him the bird, uncaring we're in public.

"Sorry," Abby says, looking all flushed. "I don't do it on purpose. When he looks at me like that, I get lost in our own little bubble."

Anderson slides his arm around her shoulders, pulling her in close. He presses a fierce kiss to her temple. "I love the fuck out of you Abigail Anderson."

"Ditto, babe." She pecks his lips softly. "I love you so much."

They wrap their arms around one another, and the biggest smile coasts over my mouth. "I love the way you guys love one another. That's what I aspire to."

"You will find that, Xavier. You're too amazing not to find it," Abby says, shucking out of her husband's embrace and reaching across the table to squeeze my hand.

"You're probably biased, but I'll take the compliments where I can get them."

"I'm sorry," Abby says, squeezing my hand one more time

before letting it go. "We didn't ask you to dinner to give you the third degree on your love life. I just don't want to see you getting hurt again."

"Don't worry. It's not like that with Jamison. It's casual and fun."

Footsteps thump in our direction, and we swivel our heads as one.

"What are you doing here?" Abby asks as Drew approaches our table.

"Scoot over," he tells me, and I move into the empty seat by the wall.

"Thanks for the invite, by the way." He levels Anderson with a cutting look.

"We thought you were catching a movie with Shandra tonight," Abby says, looking perplexed.

"Change of plans," Drew says in a clipped tone.

"Andrew." Abby gives her brother some serious stink eye. "If you stood my friend up, I will throw you out that window. I'm not joking."

"If you must know, she stood *me* up." Lifting his hand, he calls the waiter over, ordering the surf and turf, like Kai, and telling him to ensure it comes out the same time as our entrées.

These Rydeville heirs are such bossy pricks. Sawyer is too, but it's one of the things I love most about him.

"No way." Abby shakes her head. "Shandra wouldn't do that."

"She did, and I don't want to talk about it." Drew swipes my beer, draining the rest of it. His lips twitch as I glare at him. "Now, now. Don't be like that. I'm doing you a favor. You can't drink any more. You need to hightail it back to New York."

"Why?"

"My contact finally came through. You and Hunt are paying a visit to the Otisville Correctional Facility in the morning." He slaps a folded piece of paper at my chest. "Don't be fucking late."

CHAPTER SIXTEEN

Sawyer

I STIFLE A yawn as I step out of my bedroom, carrying my shoes along the hallway, trying to be quiet so I don't disturb Sydney. It's still early, and she won't be up for a while yet. I'm meeting Lauder for breakfast before I collect Xavier from his apartment. We are driving together to Otisville to visit Roland Murtagh at the correctional facility, which should be fun.

Jackson is waiting for me outside my building, and we hug briefly, slapping each other on the back. "How was Italy?" I ask as we set off on foot in the direction of our favorite breakfast place.

"Amazing. The weather was fantastic, as was the food and the beaches, and the people were very friendly. I didn't want to come back."

"I'm surprised you ventured outside of your hotel room," I tease, removing my jacket and draping it over my arm.

"We still found plenty of time for sex." He waggles his brows. "But my wife had a list of things she wanted to do and places she wanted to see, and I ensured she got to do all of them." He smiles, and it's good to see him looking so carefree. Lauder was troubled for so long, and Vanessa helped to bring him back to life.

I see how much my two best friends have changed since falling in love, and I crave that as much as it terrifies me. "I'm glad you had a good time."

"What did I miss while we were gone?" he asks, and I bring him up to speed, finishing just as we reach the café.

We are shown to our usual table in the back by the window. The waitress runs off to place our regular orders, and we settle into our seats, drinking freshly squeezed orange juice as I contemplate the prison visit. A yawn slips out of my mouth, and I place my hand over my lips.

"Is your new bride keeping you up at night?" Lauder asks, drumming his fingers on the table.

"Why would you ask me that?"

"I heard a rumor." He props his elbows on the table. "Are you fucking Sydney now?"

"Where the hell did you hear that?"

"Anderson. And he got it from Daniels."

"You lot gossip like a bunch of pussies, and how did Xavier know?" I shift uncomfortably on my chair.

"He saw you had a hickey and put two and two together." Jackson runs a hand through his blond hair. "Unless he was wrong?"

"I made a mistake," I admit. "She was crying, and I felt like shit because it was my fault."

"Ah, I see. It was a pity fuck."

The waitress's brows climb to her hairline, but she says nothing as she sets coffee and silverware down on the table before leaving.

"It wasn't. It was a spur-of-the-moment thing." I rub the back of my neck, wondering if I really want to have this conversation, but it feels like I'll burst if I don't talk to someone. And I know Lauder won't judge. I tell him about showing up drunk at Xavier's apartment and Jamison being there.

"I knew I didn't like that nerd for a reason." Jackson narrows his eyes. "You should fire him for insubordination. He can't speak to you like that. You're essentially his boss."

"I'm not really, but I could get him fired. If I want to lose Xavier forever."

"I know we don't talk about feelings a lot, but you can talk to me, Hunt. I won't tell a soul. Well, except Nessa. But she loves you, and you can trust both of us to keep your confidence."

"I have made such a mess of everything, Jackson. I should've had the balls to tell my parents about Xavier when I realized I was serious about him. But I was too afraid, and I hurt him. Now, it feels like I have betrayed him again by fucking Sydney, which is crazy because he's been fucking Jamison for weeks—and it seemed easy for him to move on. Meanwhile, I'm over here beating myself up and unable to sleep, thanks to an overwhelming sense of guilt, because I slept with my wife the night of our wedding."

I clam up as the waitress delivers our breakfasts, waiting for her to leave before speaking again. "I miss him so much." My heart slams against my rib cage as a tight pain spreads across my chest. "Even though I see him most days at work. It's torture working beside him and Jamison knowing I lost the best thing to ever happen to me and I have no one to blame but myself."

"Look at me and Nessa. I fucked up spectacularly, but I got her back, and you'll get Xavier back. The best thing you can do right now is find out who is responsible for the breach and plug that hole. Then you can start rebuilding your life and repairing the damage done to your relationship."

I'm not feeling as confident as Lauder, but I haven't given up all hope. I was wrong before. All isn't lost, provided I don't take any more missteps. And getting to the bottom of the Techxet riddle is the priority because nothing will change unless we find the culprit and reclaim the stolen money. "I have a good feeling about today," I tell him. "It feels like it might be a turning point, and I hope I'm right, because the longer I stay married, the less chance there is of me winning Xavier back."

"So, how is married life treating you? How is Sydney?" Xavier asks after a deathly quiet half hour in the car.

I've spent the entire time navigating early morning traffic in the city, not knowing how to break the silence. Now we're cruising on the Palisades Parkway for the next couple of hours until we hit Otisville. It's pretty much a straight run all the way from here.

Gripping the wheel tighter, I cast a quick glance in his direction. "We're really doing this?"

"What?" He feigns innocence, kicking off his sneakers and lifting his feet onto the dash. "I can't ask my colleague how his sexy new bride is?" It could be my imagination, but his face turns a little green as he says that.

"I fucked her one time, and it was a mistake," I admit. "It won't be happening again." Something I had planned to make clear with Sydney last night when I returned from the office, but she was already in her bedroom. "I don't think you can say the same," I add, narrowing my eyes at his feet. He is wearing two different ankle socks, and the sight brings a pang to my chest. Xavier and his zany sense of style was always one of the things I loved about him. Didn't stop me giving him shit for it though.

"What have *I* got to do with this? I'm not the one who cheated, and I'm in a committed relationship. I'm not the one saying my marriage is fake and then fucking my bride on our wedding night. Unless you're trying to say that was fake too?"

I level him with a dark look. "How the hell do you fake fuck someone? Please tell me as I'd love to know how that works."

"You're splitting hairs, Hunt. You know what I mean."

"I just told you it was a mistake! What more do you want me to say?"

"I don't care. Fuck her or don't fuck her. It's none of my business."

"Then why the fuck did you ask?" I shout.

"I'm just trying to make polite conversation," he retorts.

"By asking me if I'm fucking my wife? You are so exasperating. And get your damned feet down off my dash!"

He smirks. "Was wondering how long it would take you. You lasted five minutes. I might be impressed if you weren't such an asshole."

"Because I'm trying to help my dad and keep everyone in their jobs? Including your boyfriend, I might add."

"Oh, please. Don't try to pretend like you're doing me any favors. I have always been at the very bottom of your priority list."

I take a few seconds to calm down before I reply. "That is not true, and you know it."

"Then why, Hunt? Huh?" He swivels on the seat, the leather squelching with the motion. "Why did you keep me a secret if it wasn't because you were ashamed of me?"

Tears glisten in his eyes, and I'm horrified. He thinks I was ashamed of him? God, I have really fucked up. "Xavier. I was never ashamed of you. Never." I hate that I'm driving on a highway because he needs to understand it was never about that. As luck would have it, I spot a rest area just up ahead. "I want to stop. We need to talk about this."

He doesn't object, so I take that as a yes. Maneuvering into the right-hand lane, I pull off the highway and drive into a vacant spot in the mostly empty parking lot of the gas station and restaurant. I kill the engine and unbuckle my seat belt, turning to face him so I'm giving him my undivided attention.

"Xavier. I was never ashamed of you. I could never be. You are the most brilliant, creative, compassionate, witty man I have ever met. I was proud to be with you, and I'm sorry if you ever felt differently."

His gorgeous sage-green eyes drill into me as he tugs on his lip ring in an obvious nervous tell.

"You drive me fucking insane, but I wouldn't have it any other way," I continue. "I love your heart, your intelligence, your humor. Life was never dull with you around, and your presence is the very definition of larger than life. You filled up my world, Bright One, and now it feels so empty without you in it."

"Pretty words, Hunt. You have lots of them. But you still

haven't answered my question."

My Adam's apple bobs in my throat as I prepare to give him some of my truths. "You have met my parents, and I'm sure you've formed your own opinions. Appearances matter hugely to them. When I told them I was bi, my father said he'd tolerate it provided I was discreet and I understood when the time came I would marry a woman. Someone well connected within our social circles."

"And you let him get away with that?" Disbelief radiates from his every pore.

"You don't understand, I—"

"I understand it more than you realize."

"What does that mean?"

A muscle clenches in his jaw. "My parents are middle class, but it seems they share some of the same values as your parents. Mom is a nurse. Dad is an accountant. I was an oops baby. Mom had me when she was forty-two, and I don't think they ever knew what to do with me. My brother and sister were seventeen and eighteen when I was born, so I never really knew them. Not like most people know their siblings. My father was disgusted when I told them I was gay, when I was thirteen, and yeah, it was pretty much downhill from there." He sighs, looking out the window.

Reaching out, I take his hand, pleased when he doesn't automatically pull away. "I'm sorry. How come I didn't know this?"

He grunts, removing his hand, and it hurts. "Because we didn't open up to one another, Hunt. We bickered, we worked, and we fucked. But we never shared emotional truths because, anytime I tried, you clammed up tighter than a nun's vajayjay."

"They have never loved me," I blurt, and it hurts to say those words. "Not in the way a parent is supposed to love their kid, and I tried so hard to get them to love me." I swallow over the messy ball of emotion in my throat. "I had two choices, as I saw it. I could rebel and act out and try to get their attention that way. But I figured that would just anger them more. If they got pulled away from work to deal with my shit, it would piss them off. So, I chose the other option. I have tried to do what they wanted me to do, even if I don't agree with it. I bite my tongue and do their bidding, hoping one day I will make them proud and they will love me."

"Sawyer." His features soften, and he leans in closer.

Unable to resist any longer, I thread my fingers through his messy hair. "I love your hair like this."

"Don't do this. Don't shut down after opening your heart."

Removing my hands, I swipe at an errant tear rolling out of one eye, horrified to discover it. "I was wrong," I tell him, peering deep into his eyes. "I should've told them how much you mean to me. I should have told my dad no when he said I had to take Sydney on a date. I should have done so many things differently."

"You should have," he agrees. "And I know you have tons of inner strength. The Sawyer Hunt I know bows down to no one. He walks to his own beat. I had no idea you were letting your parents do this because you gave me no indication. I thought they were decent people, but they are fucking assholes. How could they treat you like that?"

"They don't see anything wrong with their behavior. There are a lot of parents in our social circle who are the same. Plenty who don't have the excuses of work and career when they hand their kids to nannies to raise them."

"Thank you for telling me. I wish you had told me sooner. I have some experience in telling parents to go fuck themselves. Experience that might have helped, but you didn't confide in me, and that hurts, Hunt."

We're back to Hunt, and I know what that means. He only calls me Hunt when he's keeping me at arm's length. I straighten up and stuff my emotions back down deep inside. For a few precious minutes, I thought I had a chance. That there was some way of salvaging things, but he's preparing to let me down.

"I wish I had, but it's too late now, right?" I say, getting in there first.

"You're married." He tugs on his lip ring, and my eyes lower to his mouth.

I miss kissing him. He always kissed me with so much passion, and I didn't properly appreciate it. I'm ashamed that I took him for granted. That I made him feel like he wasn't important to me.

"And you had sex with her. Next you'll be telling me she's pregnant with your kid."

"How stupid do you think I am? I used protection. And I'm never having kids," I blurt.

"Wow. Really?"

I nod, not supplying an addendum. If I was with Xavier, and he wanted kids, I'd be willing to try with him. I don't say it though. What's the point when we're no longer together and it's clear he has already drawn a firm line under our relationship. I thought there was hope, but there is none. Pain stabs me in the heart, like a multitude of tiny needles are being slowly pushed into the organ.

"I think I have learned more about you today than a year of dating," he says, and that annoys me.

He's making out like we never confided things in one another, when it's not true. I told him stuff I haven't told anyone else. Okay, I never fully allowed myself to be vulnerable, but to insinuate he knew nothing about me is fucking crap. "That's bullshit, and you know it."

"Is it?" His tongue darts out, wetting his lips. "We didn't have meaningful conversations unless it was about work or elite shit or our friends. We never talked about us."

"That's not true. I think your memory is selective, and there were two of us in the relationship, yet I'm the one being blamed. You told me nothing about your family either. If you wanted me to open up, why didn't you ask me stuff?"

He shakes his head, looking torn between anger and sadness. "No one should be forced or coaxed into opening their heart. It's what happens when a couple is in love. They want to share every part of themselves with their partner. Even the scary parts."

"So why didn't you?"

"I don't know." He tugs his lip ring between his teeth. "Maybe you're right. It wasn't just you. Maybe our relationship was completely different from the vision I had in my head. Maybe we just weren't right for one another."

"Wow. Way to shit all over every good memory I have of us."

"The truth hurts, Hunt. You should try to make things work with Sydney, because there is no future for us."

And he drives the final nail in the coffin. I'm an idiot for continuing to hope. My head and my heart hurt, and I can't do this. "I'm not doing this with you now. We shouldn't even be talking about it."

"No, we shouldn't." He looks at the clock on the dash. "We need to get back on the road. Drew will bust our balls if we're late."

I turn the key and start the engine. "Let's just keep all conversation strictly professional and leave our personal lives out of it from now on," I suggest, driving back out onto the highway.

"I agree." He folds his arms and purses his lips, staring straight out the window, and we don't talk for the rest of the journey.

CHAPTER SEVENTEEN

Sawyer

"Wait here. The prisoner will be brought to you shortly," the portly prison guard says, ushering us into a small square room. Xavier and I claim the seats in front of a small table, waiting for Techxet's disgraced ex-CFO to be delivered.

"The camera just died," Xavier says, his eyes flicking to the wall-mounted device in the corner of the room.

"Drew said he'd arrange that," I explain, glad he came through for us.

"I'm going to check for bugs or other listening devices." He removes one of the latest Techxet security gadgets from a hidden panel in the side of his bag. I extract the paperwork from my messenger bag as Xavier scans the room.

"It's clean," he confirms. "We have privacy."

"Good." I smooth a hand down the front of my suit jacket and wet my lips.

"Drew seems to have some powerful contacts." Xavier drops back into the seat alongside me.

"He's elite. Are you really surprised?"

He rummages in his bag. "He's acting more cagey than usual."

"He's always kept his cards close to his chest," I say, holding my hand out. He drops two small silver chips in my palm.

"Like someone else I know." Xavier lifts a brow as he stares at me while I press the egg-shaped chip into my ear and the circular one just under the collar of my shirt, out of sight. I don't dignify that with a response because I don't want to start arguing with him just before Murtagh arrives. I press in on the circular chip, and it's warm against my skin as the recording-slash-listening device powers on. Xavier does the same.

These new Techxet devices, part of the security products Dad developed, that will be sold on the market next year, have come in handy in recent times. Our friends aren't listening in, because they are outside the range, but this entire conversation will be recorded and stored in the cloud.

"Let me take point, and follow my lead," I caution him, just before the door is opened and the prisoner is led into the room.

I have seen pictures of the man, and he has aged considerably in the years since his confinement. His hair is now fully gray, cropped tight to his head. He's sporting at least a few days' growth on his chin and cheeks, and the lines around his mouth and his eyes are more pronounced. He says nothing, watching us with wary eyes, as the guard removes his handcuffs and pushes him down into the chair across from us. "Don't cause any trouble," the guard warns before tipping his head at me and leaving the room.

"If it isn't the prodigal son in the flesh," he sneers, leaning back in his chair and crossing his arms. "What do you want, kid?"

"Answers," I say, "and you're going to give them to me."

His gruff chuckle bounces off the dull blue walls. "I ain't telling you shit, boy."

"I think this will change your mind." I slide the paperwork across the table to him.

His eyes dart between me and Xavier, and I know he's dying to ask who he is. "What is this?"

"Proof I paid off the arrears and cleared the mortgage fully on your family's home."

His eyes race across the page as he reads the statements.

Xavier retrieves the hidden cell phone from his bag, preparing the recording.

"How do I know this isn't falsified," he says, proving he's not as dumb as he appears to be.

"We figured you wouldn't believe us, so I paid your wife and kids a visit." I nod at Xavier.

Xavier plays the message his wife recorded, holding out the phone to him.

Tears well in his eyes, and he gulps as he listens to her happy voice confirm they are no longer being evicted.

Xavier takes the cell back as I slide the second set of paperwork across the desk. "Sign that and I will deposit half a million dollars into your wife's bank account by the close of business today. I know your eldest son is graduating next year, and this will ensure he gets to go to NYU."

"What do you want from me?"

"I already told you. Answers."

"Why do you need me to sign?"

"Because we're recording this," Xavier says, "and you'll agree to testify against the elite if it comes down to it." He throws out the first bait.

Roland shifts uncomfortably on his seat. "You don't want to mess with these people. I did and look where it got me."

There's the first confirmation we need. "We know how to handle the elite," I supply. "You just worry about yourself."

"If I talk, they'll come after me."

"We'll ensure you have protection," I coolly lie.

"How?"

"How do you think we are sitting here today?" Xavier says, because he just can't keep quiet, even though I asked him to let me lead. "In a room with no guard and the camera switched off?"

Roland shifts on his chair, inspecting the camera, before he turns back around. He scratches the scruff on his chin. "People have been murdered in here. I don't know."

I shield none of my disgust when I look at him. "This is for your family. The family you basically abandoned when you chose to defraud my father's company. You should be spilling your guts already, not worrying about your pathetic ass. Or don't you care about your kids?"

"Of course, I do. I love my family."

"Then prove it," I snap, pushing the contract at him again.

He bobs his head. "You're right. And you're going to protect me." His hand shakes as he scribbles his signature on the dotted line.

I take the document, setting it down on top of the other paperwork.

"What do you want to know?"

Xavier presses the record button on the cell, but it's purely for show. I clear my throat. "Why did you steal from Techxet, and who was really behind it?" I ask.

"I'd been stealing small sums for years. Completely undetected because I knew how to cover my tracks. I had a gambling problem, you see. Every time I ran into trouble, I dipped into Techxet's funds."

He doesn't even look apologetic, but I keep a neutral mask planted on my face, urging him to continue.

"I was waiting for my kid to finish football practice one evening when this guy accosted me in the parking lot of the school. Said he knew what I'd been doing. Showed me paperwork that could send me to jail. He gave me a burner cell and told me to wait for instructions. A few days later, he sent me coordinates to a meeting location and told me to come alone."

"Who was it?" Xavier asks.

Murtagh scratches the back of his head, looking anxiously around. "Mathers. His name was Denton Mathers."

Can't say I'm hugely shocked. "Go on."

"I nearly died when I showed up to find Vincent Becker there."

"Techxet's chief technology officer at the time," Xavier confirms.

"Yes. We knew each other, of course. He was just as shocked to see me there."

"What did Mathers have on Becker?" I inquire.

"I don't know. He made it clear he had eyes on both of us and that we weren't to discuss our individual circumstances. I have no clue what he had on Becker. Frankly, the guy was straight as an arrow. I can't imagine he did anything illegal, but he was holding something over his head. He gave each of us a sealed envelope and told us he would use the contents if we talked to anyone or didn't do as he asked." Sweat beads on his brow. "He had his men hold guns to our heads the entire meeting. I was sufficiently scared."

"What did he ask you to do?"

"He wanted us to work together to find some evidence your father had on the elite. He didn't say what. Becker gave him access to the Techxet system when his searching came up empty-handed. Becker came to see me a few nights later. He wasn't in a good place. He said he couldn't do it anymore. That the guilt was crippling him. He was going to fess up. I tried to talk him out of it, but he seemed determined." He shakes his head. "A few hours later, Becker, his wife, and his daughter died in a car crash. I was fucking terrified, because I knew it was no accident."

He blows air out of his mouth, and he drums his fingers on the table. "Denton hauled me in shortly after that. He confirmed he had taken Becker out. Said me and my family would be next if I even attempted to open my mouth."

"So, you kept quiet, and then what happened?" I coax.

"I gave him copies of the bank statements every month, and I knew his team was in the system, looking around, but nothing happened for almost a year. I kind of hoped they had found what they wanted or given up. But then your father and his lawyers called me into a meeting. They told me serious fraud had been committed, and they wanted to know how it had happened and I hadn't noticed anything was amiss. I was shitting bricks. I swear I had no idea Mathers was going to steal all that money."

I doubt it would have made a difference if he did.

"I was suspended while an investigation was being carried out. I knew shit was about to hit the fan, so I tried to run." He swipes at his sweaty brow. "I was an idiot to think he'd ever let me get away."

Xavier and I exchange wary expressions. "What happened next?"

"Mathers caught up to me less than twenty-four hours later. I was taken to some underground basement and interrogated. He told me I would take the fall for the missing money and I would tell them Becker had been involved too. Mention how unhinged he was. Insinuate the accident was more like suicide."

"And he used your family to force you to cooperate," I guess.

He nods. "He told me as long as I kept my mouth shut, he would look after my family, and he did."

"Until he died," Xavier says.

He sits up straighter. "You know about that?"

"Like I said, we know about the elite." I fucking knew the elite were involved. I knew my gut instinct was correct and we've been going about our investigation all wrong.

"Why didn't you come forward if you know he's dead?" Xavier asks.

"That fucker wasn't working alone. I knew he had a team. Word was sent through to me to keep my mouth shut or they'd murder my family. They stopped putting the monthly deposit into my wife's bank account. Motherfucking assholes." His nostrils flare. He's obviously never heard there is no honor among thieves. "But I was too scared to say anything."

What a dumb fuck. He deserves to die for his stupidity, and I have no qualms about lying to him on the protection front. As soon as we walk out of here, dude is on his own.

"Has anyone named Hamilton ever paid you a visit?" I ask.

He shakes his head. "The only one I ever saw or spoke to was Mathers. I don't know who the others are."

"If I find out you're lying, I will retract my protection and let the elite hounds go at you," I threaten.

"I swear I don't know anything else. I have told you everything."

"What about the stolen money?" I ask. "Where is it?"

"I don't know. I had nothing to do with the theft."

"Of course, you didn't," I sneer. "You just showed him where all the money was kept, both onshore and offshore, and Becker gave him access to the entire system." I gather my documentation, placing it back in my bag.

"For what it's worth, I'm sorry, okay?"

No, it's not okay, dipshit.

"Were you involved in the most recent theft?" I ask, zipping my bag.

His brow scrunches up. "What recent theft?"

"Someone stole more money recently."

His eyes pop wide, and unless he's a great actor, he looks genuinely surprised. "I had nothing to do with that. I swear!"

"You better pray you didn't," I warn, standing.

Xavier shuts off the recording and seals the cell back in the hidden compartment of his bag.

"You'll send the money to my wife. Like you promised," he says as Xavier goes to get the guard to tell him we're done.

"I will. She will have the money by the end of the day."

That is one promise I will keep. It's not her fault her husband is a lying, thieving bastard. She's a victim too. If my father was aware of what I'd done, he'd be disgusted because he would see her and her children as an extension of the man who defrauded him. I see it differently. She has paid the price for his sins, and if this is what it took to get the man to tell the truth, then it is money well spent.

The guard enters the room, and I walk away without giving the asshole another passing glance. He has served his purpose and served it well.

CHAPTER EIGHTEEN

Sawyer

"We've been approaching this all wrong," I say into my phone as I drive us away from the correctional facility. We called the crew and updated them on our conversation with Murtagh as soon as we walked out of the prison gates. "We need to trace the money from the other end, starting with Mathers."

"I'll get on it immediately," Charlie says.

"Dig into Hamilton's financial affairs too," Drew says.

"Be careful." Xavier pulls his Mac out of his bag. "Ensure whatever you're doing is hidden and no one makes a move until Hunt and I have hacked into their systems."

"You probably won't find anything," Anderson says.

"And that's if you can even get into their stuff," Drew adds. "If they are behind this, you probably won't be able to get past their firewalls."

"I think we need to prepare for a recon mission," Anderson says, taking the words right out of my mouth.

"I'll put the Manning Motors jet on standby," Drew replies.

"No," Xavier and I say in unison. "We can't tip anyone off we are coming," Xavier says.

"We'll drive," I confirm, pulling out onto the highway.

"I'll call my dad," Lauder says. "See if we can line up those same guys we used when we hit Bama the last time. They knew their stuff."

"Wasn't one of them on the inside?" Xavier says. "Is he still on their payroll?"

"Good question," Lauder says. "I'd say it's unlikely, but I'll check. Even if he's no longer on the detail, having him on our side would come in handy. He'll know the layout of the property and the house."

"We need those guys," I agree. "The more hands we have on deck, the better. I'll grab equipment and attire from Techxet."

"The girls stay out of this," Anderson says.

"Agreed," Lauder says. "It's too fucking dangerous."

"I'll have no issue with Demi," Charlie says. "But how the hell do you intend on keeping Abby and Nessa out of this? They'll want in."

"Shandra too," Drew says.

"Abby has performances coming up. She won't like sitting this one out, but she won't let Madam or the other dancers down."

"Nessa won't want to go anywhere near that house," Jackson quietly says. "She won't have an issue sitting this one out."

"And Shandra will be fine if the other girls aren't coming," Xavier supplies, tapping away on his laptop.

"Okay. We've got a plan. Let's take a couple of days to see what we can dig up, and if we come up empty-handed, we drive to Bama on Thursday," I say.

Everyone agrees and we hang up.

I keep music on low as we drive back to the city. Xavier has his head buried in his computer, already working some angles.

"Are we going to your place or HQ?" I ask when we enter the city limits a couple of hours later.

"Go to my place." He lifts his head, piercing me with sharp eyes. "I'll kick the others back to the office so we can work in privacy. No one else can know what we're planning."

"Agreed." We still haven't discovered if there is a mole in the company, but it seems like the only logical explanation. No one outside of our crew knows we are working an elite angle, and we need to keep it that way.

I make good time, and we pull into the underground parking lot of Xavier's building thirty minutes later. Gathering our shit, we climb out of the car and head to the elevator. "At least it feels like we are finally getting somewhere," Xavier says, his foot tapping impatiently off the floor.

"It's great to get confirmation we were right, but we need proof."

"And we need to find the money," Xavier adds, rushing past me when the elevator pings and the doors open.

"You focus on Mathers," I murmur as we stride along the hallway toward his apartment. "And I'll look into Hamilton."

Slotting his key in the lock, he opens the apartment and we walk inside, slamming to a halt at the sight of Jamison and some stranger with cropped blond hair bent over a computer screen.

"What the fuck is going on?" Xavier says, eyeing his lover suspiciously. The other guy turns rigidly still, lowering his eyes to the desk.

"Xavier." Jamison straightens up, smiling widely. "You're back early. I wasn't expecting you until much later." He scowls as he notices me. "I thought you were meeting your boss in Boston?"

"I was," Xavier lies. "I called Hunt on the way because we need to work on something."

"Who are you?" I ask, stepping forward as I drill a look at the young guy.

"He's one of the student interns," Jamison says, slapping the guy on the back before he can answer me. He smiles at him. "Thanks for bringing me lunch. I'll continue your training some other time. Head back to the office."

The guy bends down, collecting a backpack off the ground. He clutches it to his chest and moves around the desk. I slam my hand down on his shoulder as he moves to brush past me. "You don't come here again. This place is off-limits."

He lifts his chin, piercing me with startling blue eyes behind stylish black frames. "Apologies, Mr. Hunt. It won't happen again." Removing my hand, I let him leave, staring after him for a few seconds.

"Why was he here?" Xavier throws his bag down on the couch and stalks toward his boyfriend. He whips his head around. "Where's everyone else?"

"Argon brought me lunch, and everyone else went to the sushi place around the corner."

"My father was implicit in his instructions. Complete privacy means no one else is permitted to know what we are doing here or come here." I fold my arms, narrowing my eyes at Jamison. He might have compromised the project, and he'll have to be removed. Xavier won't be happy, I'm sure, but I'll try to contain my glee when it happens. I make a note to talk to Dad.

"You could've ordered delivery," Xavier says.

Jamison's nostrils flare. "You're making a big deal out of nothing. The guy has been hanging off my coattails since he started his internship. I've been showing him stuff in the evenings. He's a good kid. Super smart with amazing skills. He offered to bring me lunch, and I didn't see the harm. I've just made a breakthrough, and I didn't want to stop to grab food."

"You couldn't have led with that?" Xavier asks the same time I say, "What breakthrough?"

His eyes light up. "I found a digital footprint, and I was able to trace it. I got a name. Hang on. I'll print it out."

Goddamn it. Dad won't agree to remove him from the team now. Still, he deserves to be cautioned for letting an outsider in.

The printer spits out a few pages, and he hands it to Xavier, excitement burning in his eyes. I lean over Xavier's shoulder, my brows climbing to my hairline as I read the report. Xavier and I exchange a look, and Jamison scowls again. "You know this Hamilton guy?"

"We'll take it from here." I don't trust him anymore, and I don't want to divulge any further information.

"You can head back to HQ," Xavier says. "We need the place to ourselves."

Jamison frowns, stepping around the desk. He places his hands on Xavier's hips. "Why does it feel like I'm in the doghouse? I got a lead. This is what we've been looking for. You should be happy."

"I am happy." Xavier steps back, and Jamison's hands drop from his hips. "This is good work. Thanks, Jamison. We'll take it from here."

Hurt glimmers in his eyes, and he crosses his arms over his chest. "Is there something I don't know, X? You have something to tell me?" Accusation is crystal clear in his tone.

"It is nothing like that," Xavier says. "Let's just keep work stuff separate from our personal stuff. I'll call you later when I'm done, okay?"

"Sure." Leaning in, he grabs the back of Xavier's head, planting a hard kiss on his mouth.

I visualize slamming his face into the wall, but it only makes me feel marginally better.

I glare at him as he grabs his bag and his jacket, tempted to trip him as he walks by me with a smug smile on his face. How did I ever like this guy? I can't fucking stand him and his arrogance.

"What was that about?" I ask after Jamison has left the apartment. "He knows not to bring anyone around here, and he's never been the rule-breaker type."

"I know." He flops into his chair, logging in to the computer. "I don't know what he was thinking."

"I'm thinking maybe we can't trust him." I take a seat at the desk beside him, powering on the computer.

"Hang on here a second, Hunt." Xavier pins me with a ferocious look. "I know he shouldn't have let Argon in here, but let's not overreact. He has just uncovered the first lead, and last year, he helped you discover Nessa was Montgomery's daughter and he came through with other intel that helped in taking down Mathers and Montgomery. He's not our enemy."

I harrumph. "I'm pretty sure he's mine."

Xavier sighs, clawing a hand through his hair. "Don't let your personal feelings get in the way of what we need to do."

"I could say the same to you." I tap in my details and wait for the screen to load.

"I'm not arguing with you over this. We have work to do. Let's concentrate on that."

The first thing I do is check out this Argon intern, but I find no red flags. Argon Sanderon is a straight-A student from a local private school. His parents are of Greek descent, hence the weird name. His father died when he was a kid, and he's an only child.

Leaning back in my chair, I tap my pen on my chin. Something tickles my awareness, but it's just out of reach. There is something about that guy that has my spidey senses on full alert. I snort out a laugh, ignoring the side-eye Xavier throws my way, even if I know he'd get a kick out of my thought.

SEVEN HOURS LATER, we call it a night. Both of us are tired and cranky. While we managed to hack into Hamilton's and Mathers's home computers, the investigation yielded nothing. We figured as much. These guys don't hide shit in plain sight. The fact we easily broke through their firewalls implies we were let in. "We need to search their homes and offices," I say, stifling a yawn as I switch off my computer. "A lot of the elite are old school when it comes to hiding shit they don't want discovered." I stack up the empty takeout containers, carrying them into the kitchen and dumping them in the trash.

"I think you're right." Xavier yawns, rubbing his tired eyes. "Hamilton will be tricky to get to. He's the elite president. His home and his office will be heavily guarded."

"We start with Mathers, and that may give us everything we need."

He nods, yawning again as he stands. "I'm beat." He stretches his arms over his head and arches his back. His shirt lifts, exposing a strip of toned stomach, and my eyes linger.

"Me too. It's been a long day."

He clears his throat, and I jerk my head up, embarrassed to

be caught ogling him. We stare at one another. The weight of everything that is unsaid bearing down on both of us. I would love nothing more than to collapse into bed with him and hold him during the night.

    Xavier is a snuggler. Something I never thought I'd like, but waking up with us draped around one another was my favorite way to wake up.

    A pang of nostalgia slaps me in the face, and I force my feet to move before I do or say something I'll regret. "Thanks for everything today. I'll see you tomorrow." I stride toward the door.

    "Sawyer?" he calls out when I have my hand curled around the door handle.

    I turn around, hopeful for some stupid reason. "Yeah?"

    Silence engulfs us as simmering electricity crackles in the air. "Night, dude."

    My heart sinks, and I'm not sure I'm quick enough to hide the disappointment from my face. "Night, Bright One. Sweet dreams," I say, before exiting the apartment.

CHAPTER NINETEEN

Sawyer

"Sydney." I rap on her bedroom door again. "Can I come in? We need to talk." I've been trying to catch her for days, but I'm usually up before she's awake, and she's generally in bed when I return at night, so there hasn't been time. I purposely left Xavier's place early tonight, determined to speak to her.

"I'm not really in the mood," she calls out.

"It's important," I shout through the door. "Either I'm coming in or you'll have to come out."

The door swings open, revealing a pouting, disheveled Sydney. Strands of matted hair cling to her clammy brow. Her eyes are bloodshot and red rimmed, and her skin is all splotchy. "What's wrong? Are you sick?" I ask, spotting the copious used tissues littering the floor and the pain meds on her bedside table.

"I've been better," she cryptically says, stepping aside to let me enter. "You might as well come in."

Tiptoeing around the half-emptied boxes, I make my way to the couch, opening the window to air out the stuffy room. I push some magazines and papers to one side to make room on the couch, sitting down as she drops into the recliner, pulling her knees into her chest. She's wearing wrinkled pajama pants and a white tank with obvious stains. "Can I do anything to help?" I ask, wondering what is up with her.

"You've already helped me enough." Her features soften. "Charlie sent me my new bank details and card, and I know you did something to get me that interview at the gallery."

"Are you mad I interfered?" I only did it because I want her to get the job and to have some kind of purpose. I'm not around much, and she must be lonely.

"I was a little, at first, but I got the job and I start Monday, so I guess thanks is in order."

"That's great. Congrats." I rest my ankle over my knee, leaning back in the couch.

"What did you want to talk about?" She nibbles on her lower lip.

"I'm going away for a few days. Not sure when I'll be back, but it should be by Sunday. Florentina will be here tomorrow, and I put money into your new account and ordered groceries to be delivered."

An amused grin spreads over her mouth. "I'm twenty-four, Sawyer. I can look after myself, but I appreciate the gestures."

Placing my foot on the ground, I lean my elbows on my knees and clasp my hands. "There was one other thing. I know we agreed to a 'friends with benefits' arrangement, but I've changed my mind. It's not what I want. Us sleeping together was a one-time thing, and I'd prefer it if we kept it strictly platonic from now on."

"It's okay, Sawyer. I figured as much." She brushes knotty hair out of her face. "I'm guessing you're still hung up on Xavier."

I nod. "I'm not ready to move on in any capacity," I truthfully admit. "And I don't want to hurt you. I don't think sex is a good idea between us."

"You're probably right." Her eyes flit to the stack of magazines beside me, and pain is etched across her face. She stands. "Was that everything? I need to shower and clean up this place. I know how much my mess must be getting to you."

I rise to my feet. "Honestly? Yes, but it's your room. At least you're not trashing the apartment the way Jackson used to." A full-body shudder works its way through me. "I love the guy like a brother, but he's one untidy bastard."

She giggles before her gaze drifts again to the pile of magazines on the couch. Darting forward, she scoops them up, thrusting them into my arms. "Dump those, please." She gives me a quick hug. "Have a good trip. I'll see you when you return."

I walk to the kitchen to dispose of the recycling material, scanning the headline on one of the celebrity magazines. It seems Jared Dempsey—drummer for Ruminate, the band Ryder Stone's little brother Wilder is a member of—is engaged to be married to some up-and-coming supermodel. I wonder why Sydney has scribbled all over their faces?

"THIS IS LIKE déjà vu," Lauder says, keeping his voice low as we scan the grounds of the Matherses' estate from our perch in one of the trees at the forest edging the property, using high-tech binoculars courtesy of Techxet. We have split into groups of two. I'm with Jackson. Anderson is with Xavier, and Drew is with Charlie. Diesel has a crew of six who is currently clearing a path to the house, while we scope out the grounds for unanticipated threats. "I'm just waiting for Daniels to confirm the deranged sociopath is on the move," Lauder quips.

"That would be a tad difficult," Xavier says through our earpieces, "considering said sociopath is now dust in the wind."

"He wasn't the only Mathers with sociopathic tendencies," Anderson says in my ear. "I'm pretty sure Alessandra shares the same traits."

"Truth," Drew says. "She's definitely his mini-me in the making."

"Concentrate on the task at hand," Diesel commands in an authoritative voice. "We need to get in and out before the ladies return from their gala event."

"They are no ladies," Drew says. "But we hear you loud and clear."

We arrived in Bama late last night, holing up in some skeezy motel on the outskirts of town. We need to keep our presence on the down low, so staying in one of the five-star hotels was out of the question.

I'm glad I chose to bring my own bedsheets. There is no way I would've gotten any sleep on the hard, stained sheets of the twin bed I ended up in otherwise. Anderson was in charge of the room bookings, and of course, he put himself with Lauder and me with Xavier. Meddling asshole. Xavier, being the diva he is, claimed the double bed, leaving me with the tiny twin. It's a miracle I managed to grab any sleep with my feet poking out the end of the bed, and I kept falling off the side every time I turned over.

I don't care what he says—I'm taking the bigger bed tonight.

We spent all day running over plans with Diesel and his team. Johnson has a map of the entire place from his time spent on Denton's security detail. He was also able to tell us the layout of Mathers's office, including the hidden room behind the bookcase. A friend who is still on the security team confirmed Denton hasn't been seen since the night we broke Van out of here. Obviously. 'Cause he's currently languishing in hell. What is interesting is the fact they've been told Mathers is overseas on extended business and Alessandra is running the ship in his steed. I'm sure she's in her fucking element and enjoying lording it over everyone. A bitch like her given access to power is dangerous, in the extreme.

There is a reason they are keeping his death a secret, and I want to know why.

"Exterior and interior has been cleared," Diesel says, and we start making our descent from the tree. "Let us know when the cameras are down, Daniels," he adds as we race across the grounds toward the side entrance.

"Done," Xavier says. "We're good to go."

"The gas gives us one hour max," Diesel reminds us.

We chose to deploy the same strategy we used when rescuing Anderson from Hearst's house after the bastard had kidnapped and tortured him. It's the easiest way of disarming the staff and the guards inside the mansion. The guards patrolling the grounds were taken down the usual way. "Johnson and Travers will escort you inside. The rest of my men will patrol outside. We don't know what contingency plans might be in place, so hurry."

We regroup with the others, following Johnson and Travers inside the vast property.

Everyone is decked out in Techxet's all-black combat ensemble. The lightweight pants and long-sleeved shirts are resistant to infrared laser and bulletproof, and we are all carrying a gun and several knives. We know from experience not to underestimate any elite, and to expect the unexpected.

Alessandra Mathers might be a giant cunt, but she's smart, and she has huge lady balls. Although we've gone to great lengths to hide our presence from her, we can't rule out she knows we are here and was anticipating an attack.

Racing past sleeping employees and guards, we follow Johnson directly to Denton's office.

Johnson slams to a halt outside a large mahogany door, holding up one hand. He wiggles the door handle, but it doesn't budge. With impressive speed, Johnson picks the lock, and we hold back as he and Travers clear the room. "We'll stand guard out here and give you a five-minute warning before we have to leave."

I nod at him as we dash past, heading straight toward the wall of books, finding *Oliver Twist* on the second shelf, where Johnson said it would be. The guys stand behind me as I remove the book and press the hidden switch. We aren't bothering to search the exterior office; Mathers wouldn't hide anything of value in such a visible manner, and we've already hacked into the computer sitting on that desk and found nothing of interest.

Whatever we seek will be in the hidden room.

We stand back as the shelving unit retracts into the wall, revealing a spacious office-slash-den. "Stay back," I command, holding out my arm. "This will work best with no heat signatures in the way." Extracting the device from my front pocket, I press it on and hold it out, letting it scan the room. A thin red line spreads out, expanding like a blanket, as it sweeps the room for bugs and other electronic devices. It picks up two signals: one behind the monstrous family portrait residing over the ornate fireplace and a second one in a panel on one of the bookshelves.

Anderson and Lauder head for the oil painting, pulling it away from the wall. "Bingo." Anderson grins as they reveal the safe.

"Hidden camera." Xavier plucks a book from the panel. "What did the man have against books?" he mumbles, examining the camera built into the center of the book in his hand.

"Disable it and put it in the bag. That might contain some useful footage."

"No shit, Sherlock," Xavier says as I head to the desk and Charlie and Drew start taking photos of the rest of the space before rifling through drawers and shelves.

"Photograph everything," I say as I sink onto the chair and power up Denton's secret computer.

"Let me do that," Xavier says, appearing a few minutes later as I've logged on to the computer and I'm preparing to run the software to get me into his system.

"I know what I'm doing." I shoot him a glare.

"I know you do, but I'm faster." He waggles his brows, and I purse my lips. My stubborn streak demands I tell him to fuck off, but time is of the essence, and the truth is, Xavier is better than me.

"Fine." I stand, slapping the USB key into his hand. "Prove it."

"You have twenty minutes left," Diesel says a while later. "All is clear. We still have eyes on the gala event, and the van is waiting for you outside."

"We need some help." Anderson pants, and I stop rifling through Mathers's desk drawer, running to help my two friends. "Fuck, this thing weighs a ton." Anderson and Lauder are struggling to hold the safe now they've extracted it from the wall. Removing it and taking it with us was the safest option with the limited time we have. I lend a hand until Johnson and

Travers come into the room, helping Lauder and Anderson carry it outside to the van. I close the painting and return to the desk, grabbing the paperwork and shoving it in our bag.

"Get ready to wrap things up," I tell the others as Xavier finishes the file download and secures the digital key in the zipped pocket of his pants.

"We're done," Charlie says, holding his cell out as he takes some final photos of the framed pictures on top of the grand piano at the far end of the room.

"Guys. You need to get out of there." Diesel's urgent tone filters into my ear. "We have incoming vehicles approaching from the front entrance. I have two men on the roof. They will cover you, but you need to get to the van and get the hell out of here!"

We don't need to be told twice. The only sound in the eerily quiet hallway is the sound of our feet as we sprint through the house toward the door. "Shit," I curse as we approach the doorway and the screeching of tires alerts us to enemy arrival. "Get ready," I say, removing my gun. I turn to Xavier. "You remember everything I showed you at the gun range?"

"I know how to pop bullets in the baddies, Hunt. Don't treat me like I'm an idiot."

I drill him with a look. He is so fucking infuriating at times. I know he knows how to shoot. I was the one who fucking taught him. But he's never killed anyone before. He's never even fired a weapon at anyone, and shit is about to get real. I don't want anything happening to him. "I know you're not an idiot, but you're not experienced like us three. Don't do anything stupid. Stay back and keep your eyes peeled."

He gives me a curt nod, but I don't trust him. Gripping both sides of his face, I peer into his eyes. "If anything happens to you, because you are reckless, I'm holding you fully responsible and I will not go easy on your ass. Be careful." I press a quick, hard kiss to his lips, without thinking about it, just as gunshots ring out from outside.

"Let's go," Drew says, barreling out the door with a gun in

each hand.

"Showtime." Charlie grins, looking way too gleeful, and it's a timely reminder these guys have seen and done a lot of bad shit.

The pop of gunfire being traded signals it's time to make a move. "Keep behind me," I tell Xavier as we move slowly outside.

"Holy shit," Xavier exclaims as we watch Drew and Charlie take guys down like bowling pins. Shots whizz over our heads as Diesel's men take aim from the roof. Anderson and Lauder are behind the van, ducking and diving, as they take shots at a Land Rover. A familiar brunette pops her head up, returning fire as the men Alessandra brought with her drop like proverbial flies.

"Surrender," I say, stalking toward her with my gun raised as Charlie takes down the last man standing. "Or I'll happily let Manning put a bullet in your skull."

Drew creeps up behind her, disarming her in seconds. "I would love nothing more," he hisses, yanking her hands behind her back, slapping cuffs around her wrists.

"If I'd known you were into kink, we could've had so much fun," she purrs, looking way too unruffled for a prisoner.

"Get out of here," Diesel commands, racing around from the side of the house. "We'll clean up, but you need to go now."

"What about the slut?" Anderson asks.

"Put her in the van," I say, tucking my gun into the belt around my waist. "I want to ask her a few questions." We might as well try to get something out of her now she's caught us in the act.

"I'm telling you nothing." She flashes me an arrogant grin.

"Famous last words, sweetheart," Drew says, pushing her toward the vehicle.

CHAPTER TWENTY

Sawyer

Johnson drives us to an outbuilding on the very far side of town. One they had scoped out before coming to Alabama, in case we needed a place to lie low. Or somewhere to interrogate a haughty bitch. Clever planning like this is why Diesel and his crew are worth every penny I'm paying them.

"Start talking," Drew says when he has secured Alessandra's wrists and ankles to the chair. We've already checked her for recording devices and weapons.

"Fuck you."

"How original," Xavier drawls, not lifting his head from his Mac. I know he's embedding a virus into the camera system back at the house, just in case they had any backups.

"Shut your mouth, faggot."

My hands are around her throat in a flash. "I don't give a fuck if you're a woman. I'll snap your neck in a heartbeat if that word leaves your mouth again." I apply more pressure to make my point before reluctantly letting her go.

She coughs, stabbing me with venomous eyes. "You're very territorial about your ex-lover for a married man." The knowledge she's been keeping tabs on us is alarming if not surprising.

"Why weren't you at the gala ball?" Anderson asks, tossing a knife back and forth in his hand.

"I was, but I left early. I had better things to do with my time."

"Like spy on us," Charlie says.

She smirks, and I grow uneasy.

"Why haven't you reported your father as a missing person?" I ask.

She barks out a laugh. "I told you I'm not telling you dick. We can do this all day. It's no skin off my back."

"Fuck this shit." Drew snaps, snatching the knife from Anderson and pressing it to her crotch. "Unlike Hunt, I have no qualms about torturing or killing a woman like you. I wouldn't lose a wink of sleep over it." He presses the knife down, and a shrill cry leaves her mouth. "How valuable would you really be without this weapon between your legs. Huh?"

Charlie steps forward, knife in hand, and he yanks her head back by her hair. "Who would want you if we mess up your pretty face and cut off your hair." He lops a chunk of her hair off, dropping it on her lap, before trailing the edge of the knife down the side of her face.

"Okay! Stop! I'll tell you."

Anderson and Lauder grin at Drew and Charlie. Anderson is recording this on his cell, to show Abby, I'm guessing. She'll get a real kick out of this.

Charlie releases her hair, but he doesn't step back, hovering over her with a menacing look on his face that gives me chills. Drew eases the knife back a little but keeps it pressed to her pussy. "Talk, cunt. I'm low on patience."

"I want the money," she spits out. "If we report him as missing, his bank accounts will be frozen, we'll have the authorities breathing down our necks, and the elite will force me to take Daddy's place."

"Why would that be an issue for you?" I ask, watching her scowl in Xavier's direction. "You love every sick and twisted part of that world."

"You know jack shit, Hunt." A muscle pops in her jaw. "They'll never let a woman have any real power despite

Hamilton's promises. I'll be their fuck toy. Nothing more, and I'm done being tossed around by those pricks. I hate those fucking bastards as much as I hated my father." She stares me straight in the face. "I guess I should thank you for taking care of that problem for me."

"You mean to say you didn't enjoy opening your legs and your ass for your father and his friends?" Drew drags the tip of the knife across her crotch, and she jumps a little.

"Rape. The word is rape, and of course, I didn't enjoy it."

"You know what I think," Drew says, putting his face all up in hers as Charlie crowds her from behind. "I think you loved every fucking minute of it."

"Where is the money?" I ask, growing tired of this.

"If I knew, I'd already be a million miles away from here," she hisses. "You can forget about getting into Daddy's safe. It's impenetrable. It's fitted with a safety feature that will set it on fire as soon as you attempt to open it. You'll burn the contents, and they'll be lost to you forever."

I keep a neutral expression on my face as I tilt my head to the side, staring at her. She doesn't know Techxet has developed a tool for opening every type of safe. Dad commissioned it after the issues we had getting into Hearst's safe. As soon as Diesel organizes shipping the safe back to Xavier's warehouse in Rydeville, we'll have that baby open in a couple of hours.

"Hunt. You need to see this," Xavier says, his gaze swinging to mine. He's wearing his shitty poker face, barely concealing his obvious delight.

I walk toward him, leaning over his shoulder. "What is it?" I whisper.

"The code is the same as that code Jamison found the other day," he explains, meaning whoever hacked into Techxet's system also helped to set up Denton's secret home computer.

"Can you unscramble it?"

"Does a bear shit in the woods?" He grins, his green eyes sparking to life.

"Keep at it."

I return to Alessandra, watching her glare at Xavier with undisguised disgust. I find it hard to believe she's that homophobic, surrounded by the world she lives in. Guy on guy action is not unheard of within elite circles.

"Why did your father go after mine?" I stand in front of her with my arms folded across my chest.

"I'd think that's obvious. He was acting on Hamilton's instructions, and Hamilton knew your father had evidence on the elite that could cause a lot of problems." Angling her head, she smiles at Lauder. "Hamilton targeted your father first because it was just too easy to get to him." She barks out a laugh as Jackson stiffens. "I met her, you know. Your sister. I attended a party on the island one time. Well, it was more of an orgy. Dani was chained to Montgomery's side at the banquet. Naked as the day she was born. He fed her his leftovers. Like you would a dog."

The smile is wiped off her face when Charlie yanks her head back and slices a line across her right cheek. Piercing screams reverberate around the derelict barn as blood drips down her face and over her chin.

Lauder stalks forward, calmly taking the knife from Drew before he drives it straight through her crotch, embedding it in the chair. The smell of urine perforates the air and Alessandra's painful howls are animalistic as she screams. "This is a waste of time," Lauder says. "She's not going to tell us anything of value."

"Even if she does, we can't hang around to interrogate her. We need to get the fuck out of Dodge," Anderson adds.

"We can't let her live," Charlie says, releasing his hold on her hair. "She'll go straight to the elite."

"No," she whimpers in between sobs. "I won't tell them because then I'll lose the money."

A dark chuckle rumbles from my chest. "You'll lose the money anyway because we're going to steal it back."

I nod at Drew, and he withdraws his gun.

"We can split it!" she cries. "We can work together to locate the money and share it."

"Nice try, but I'm not buying it," I say. "We don't trust you or like you."

Drew turns the safety off and readies his gun.

"He'll come after you!" she screams. "If you kill me, he'll take you all down."

She must be fucking him if she is this delusional. Hamilton won't give a shit about her, except for the inconvenience of having to recruit another lackey to replace her.

"He's gunning for us anyway, sweetheart. One more kill won't make a difference." Drew tilts her head up, staring straight into her eyes. "You should count your blessings we don't have time to prolong this. If I had my way, I'd kill you slowly over the course of a week. Bringing you to the brink, over and over again. Inflicting unimaginable pain that would have you pleading for death." He straightens up, pointing his gun at the center of her forehead. "Enjoy your reunion with Daddy in hell." Drew pulls the trigger, and the light instantly goes out in her eyes before her head slumps forward.

"Pity we couldn't take her with us. I would've enjoyed watching you destroy her," Charlie says, staring at her with a face devoid of emotion.

Every so often, these guys provide a glimpse into the dark malevolence hiding inside them, and I never want to find myself up against them. I know this is only the tip of the iceberg in terms of what they are capable of. No one could endure the shit they endured as kids and not be at least a little fucked in the head.

"You know what to do," Drew tells Charlie, tucking his gun away and turning his back on Alessandra's lifeless body. "Let's wait in the van while Charlie burns the body."

"THAT WAS SOME heavy shit back there," Xavier says after we have both showered and changed in our motel room. "I knew Drew hated her, but I'm still a little shocked he went through with it."

"I'm not. She was an evil bitch. She called you a faggot, and she taunted Lauder about Dani. She deserved to die." I pack my stuff neatly in my duffel bag. Diesel suggested we take an alternate route home, and he organized new hotel rooms in Knoxville for us before he took off with his crew. It's approximately a four-hour drive, and it won't be pleasant; it's almost midnight, and we're all pretty drained. But we can't risk hanging around.

"Do you think she was bluffing about Hamilton coming after us?" Xavier says, zipping up his bag.

I shrug, slinging my bag over my shoulder as a knock sounds on the door. "We know he's coming for us. I'm guessing she was trying to save her ass by implying she's important to him or she was deflecting the responsibility in his direction. Hamilton wasn't a player until after Hearst was killed," I remind him, opening the door to Drew.

"That's only assumption," Drew says, entering the room, picking up on the tail end of my statement. "For all we know, Hamilton was the one helping Atticus. Hamilton could have a lot more reasons than we know for wanting us dead."

"Whatever the reason. We need to take him down now," Xavier says, propping his butt against the small desk by the wall. "It's all coming to a head. I feel it in my bones."

"Was there a reason for your visit?" I ask Drew, checking the time on my watch. We're not due to hit the road for ten minutes.

He nods, clearing his throat as his gaze bounces between us. "I was skimming through the photos we took in Denton's office, and I came across something you need to see." Pulling Charlie's cell from the pocket of his jeans, he opens the screen and hands it to Xavier. "Zoom in on the top left."

Xavier pulls his fingers across the screen, and his face gets paler and paler as he stares at Drew's phone.

"What is it?" I walk to his side and snatch the phone. The screenshot is an image of the framed photos on top of the piano, and it's zoomed in on a photograph of four men. Denton and William are in the middle with a familiar younger guy on

Denton's other side and an unfamiliar older man on the far side of Hamilton. I stare at the pic for a few seconds, but there is no mistaking his scrawny, nerdy ass. "Holy fuck. We've been royally played."

"You mean *I've* been played." Xavier's shoulders slump as he stares with downcast eyes at the threadbare carpet.

"It gets worse," Drew adds. "Look at the next screen."

Xavier lifts his head, pinning troubled eyes on me as I swipe right. He stuffs his fist in his mouth at the image of Jamison and Alessandra with their arms around one another. Jamison is kissing the side of her face, and she's smiling at the camera, looking genuinely happy. "Motherfucking asshole," I hiss, handing the cell back to Drew. I stand in front of Xavier, placing my hand on his shoulders. "Xavier. Look at me."

"Don't, Sawyer." He shoves my hand away. "Don't try to make this better when there are no words in existence in the English language that could ever make this okay." His Adam's apple jumps in his throat as he lifts his face to mine. I see so many different emotions on his face, and I know he's beating himself up for this.

I need to do something, say something, to make it better. "If this is anyone's fault, it's mine. I recruited him last year to help me and Lauder. I'd known him for years. He'd been interning from the time he was seventeen. I was the one who recommended him for this project."

"Stop it, Hunt!" Xavier shouts. "You weren't the one fucking him!" he yells. "You weren't the one working closely beside him every day. Showing him exactly what you were doing and what you were planning to do! No wonder I couldn't make any progress. He was watching everything I did and covering his tracks any time I got close to uncovering the truth." Picking up a bowl on the desk, he throws it at the wall.

"Xavier." I reach out for him, but he swats my arm away.

"Just don't." He grabs his bag and swipes the keys from my hand. "I'm going to wait in the car. I need a few minutes alone."

The door slams as he leaves, and I have never felt more

helpless.

"I'm going to string that double-crossing bastard up by the balls and gut him like a pig," Drew snarls.

"You'll have to get in line." I crack my knuckles. "I hate that prick, and I sensed something was off with him, but I didn't listen to it."

"You thought it was jealousy," Drew guesses, and I nod.

I scrub a hand over my smooth jawline, pondering so many questions and what-ifs. But all of that takes a back seat to my concern for Xavier. The look of horror and shame on his face when he looked at that picture said it all. "This is going to devastate him. I know he was already internally critical of his inability to locate the hacker. Finding out—"

I'm cut off by a massive explosion that rattles the walls and shakes the floor. Drew and I trade terrified expressions before racing out of the room.

Anderson, Lauder, and Charlie emerge from their rooms at the same time, and I collapse against Drew, my knees buckling as I stare at the remnants of my SUV. Thick black smoke spirals into the sky as flames lick what remains of the frame of my car. "No!" I shout, clutching Drew's shirt as tears stab my eyes. Anderson looks at me with fear in his eyes. "He was in the car! No! Xavier! Please, God, no!" I roar, staggering away from Drew toward the wreckage. "I need to get him out. Call an ambulance," I bark, my face heating as I approach what's left of my car.

Lauder reacts fast, yanking me back, wrapping an arm around my chest to stop me from moving. "He's gone, Hunt. No one could have survived that." He holds me closer. "I'm so sorry," he chokes out as I sag against him.

CHAPTER TWENTY-ONE

Xavier

"I GUESS IT'S good I was salty and went to buy booze," I deadpan, stepping out onto the path, waving a bottle of gin at my shell-shocked friends as they all whip their heads around in my direction. Behind them, what's left of Hunt's luxury SUV crackles and burns, sending billowing dark smoky clouds shooting into the nighttime sky. Thank fuck, this place is a shithole and we're the only residents.

When the explosion went off, the old broad behind the reception desk barely batted an eyelash. Like car bombs and attempted murder is the norm around here.

Who the fuck knows? Maybe it is.

Sawyer's face is ghostly pale, and his eyes are suspiciously glassy as he blinks profusely, staring at me like I'm an apparition. Or Jesus Christ come back to life. Then he's running toward me, throwing his arms around me, and nearly squeezing me to death. "Ugh, can't breathe." My words are muffled against his chest as he clings to me like he's afraid to let me go. A messy ball of emotion clogs my throat as I place my free hand on his chest. His heart beats erratically under my palm, and the pulse in his neck is throbbing at inhuman speed.

"I thought you were dead," he croaks, his voice all choked

up.

"Surprise. I'm alive!" I shuck out of his arms, instantly missing his warmth and the comforting spicy scent of his expensive cologne.

"Xavier." Sawyer grabs my head in both hands, peering deep into my eyes. "Do not fucking joke with me right now. I thought I'd lost you." Tears pool in his eyes, and he's shielding nothing from me. "Fuck. It feels like I'm having a coronary."

"Or an epiphany," I say because joking around in serious situations is my default setting.

"Yes." He nods, surprising me with his agreement. "I think that's it."

I arch a brow, opening my mouth to retaliate when he brushes his thumb across my lower lip, effectively silencing me. His touch reverberates in every part of me, and my heart picks up pace as adrenaline floods my system.

"I love you," he blurts, his face awash with emotion. "I love you so much, Xavier," he adds before his lips crash down upon mine.

Sawyer's kisses always have the power to render me senseless, and this time is no different. Using my free hand, I fist a hand in his shirt, pulling him as close as humanly possible. Tilting my head, I let him deepen the kiss, moaning into his mouth at the familiar taste of him against my lips. No one has ever kissed me as good as Sawyer Hunt. His tongue flicks out, demanding entry, and I can't deny him anything right now. Even though this is probably the worst decision.

But right now, I need him, and I'm going to be fucking selfish and take what I want.

We devour one another, and all the blood in my body pools in my crotch. Sawyer drops one hand, grabbing my ass and grinding his hard-on against me. Precum leaks from the tip of my straining cock, and I rock against him, wanting nothing more than to lose myself in him and not think about the asshole who has made a fool out of me.

"Guys, as much as this is awesome—and weirdly arousing,"

Jackson drawls. "Can you take a rain check?"

Reluctantly, we break apart, but Sawyer keeps one arm around my back.

"We need to get the fuck out of here," Jackson adds. "And we need to find ourselves some new wheels cause I'm guessing that chargrilled bitch planted a bomb in my car too."

"Let me call Diesel. They can't be too far away. Maybe we can take one of their vehicles," Sawyer says.

I shuck out of his hold and take a step back, opening the bottle of gin and drinking a healthy mouthful. Hunt glances at me, concern etched on his face as he makes the call. He jerks his head at Anderson as he walks off to speak to Diesel.

Anderson, Jackson, Charlie, and Drew approach, taking turns slapping me on the back. "Thank fuck, you're okay. I was not looking forward to calling my wife and telling her the news," Kai says, squeezing my shoulder like he needs to reassure himself I'm a real boy.

"I wish we'd tortured the slut now," I say in between mouthfuls. "She got off way too lightly."

"We don't know it was her who did this," Drew says. "It could've been Jamison. Did you tell him where you were going?"

I shake my head as pain presses down on my chest. "I have told him nothing about our little side operation." Not that it appears to matter much. He has still run circles around me and made me look like a bumbling idiot.

"They must've been working together," Charlie says. "She had to have been tipped off."

"Give me your cell," Drew demands, holding out his hand. "I bet it's bugged."

I glare at Abby's brother. "My cell is not bugged. I check it regularly. But have at it." I slap it down on his palm, grinding my teeth to the molars.

"Alessandra could have found out any number of ways," Sawyer says, rejoining the conversation. "This is her home turf. She probably has spies everywhere. Someone must have spotted us and notified her. We know she slipped out of the event, without

Diesel's men seeing, so it's logical to assume she came here, planted the bombs and then showed up at the house, thinking she could take us out or scare us into running straight home."

"Your cell is clean," Drew says. "But I'm betting he has a tracker on you someplace."

"It's not possible. I'm all over that shit on a daily basis."

"Drew, man. Just drop it," Sawyer says. "However it happened, she hasn't succeeded." Pushing the guys aside, he stalks to my side, threading his fingers in mine. "We're all okay. Diesel is sending a bomb expert friend of his to check out Lauder's SUV, and he has a vehicle on the way we can use to get home." He squeezes my hand.

"He probably has your computer bugged," Jackson supplies, earning a dark glare from Sawyer.

"I said drop it," Sawyer hisses through gritted teeth. "I know we need to discuss these things, but not now. We'll figure it out later. Let's get the fuck out of here."

Twenty minutes later, we are on the road. Diesel gave us one of his blacked-out seven-seaters, so at least there's room for all of us. Drew is driving, and Charlie is going to take over in a couple hours. They are up front, quietly talking among themselves. Anderson is messaging Abby. Lauder is asleep with his head against the window. The mood is low. We're all on edge and tired. I'm pissed. So fucking mad at myself and struggling to silence my thoughts.

"It's not your fault," Sawyer says, pressing his mouth to my ear. "Stop beating yourself up." He must be worried about me because he crawled into the smaller two seats at the very back, beside me, with none of his usual grumbling. His legs are a few inches longer than mine, scrunched up against the seat in front, and I can tell he's not comfortable.

"Don't pretend you know how I'm feeling," I snap, my skin itching with a blistering rage I need to expel. I swallow another mouthful of gin, but it's not hitting the spot. Recapping the bottle, I toss it on the floor and quietly seethe.

"Take it out on me," he says. "Get it all out. I can handle it."

He reaches for my hand, but I push him away.

"Stop, Hunt. Just stop." I know he's trying to comfort me, but my emotions are veering all over the place, and I don't know what the fuck to do with his declaration of love. "I don't want to talk about it."

Remarkably, he stays quiet, and somehow, I fall asleep.

CHAPTER TWENTY-TWO

Xavier

Hands shaking my shoulders wake me sometime later. "Xavier. We're at the hotel," Sawyer says, gentling his tone. "Come on. I got us a room."

Not sure how we ended up roomies, but it beats sharing with Anderson or Drew. Drew snores like a freight train. And Anderson is prone to moaning in his sleep, calling out for Abby.

Hunt has already checked us in, and the others are nowhere in sight, so I'm guessing they've crashed. I stifle a yawn, clutching the bottle of gin in my hand as we ascend the floors in the elevator. I lost all my stuff in the explosion, and I'm just grateful Sawyer had insisted on storing all the evidence from Mathers's office in his bag or we'd have lost the computer data. I back up everything to the cloud, but I'm still pissy I lost my shiny new red MacBook Pro.

"I got us a suite, but they only had one-bedroom suites available," Sawyer says as we walk along the hallway toward our room. "I can sleep on the couch," he tacks on the end, not sounding very committed.

I shrug, because our sleeping arrangements are the last thing on my mind right now.

He opens the door to our room, letting me walk in first. It's pretty spacious with a separate living space, large bathroom with a tub, and a generously proportioned bedroom with a comfortable-looking king-sized bed and an en suite shower and toilet. "I'm gonna take a shower," I say, hating how the smell of smoke clings to my clothes.

I strip out of my smoky clothes as I turn on the shower. Getting in, I stand under the steaming water, trying to evict past errors from my mind, but my mistakes enjoy taunting me when I'm feeling low. I wash my hair and my body as if on autopilot, wishing I had a magic carpet so I could zoom home, crawl into my own bed, lock the door, and shut out the world.

Eventually, I get out when I can't take my errant thoughts anymore and my skin is starting to wrinkle. The bathroom is well equipped, so I brush my teeth and take a piss, before I realize I have nothing to change into. That's just super duper. Wrapping a towel around my toned waist, I wander out to the bedroom.

Hunt is sitting on the bed in light sleep pants, scrolling through something on his phone.

I flop down on the bed beside him, and he lifts his head, immediately setting his phone on the bedside table. Slowly, his gaze roams my body, his intense stare growing more heated as he drinks his fill.

Sawyer has this way of looking at me that melts all my body parts. Except for the one between my legs. His dark gaze always turns my dick rock hard, and now is no different.

Sex was never an issue with us. Communicating was the blocker in our relationship.

He clears his throat, lifting his hungry eyes to mine. "I can grab you something to wear from my bag."

I shake my head. "I'll sleep naked, but I will need to borrow some clothes tomorrow. Mine reek of smoke."

"No problem. I have spare shit."

I smirk. "I know. Packing light is not in your vocab." I lie back against the headboard, hating how I'm wide-fucking-awake now at four thirty a.m.

"Are you okay?" he asks, and I twist my head to look at him.

"Honestly? No."

"I'm here for you. Whether you want me to listen or just sit in companionable silence." He runs a hand through his hair in a nervous tell. "I can sleep on the couch, but I was hoping you might let me sleep in here with you. I don't think you should be alone."

My lips fight a twitch as I lie down on my side, facing him. "Are you hitting on me? Whatever would your wife say?"

"I set Sydney straight. As much as I want to hit on you, I would never take advantage of you when you're vulnerable. I'm worried about you. Don't let him fuck with your head. He's not worth it."

"I feel like such a fool, and now everyone is going to know and judge me. It's like I'm seventeen again and my parents have just discovered my affair with a married man." Sawyer's expression showcases his surprise, but he doesn't interrupt, reaching out and threading his fingers in mine. I hold his hand, needing his touch. "The guy told me he was separated but he couldn't afford to pay two mortgages so that's why he was still living in the family home."

I shake my head as a familiar wave of self-loathing crests over me. "I was such a naïve fool to believe him."

"You always want to see the good in people. That's a good trait, Xavier."

"I've lost my faith in humanity," I truthfully admit. "There are too many self-serving evil bastards in the world for me to buy into that bullshit anymore." I sigh heavily, wanting to tell Sawyer this. Needing to get it off my chest. "I can't help but draw comparisons. I still remember the look of disgust on my father's face and the disappointment on my mother's when the dickhead's wife secretly filmed us fucking and released it on the local town online forum."

"Fuck. That was a shitty thing to do, even if she was hurting."

"It was gross stupidity too. Age of consent is eighteen in North Dakota, and the police prosecuted her husband. He was sent down for ten years and his name will forever exist on the sex-offender's list."

"Can't say I feel any sympathy," Sawyer says.

"I didn't either. He couldn't dump me fast enough. Backtracking and trying to make amends with his wife. He tried to deflect all the blame on me."

"What a jerk."

"I thought I was in love with him." It seems there is no end to my stupidity. "But I meant nothing to him. He abandoned me when I needed him the most. Senior year was sheer hell because every one of my friends abandoned me and the jocks and popular kids loved taunting me. Stuffing my locker with lube and gay magazines. Some asshole even printed a screenshot from the video and plastered it all over the town."

Sawyer pulls me into his arms, and I go willingly. "I'm sorry you had to deal with that."

I let him comfort me for a few seconds before I pull away. Pain tears strips off my fragile heart. "I swore when I left North Dakota behind for good that I would never again be duped. That I would only give myself to someone who was worthy of me. Someone who genuinely loves me. Yet, I keep making the same fucking mistakes. I never learn." I slap a hand to my brow. "I'm so fucking dumb."

"I'm the dumb one," Sawyer says, gripping my wrist and pulling it away from my face so he can see me. "I'm the one who was never worthy of you. I was too scared to open up and let you in, and I hurt you in the process. As long as I live, I will never forgive myself for that." Fierce determination slants across his face as he moves closer, sliding his arm around my back. "I'm so fucking sorry, Xavier. I'm sorry I let you down, but I meant what I said earlier."

His features soften, and deep emotion shimmers in his eyes. "I love you, Bright One. I love you more than I have ever loved anyone, and that terrifies the fuck out of me. Deep down, I have known that for some time, but I was too much of a chicken shit to confront it, let alone admit it to you or tell my parents. If you give me another chance, I promise I will put you first. I promise

I will make everything right."

I want to believe him. So bad. But I don't trust my judgment anymore. And I don't trust his words because it would be too easy to wrap them around my heart in an attempt to paper over the cracks. "Words aren't enough, Sawyer. And it's too late. You're married."

"I'm divorcing her," he says, holding me closer. Our chests brush, sending a wave of desire pooling south. My dick thickens, and I feel his cock hardening too through the flimsy pajama pants he's wearing. "I don't care about anything but you. I'm sorry it took tonight for me to wake the fuck up. Thinking you were dead." His voice cracks, and tears pool in his eyes. "It destroyed me, Xavier. All I could think was you died not knowing I love you." He presses his brow to mine. "I know I need to prove to you I'm sincere. I understand it more now you've explained about your past. I know it will take time, but I'm not giving up." He presses a hard kiss to my mouth, and I groan as his erection brushes against mine, sending fresh need shooting through my veins.

I'm hard as a rock now and ready to fuck all these pent-up feelings out.

"I'm going to fight for you, Xavier."

I thought he looked determined before, but that's nothing on the look of dogged resolve on his face now.

"And I'm not giving up until I get you back. We belong together, and I won't rest until you believe it's true."

CHAPTER TWENTY-THREE

Xavier

"You say you've changed?" I challenge, pushing him flat on his back, throwing my towel aside and straddling his hips. "Then prove it. Let me take my pleasure from your body because that is the only thing I am willing to offer you."

"I'll take you however I can get you," he says, reaching out to cup my face. "Do what you want to me. You know I'll love it."

I arch a brow and chuckle as I move my hands along his warm, bare chest. "Now, now, Sawyer. Don't lie. We both know how much you love to dominate me. How much you need to be in control."

"That doesn't mean I'm not prepared to relinquish control or I didn't enjoy bottoming with you." He wets his lips, looking nervous. "I never told you this. I should have. But you were my first."

"Bullshit." I narrow my eyes, wondering what game he's playing. "Don't fucking lie to me. You were tight, but not that tight."

"I've used my fingers and toys. A lot. On my own and with previous partners. I like having a cock in my ass, but I never trusted any man to fuck me with his dick until you."

I know he's not lying. The truth is written all over his face, and I get an enormous thrill from it. Bending down, I smash my lips to his as I grind on top of his dick through his light pants. Something hard brushes against the metal of my dick piercing and I stall, pulling my mouth back and straightening up. "What was that?"

A wide grin spreads across his mouth, and it's like getting sucker punched in the nuts. Sawyer is gorgeous. Hot as fuck. Sexy as fuck. Best lay I've ever had. I'm horny as fuck and if this is what I think it is, I'm likely to shoot my load in seconds. "Take off my pants and see," he purrs, using that hypnotic sexy deep voice of his.

I scramble off his legs in record time, yanking his pants down and quickly getting rid of them. Leaning down, I inspect his magnificent cock up close and personal. "Holy fucking shit, Sawyer. You did it. You got your cock pierced." He has a Prince Albert piercing at the crown like me. Unlike me, he also has four ladders down his shaft. I trace my finger down his length, and he hisses.

"Before you ask," he says, his cock bobbing as my tongue darts out, licking his hard, warm flesh and the cool metal of his many piercings. "I did this for you. It was just before everything went to shit, and I hadn't had time to show you."

I climb over him, straddling him again, skin to skin. "Is that the truth?"

"One hundred percent."

"Why?" I teased Sawyer mercilessly over being pure because he has no piercings and only one small tattoo on his arm.

"Because your dick feels incredible sliding in and out of my ass with the piercing and I want you to experience the same."

"Fuck me taking pleasure from your body," I murmur, pressing kisses all over his chest. "I need your dick in my ass. Stat."

Sawyer grabs the back of my head, pulling me down hard on top of him, as his mouth fuses with mine. His tongue plunges into my mouth, and we grind against one another as we ravage each other with our lips and tongues. My hands roam his gorgeous body, reacquainting myself with every chiseled dip and curve. Sawyer flips me onto my back, and I scrape my nails down his spine and knead his ass cheeks as he thrusts against me. "Fuck. I have missed sex with you," he rasps in my ear before biting my neck like a vampire.

I lick my fingers before finding his puckered hole. I push two digits in, enjoying how his cock jerks against mine, and he curses against my lips. I pump my fingers in and out of his ass as my hips thrust up and we rub against one another. Our kissing turns more frantic, our touching more wild, until I can't take it anymore.

I flip us over, pressing my ass against his cock as I sit on him. "Please, please, please. For the love of all things holy, tell me you have condoms and lube."

"Would it seem presumptuous if I said I did?"

"Completely," I say, climbing off the bed, almost taking a tumble in my haste to get to his bag. "But I couldn't give a flying fuck. Right now, I'm impressed with your forward planning," I add, rummaging in his bag, uncaring I'm messing all his shit up. He can rip me a new one tomorrow for it. "And appreciative of your need to obsessively control every aspect of your life." Finding the supplies, I get to my feet and turn around, slamming to a halt.

Hunt is propped up in the middle of the bed against a mountain of pillows, with his legs spread wide and his knees pulled up to his chest, exposing everything to me. His hungry eyes pin me in place. "I need your cock in me first."

I climb up on the bed, excitement sending shivers all over my body. I stroke my cock as I kneel between his legs. "Say please and I might give you what you want." I flash him a grin, knowing he will do and say whatever I want because he's just that desperate to please me. Sue me if I'm taking advantage. Sawyer is normally the bossy one in the bedroom, and I'm happy to go along for the ride. Tonight, I'm in charge.

"Please fuck me, Bright One."

"You don't play fair, Drill Sergeant." I waggle my brows,

grinning.

He groans. "I have *not* missed you calling me that."

I wrap my hand around his erection and squeeze. "Sure, you have. Just like you've missed drilling me with your monster cock." Leaning down, I lick a path up and down either side of his long, thick dick. "Be grateful I didn't tell the others. Especially when you let my pet name slip."

"That wasn't intentional," he says, his hips jerking when I flatten my tongue against his crown. Beads of precum wet my tongue, and I wrap my hand around my straining length, giving it a few pumps as I suck on the tip of his giant cock.

"I know," I admit, sitting up and pumping both of us in one hand, enjoying the feel of his dick pressed against mine. "That's the only reason I didn't spill the beans." I chuckle at my own joke as he rolls his eyes.

"Quit teasing me, man," he says, pleading with lusty eyes. "I fucking need you now."

"And you'll have me. When I say so." I apply some lube to my fingers and roll a condom over my erection.

He bites down on his lip, and I know it's hard for him to let go so I take pity on him. Lowering my head, I suck his dick into my mouth, sliding my lips up and down his shaft, carefully licking his piercings as I shove two fingers into his ass, prepping him. "Fuck," I hiss, as his hole clenches around my digits. I can't torture myself any longer either. I suck him off for another couple of minutes as I continue pumping my digits in and out of his ass, pushing up as far as I can, quickly stroking his prostrate. He almost jumps off the bed, and more precum leaks into my mouth.

Not wanting this to be over too fast, I let his dick go with a loud pop and remove my fingers. I lower my body flush against his, claiming his lips because I'm dying to kiss him. "I love you," he says when we come up for air. He grabs fistfuls of my hair. "I'm going to keep on telling you until you believe it."

"I love you too," I say because there's no point lying when he already knows the truth.

This doesn't mean everything is hunky-dory. Far from it.

But I suppose it's progress.

We kiss a few more times as I slather lube all over my dick, and then I position myself at his entrance, pushing his legs back into his chest, enjoying the view as I slowly thrust inside him.

"Fuck, Sawyer." I push all the way in and hold still, closing my eyes for a second, bathing in the amazing feeling of his ass hugging my cock.

"Move, baby," Sawyer says, and I open my eyes in time to see his mischievous grin. "Pound that ass!"

I chuckle, knowing what he's referencing. "What a pity Lauder and Anderson aren't outside to hear this," I pant, pulling out and then slamming back in.

"We can always invite them to watch," he teases, his back arching off the bed as I thrust in deep.

"I know that's their thing, but somehow, I don't think two dudes going at it would get their rocks off."

Sawyer grins. "Stanger things have happened."

"They have," I agree, pressing my body down on top of his. "But I won't share you."

"I'm down with that plan," he agrees.

I press a hard kiss to his mouth as I fuck him, driving my cock deep, reveling in the feel of being inside Sawyer again. Skin slapping against skin and our joint moaning fills the air as I screw him into the bed.

"Enough, baby." Sawyer says, pushing my chest. "I want to come inside you." He presses a soft kiss to the corner of my mouth. "I want you to feel what I feel when you're moving in me."

"Why, Sawyer, I believe that is one of the most romantic things you've ever said to me."

"If that's true, I'm failing miserably." He lowers his legs as I pull out.

"I want you to fuck me from behind," I say, "but kneeling up."

"I think you like being bossy," he says, rolling a condom on and lubing up.

"If it gets me your dick in my ass, then yeah," I admit, kneeling on all fours so he can get into the right position.

Sawyer parts my cheeks, and I almost come undone when I feel the wet warmth of his tongue rimming my asshole. I tug on my dick, shoving my ass back in his face as he licks me all over. A strangled cry rips from my mouth when he drives his fingers in my ass while shoving my hand away and stroking my cock. "I'm going to combust, and I'll be lost to you forever if you don't hurry the fuck up. Come on, Drill Sergeant. Drill the fuck out of me."

The bed moves, and I hiss as his cock nudges my entrance. "Remember you asked for this," Sawyer says, digging his hands into my hips as he slams into me in one deep thrust. He doesn't hold back, ramming his dick in and out of my ass, and it's fucking incredible.

I've fucked guys with piercings before but no one as big as Sawyer. The sensation is mind-blowing. "Fuck, Sawyer. You feel so fucking good. Go harder. Deeper."

Sawyer wraps his hand around my throat and sits up straighter, pulling me with him so my back is flush against his hot chest. Keeping one hand on my throat and one on my hip to keep me at the right angle, he fucks me mercilessly.

"I'm close," he says, burying his face in my neck and lightly biting my skin.

"Me too," I say, and seconds later, my head is pushed into the bed as he jerks my ass up and parts my legs wider. He covers me with his body from behind as his hand moves around to jerk me off. He strokes me hard and fast as his cock slams in and out of me, and my balls tighten, my spine tingles, and I get a three-second warning before I explode all over his hand.

Sawyer roars, thrusting his hips forward and pulverizing my ass as he milks both our climaxes with expert skill. Stars are still detonating behind my eyes as I ride out the best fucking orgasm of my life.

When we're both done, we collapse in a sweaty tangled heap on the bed, automatically pulling each other close and passing out within seconds of each other.

CHAPTER TWENTY-FOUR

Sawyer

I WAKE UP to Xavier draped around me like a spider monkey, and it puts the biggest smile on my face. Last night was amazing, and I'm kicking myself for not getting pierced sooner, because holy hell. Sex doesn't get any better than this. Or maybe it's because I'm not holding anything back now. I opened myself fully to him, and it was a lot more freeing than I realized.

I know I still have a long way to go. Like I know he's not going to make it easy for me. Nor should he. I deserve to grovel and worship at his feet.

Tightening my arms around him, I close my eyes and press my face into his gorgeous hair, inhaling the fruity scent of whatever shampoo he used last night.

Xavier stirs, blinking sleepy eyes open and yawning. He frowns for a second, looking around until he's reorientated himself.

"Morning, Bright One." I press my mouth to his, kissing him softly, pleased when he kisses me back. Our lips break apart a few minutes later, and he stares curiously at me. "What?" I ask.

He pushes down on my chest, forcing my back to the mattress. "Be gone with you, alien freak, and return Sawyer 'I don't do morning breath' Hunt to me."

A chuckle rumbles from my chest. "Did I really say that?"

He quirks a brow. "On more than one occasion, but I forgave you because you always let me snuggle."

I yank him down, pressing his face against my chest and wrapping my arms around him. "I love snuggling with you."

He lifts his chin. "I'm even more convinced now you've been the victim of a body invasion."

"It's not that hard to understand," I say, gripping the back of his neck. "I've let down my walls. I'm making myself vulnerable for you because you're worth it."

And that was clearly the wrong thing to say if the hurt-filled look on his face is any indication. Shit. I'm so bad at this stuff.

He pulls up, swinging his legs out the side of the bed. "Don't do me any favors, Hunt. I don't want you to force yourself to be someone you're not." He stands, his cock jutting out proudly.

Jumping out of the bed, I stop him from walking off. "This is scary for me, Xavier, but it doesn't mean I'm being fake with you. I'm more real with you now than I've ever been with anyone before." I clasp his handsome face. "I don't know how to love because I haven't grown up with it. I figured out at an early age that my parents' marriage wasn't the norm. They didn't look at one another like Laurena and Travis did, and they sure as fuck didn't rain love down on me."

Air whooshes out of my mouth as I let him go, flopping down on the bed. "I'm a fuck up, Bright One." I pin him with a shaky smile. "I see how Lauder and Anderson are with their women, and letting go like that terrifies me, but I want that with you. I do. I'm cutting myself open and exposing my heart and my fears because it feels right. You and me feels right. It always has. I know I've made a mess trying to figure everything out, but I will make it up to you."

He sinks onto the bed beside me, and I link our hands. "I love you," I tell him, staring into his eyes. It gets easier to say it each time those words leave my mouth.

"I think you don't really know what you want. I think what happened at the motel scared you into doing something you're not sure about. I believe you believe you love me, but it's a reaction to the car bomb. It's nostalgia."

I grind down on my teeth, working hard to contain my anger, because I don't want to argue with him. "Don't put words in my mouth. Don't tell me how I feel. Throw my words back at me if you don't want to believe them. But don't you fucking dare tell me *I* don't believe them."

"It doesn't matter anyway," he says, yanking his hand from mine and standing.

It's challenging to hold on to my anger with his morning wood practically poking my eye out, but his words annoy me. "How can you say that after last night? I know I wasn't the only one feeling it."

"Hot sex doesn't magically solve our problems, Sawyer. And I really don't think we should be talking about this. We have shit to do like finding that manipulative asshole who's been lying to me for weeks."

"Fine, but we are talking about this again."

Purposely ignoring that, he says, "Grab me something to wear, and I need the tracker scanner" before disappearing into the bathroom.

I grab my bag off the floor and hoist it onto the bed, exhaling heavily when I spot all my neatly folded clothes in a crumpled mess. "For fuck's sake, Xavier!" I yell. "Did you have to mess everything up?"

"Relax. They're only clothes," he shouts back.

I glare at him as he takes a piss with the door open.

"It's like Lauder two-point-oh," I mutter to myself as I pull out clean boxers, a plain white shirt, and a pair of dark jeans. Everything will be a little big on him, but it'll have to do.

The shower turns on as I dump the contents of my bag on the bed and fold everything neatly before putting them back in. I keep the digital device out, leaving it on the bedside table for Xavier.

He reappears a minute later, completely naked and dripping water all over the carpet. He deposits his smoky clothes on the floor and returns to the bathroom, returning a second later, still soaked. Running a towel back and forth across his back, he stares at the pile of clothes I left on the bed like they've personally insulted him.

I narrow my eyes to slits. "Is there something wrong with those clothes?"

"Nothing a splash of color and a few strategically placed rips wouldn't fix."

I roll my eyes as I stand, grabbing my bag to take into the bathroom with me. I don't trust Xavier not to mess with it again, just to rile me up. "They are a loan." I prod him in the chest. "Do not alter my clothes."

"Relax. I'm just yanking your chain," he says, rubbing the towel in and around his crotch.

My eyes greedily follow the motion as lust stirs in my loins.

"Stop looking at me like that. I'm not fucking you again."

"Did I ask you to?" I walk off, slamming the door shut, his laughter following me in. At least I distracted him from destructive thoughts.

I emerge from the bathroom fully dressed twenty minutes later to sounds of Anderson and Lauder talking with Xavier in the other room.

"What's up?" I ask, dropping my bag on the floor as I snatch the room service menu from the coffee table.

"Your dick, it seems." Lauder grins like a loon. "Have Mommy and Daddy kissed and made up?"

"Fuck off," I snipe, dropping onto the couch beside Anderson.

"You're not going to believe this," Xavier says, pacing the room as he angrily swipes buttons on his cell. "The asshole *was* tracking me." He pulls a business card from his wallet and throws it across the room at me. "That sneaky fuck had a tracker embedded in the business card he gave me. I had it in my wallet, and I never thought to scan it for bugs."

"I get why you're pissed," Anderson supplies, drinking coffee out of a paper cup. "But you put a tracker in his watch. It seems like the mistrust went both ways."

"I did that with all the guys who were on the team. I'm not letting people into my place without some insurance," Xavier says, and he's practically frothing at the mouth. Xavier is super smart, and I know this is more than his lover screwing him over. He prides himself on being the best at what he does. Jamison getting one over on him like this hurts more than anything.

I swat the back of Anderson's head. "Where's mine?" I gesture toward the coffee.

"We were going to invite you to come with, but we figured you were visiting Pound Town all night and needed your beauty sleep."

Lauder almost spits his coffee all over the floor.

"Immature much?" I'm tempted to pour the fucking coffee over his smug head.

"Can we fucking focus?" Xavier snaps as someone raps on the door.

Anderson and Lauder have their guns out in record time, stalking to the door and peering through the peephole. "It's the Kray Twins," Lauder says, swinging the door open to let Drew and Charlie in.

"Who the fuck are the Kray Twins?" Anderson asks.

"Ronnie and Reggie Kray were British gangsters who dominated the underworld in London for more than twenty years," Xavier says, not surprisingly.

"How the fuck do you know everything about everything?" Anderson asks as Lauder shuts the door.

"I had a crush on Tom Hardy in high school. He was in a film about their lives when I was a senior."

"*Legend* is one of my favorite movies," Lauder says. "That's how I know who they are."

"Fascinating as this is, can we discuss torture plans for that prick Jamison?" Drew says, blunt as usual.

"I think he's en route here," Xavier says, and all our heads lift.

"I'm logged into the tracking software. It shows he left New York seven hours ago, and it looks like he's heading this way."

"He's probably heading to Alessandra," Charlie says, swiping the second menu from the coffee table.

"The dick had a tracker in my wallet, and it's possible he's been following me for weeks. He probably knows what we've been doing all along."

"I hate that we're two steps behind. We need to get in front of this," I say.

"I agree," Drew says. "I know it's risky as fuck going after Hamilton, but he's got to be our next priority after we find the money and plug the breach in your system."

"Let's deal with one asshole at a time," Xavier says, and I can see he's itching for blood. I am too because fuck that asshole for doing this to him.

"If he knows you're not in Boston like you told him, why didn't Jamison follow us from New York?" Lauder says.

"He can't mysteriously disappear from work without giving the game away," I say. "Especially after my father ripped him a new one for bringing one of the student interns over to the office."

"We need to look into that," Xavier says.

"I already checked the guy out. He's squeaky clean."

"Ding, ding, ding." Charlie scrubs a hand over his prickly jawline. "That's a red flag if ever I heard one."

"The guy is sixteen, and his parents are from Greece."

Charlie shrugs. "Age is irrelevant. I'd killed twenty men by the time I was sixteen."

Anderson, Lauder, and I exchange looks. We knew the guys were involved in heavy shit, but that's a fuck ton of dead bodies for a teenager.

"Don't act so surprised," Drew says. "You know we're not altar boys."

"I'm just saying the guy may warrant a second look if he was hanging around Jamison," Charlie adds.

"Fair point, and I'll check him out again."

"After we've dealt with Jamison," Xavier says.

"Agreed. No matter how it has happened, and whether he's

coming here or to Bama, we have an opportunity to deal with the asshole," Drew says.

"What do you have in mind?" Anderson asks, finishing his coffee and tossing the cup in the trash can under the table.

"I'm ordering food," Charlie says. "Holler if you want anything."

We give him our orders, and he puts a call through to room service. We wait for him to finish before resuming our conversation.

Drew clears his throat. "I'm thinking we find someplace near here we can lure him to. Somewhere remote we can do our work undisturbed, but someplace that's also on the main route, so if he detours to Bama, we can go after him and snatch him. Drag him back to the place and interrogate him."

"You okay with that?" I ask Xavier.

"As long as I get to slice his dick off and watch him bleed out, I'm good." I know he's speaking from a hurtful place, because Xavier is a lover not a killer, but I wonder if he would actually do that. The thought shouldn't turn me on, but it does. Not sure what that says about me.

"Let's get to work then," I say. "We have approximately six hours to catch a snake."

CHAPTER TWENTY-FIVE

Sawyer

Jamison's scathing laughter bounces off the walls of the derelict house we located on the outskirts of Knoxville. The nearest neighbor is five miles away, so we have privacy to do what we need to do. Jamison figured it was an ambush at the last moment and took off. We gave chase. Ran his car off the road and dragged him out of his vehicle and into ours. Now we have him stripped to his boxers and strapped to a grimy chair in what used to be the living room. Wallpaper peels off the walls, and the damp, musty smell in the air clings to my clothes and crawls up my nostrils, making me gag.

"Quit laughing, and start talking, fuckface," Xavier says, kicking the leg of the chair his ex-lover is strapped to.

"Fuck you, asshole." An ugly sneer rips across his face as he glowers at Xavier. "My bad, I've already been subjected to that horror."

I lunge at him, slamming my fist in his face. Blood spurts, spraying over my black T-shirt, only adding to my rage. "I thought you were smarter than this, but, by all means, keep throwing shade and see how well that ends for you."

"I *am* smarter." He spits blood on the floor. "I'm smarter than all of you dumb fucks combined."

This time Drew punches him in the face, and bone cracks as his nose breaks. "You're the one tied to the chair, dumbass."

Jamison hisses, but he doesn't cry out. He's stronger than he led us to believe. "Not for long," he says, grinning wickedly. I'm glad I asked Diesel to return and run surveillance for us outside. We don't know if Jamison is working alone or if he has backup on the way. Better to be safe than sorry.

"If you're waiting for your fuck buddy to show up, you can forget that plan," Anderson says, removing his cell from the back pocket of his combat pants.

"I know you took Alessandra. If you've harmed one hair on her head, I'll fucking kill you."

Drew presses the tip of his knife to Jamison's bare chest. "Your feeble threats are boring me, and you don't seem to realize the power has shifted in our favor."

"You're just like all those other elite assholes. Underestimating women."

"You couldn't be more wrong," Xavier says. "But it's possible you overvalued your fuck buddy's worth." Xavier snatches the cell from Anderson's hand.

"She's not my fuck buddy." A malicious grin creeps over Jamison's mouth. "She's my *wife*."

Shocked silence rings out for a few seconds. Drew is the first to react, silently communicating with Xavier before he refocuses on our prisoner. Xavier hides the cell behind his back as Drew speaks. "Commiserations. I'm surprised you're not begging us to end your suffering."

"You're fucking your cousin? Gross," Xavier says.

We found information on Denton's computer files confirming Jamison was his brother's only child. At some point, Jamison legally changed his name, and the employee file at Techxet is clearly cleverly fabricated because he was one of the first employees I checked up on.

"First cousins are permitted to marry in Bama," Jamison confirms. "And trust me, there is nothing gross about what she lets me do to her."

"Such a charmer," Lauder deadpans.

"Does she know you were cheating on her with me?"

A dark chuckle escapes his mouth. "Who do you think came up with the idea to fuck you over? I wasn't sure how I could entice you away from Hunt until he handed me your ass on a silver platter."

I know I exposed Xavier. Made him vulnerable to this sick prick, and I'll never forgive myself for that.

"You were shit in bed," Xavier says. "And you're a lousy hacker because you left Denton's internal system wide-open for the taking."

"Your touch makes my skin crawl," Jamison snarls. "Why else do you think I always made you bottom and I insisted on fucking you from behind? I had to pour liquor down my throat and pretend you were Alessandra to go through with it."

I'm calling bullshit. I saw the way he was with Xavier. He was super handsy and affectionate, and no one is that good of an actor. I know how easy it is to fall for Xavier. How lovable he is. It wouldn't surprise me if Jamison caught genuine feelings, but the asshole will never admit to it.

"Fucking faggot."

Xavier kicks him in the face, sending more blood spraying from his nose and trickling out of his mouth. Jamison hisses in pain, blood dripping down his chin as he laughs. "You make me sick. You're so fucking pathetic. You and Hunt belong together. Two fucking inept pussies who deserve one another."

Removing my knife, I slam it through Jamison's thigh, purposely missing the artery because this skeezy fuck isn't dying before we get intel out of him. He howls in pain, and the sound is music to my ears. "This is how it's going down," I calmly say. "You are going to shut your fucking face unless we ask you a question. You will tell us everything you know, and in return, we won't let Drew and Charlie sate their bloodthirsty natures on your body. We'll make your death painless."

"I'm not telling you jack shit. Fuck you, queer," he pants.

I yank the knife out and he roars as blood oozes from the

wound.

"I bet you'll do it for your wife," Xavier snaps, shoving the screen of Anderson's cell in Jamison's face. He shows him the early part of the recording with Alessandra, cutting it off before the good part. "You're right. We do have her. We found the photo of you two and figured you'd need an incentive."

"Tell us everything and we'll let her go. That's the deal," I lie.

"I have no guarantee you won't kill her either, so why the fuck would I talk?"

"She's a cunt and everyone in this room has a reason to want her dead, but we don't murder women," Xavier lies convincingly.

"We do torture them though," Drew adds. "What condition she is in will depend on you."

"Bring her to me. Show me she's alive."

Drew chuckles. "Not a chance in hell. The slut stays where she is. We give you our word we'll let her go if you tell us what we want to know."

"No." Jamison shakes his head. "No deal. I don't believe you."

"I figured you might need another incentive," Xavier says, shoving the screen of his own cell in Jamison's face.

"You fucking asshole!" Jamison yells, thrashing about on the chair as he stares at the familiar kitchen. This was Xavier's idea, but it was a long shot. Jamison is super close to the single mom who raised him after his father—Denton's brother—died when he was a baby. We weren't sure if it was true. Everything he told Xavier might have been bullshit, but we took a chance. Diesel sent two guys to his mom's house an hour ago. They won't hurt her, but Jamison doesn't know that.

"Talk," Drew says, dragging his knife down Jamison's left arm.

Jamison grits his teeth and squeezes his eyes shut. "I'll tell you everything, but you leave my mom alone and you let my wife go."

"About that." Xavier thrusts Anderson's cell in Jamison's face again. "We lied."

An anguished howl rips from Jamison's throat as he watches Drew murder his love on the screen.

"We'll make sure your mom gets both your ashes," Xavier supplies.

"Provided she's still alive," I add, slicing my knife across his cheek. "Talk. Right now, or we'll get them to kill her while you watch."

His eyes are as black as the dark night sky outside as he pins them on me. "I will come back from the dead and haunt you for this." His gaze flits around the room. "That goes for all of you." Pain flashes in his eyes, proving he's not completely devoid of emotion.

Drew drives his knife through Jamison's ball sac, and a collective wince rings out in the room. Blood gushes down Jamison's legs as he yells. Tears leak out of his eyes, and he's panting heavily. "I'm all out of patience, dipshit." Drew looks at me. "Give the word. Let's just cut our losses and run. I'm done with this."

I whip out my phone.

"Stop!" Jamison shouts. "This was all my uncle. It was all Denton. He planned this years ago."

"Why?" I ask, keeping my phone in my palm.

"For ultimate power and control."

"He wanted the presidency," Charlie surmises.

Jamison nods as blood drips from his nose, his arm, his cheek, and his thigh, pooling on the ground. "He helped all of them because they were moves on a chess board he designed. Why else do you think I gave you that intel last year?" he says.

I had wondered about that earlier.

"Mathers wanted us to find Nessa so we'd end up taking out Montgomery," Jackson says, pushing off the wall and coming toward us. "We did his dirty work for him."

Jamison smirks, and Drew punches him in the gut.

"Everything you did played into Denton's hands."

"Except Hamilton is president and Mathers is dead," I remind him.

"It was going to be mine," Jamison hisses, and the pieces are starting to slot into place for me.

I couldn't give two fucks about Jamison and his delusions of grandeur. I want to reclaim my life, and that starts with salvaging Techxet. "Where is my father's money?"

"I don't know. Denton hid it offshore someplace. We've been searching for it but coming up blank. You won't find anything on his home network either."

"Don't fucking lie to me." I press my knife to his throat. "I know you were behind the most recent theft."

A muscle clenches in his jaw, but he doesn't speak. "Tell them to relieve his mother of her left hand," I calmly say, speaking to my friends while staring at Jamison.

"No! Stop!" he shouts, his neck moving with the motion. My knife slices through his skin, making a small cut. Blood dribbles down his neck and onto his chest.

"I did take it. We needed it to incentivize Denton's followers to switch their backing from him to me."

I straighten up and stand back, urging him to continue with my eyes.

"Only a handful of people know Denton is dead. His followers think he's overseas on business, and we've been using email to keep communication open, using it to drip feed me into the narrative. If Denton supports and trusts me, his followers will fall into line behind me when the time comes. Especially if there's a financial benefit."

It doesn't miss my attention that he's speaking in the present tense. Moving to the far end of the room, I press down on the communicator chip on my neck to speak to Diesel. I warn him to be extra vigilant for newcomers.

Drew is laughing as I step back beside my friends. "You two stupid fucks were so dumb. No one would back you. They would've taken your money and run straight to Hamilton."

"Truth," Charlie agrees.

"Where is it?" I ask.

His shoulders slump, and I can almost see the fight leave his failing body. "In an account on the Cayman Islands in the name of Arnold Bruce."

"How did you hack into the Techxet system without detection? And who else knows how to access it?"

"I put Denton onto Murtagh, and he already had Becker in his back pocket," he explains. "I didn't actually do anything. Denton didn't want me compromised. It was Becker who found a loophole and supplied the way in. He also ensured it wasn't discovered."

"We need that info," Xavier says. "I know you have it stored somewhere."

"There's a fake app on my phone called Eat4Now," he says, looking at Xavier. "I backed everything up there. You can see what has been done and reverse it, but there are others who know about the loophole."

"Which others?"

"Hamilton's men. I don't know who they are, just that they've been in the system."

"I thought you said this was all Denton?" I narrow my eyes to slits, mistrustful of every word that comes out of his scheming mouth.

"It was until Denton was gone. Now, Hamilton's running the op." He smirks, and it's creepy with blood coating his teeth and dripping off his lips. "He wants that evidence your father has, and as soon as he finds it, he's gonna hang you three out to dry." His gaze flits between me, Anderson, and Lauder.

At least he's confirmed what we have suspected. Hamilton does have a copy of the recording, and that's a big problem.

"Don't know why you're gloating," Anderson says. "You're a dead man, and we're gonna crucify Hamilton before he gets a shot at us."

Damn fucking straight.

Xavier holds Jamison's phone out, pushing it under his thumb. "Activate it."

Jamison obeys without argument, and Xavier quickly changes the fingerprint to his own. I watch over his shoulder as he opens the app and scans through the files. We're both silent as he quickly skims over the information, but it's enough to prove we have what we need to plug the hole.

A layer of tension lifts off my shoulders as I step to the side of Xavier. Yes, we don't know where the original missing money is, but this is more than enough to save Techxet and file for divorce from Sydney.

"Who is Argon, and what was he really doing at the apartment that day?" I ask, moving on to other answers we need.

Jamison's eyes move to Anderson's as a burst of gunfire breaks out outside, claiming our attention. I activate the comm channel to Diesel. "What's going on?"

"You need to get out of there now!" Diesel yells. "Two SUVs have just pulled up and opened fire."

Glass shatters as shots rip through the large window, spilling across the room. Everyone dives for cover, and I pull Xavier down with me, shielding him with my body. "Stay there." I shove him behind a moth-eaten couch because he lost his gun in the blast and he's vulnerable. I didn't think he'd need a replacement for today, considering Diesel and his crew are protecting us outside.

Xavier nods, looking a little out of his depth.

Curling my fingers around my gun, I crawl across the floor using my elbows, doing my best to avoid broken glass, and heading toward the others. The guys are nearer to the window but staying sheltered behind the dust-laden old furniture littering the room. I duck behind a worn leather chair and aim my weapon, firing outside.

More shots fly over our head as Diesel is shouting in my ear, but I can't hear him over the noise as we retaliate, trading gunfire with the unknown and unseen assailants outside.

And then it just stops.

I glance over at Anderson, and his confused expression matches my own. "What's going on?" I ask Diesel as the sound of screeching tires tickles my eardrums.

"They just up and left. Are you okay? Any casualties?"

I glance over my shoulder, my eyes instantly finding Xavier, safely tucked away where I left him. Relief floods through me, but it's short lived as I follow the line of his eyesight. "Well, shit."

"What?" Diesel asks.

"Jamison is dead." His mangled body is riddled with bullets, his head thrown back with one side of his face missing.

"I guess we know what that was about," Drew says, rising to his feet, brushing dust off his clothes.

"They wanted to silence him." Xavier climbs to his full height.

I get up and go to him. "Don't look."

"It's too late," he whispers, and I pull him into my arms. He's shaking. Probably in shock.

"He brought this on himself, and he must've known this was a possibility when he came after us." I wonder if his crew turned up late on purpose. If they wanted us to take him out. Maybe they didn't expect him to divulge trade secrets, but they didn't know we were holding his mother hostage to force him into speaking.

Either way, we got what we needed from him, even if I'm pissed we didn't get to ask him more questions.

"Let's get the fuck out of here," Lauder says, echoing my thoughts.

I rub a hand up and down Xavier's back. "I'm ready to go home."

CHAPTER TWENTY-SIX

Sawyer

WE THROW OURSELVES into work over the following days, setting up a temporary HQ in Xavier's warehouse in Rydeville because I don't want Dad to know what we've done yet. Not until I have something concrete to share with him. All he knows is we've had a breakthrough, but we need to keep it contained until we have investigated it fully.

Unfortunately, Denton's safe was a dead end. We got it open okay, but all it contained were some fake passports, bundles of cash, and the deeds to the house. The camera removed from Denton's secret room yielded no bounty either. It was wiped clean. Most likely, he had it set up to automatically wipe the footage after it had been uploaded to the cloud somewhere.

"Hunt! Come see this," Xavier says, popping his head out of the main room.

I've been working with Charlie in the main part of the warehouse, trawling through the contents of Mathers's computer, as well as bank statements for Techxet, Mathers, and Jamison, trying to find some clue as to where the first stolen haul is. We are also trying to locate Jamison's Cayman Island account while Lauder and Anderson are meticulously examining the intel we have compiled on Hamilton to see if they can find something we can use or some kind of lead. Xavier has been focusing on the files on Jamison's cell, trying to trace the path they took to infiltrate Techxet's system so we can work out a way to shut them out before they realize what's happening.

Abby is pissed she can't help, but she's working hard with ballet rehearsals, and Van has her brother and sister staying for a few days. Shandra has been dropping by with food and drinks, but she doesn't hover because things are strained between her and Drew again.

Getting up, I walk across the space and into Xavier's office-slash-meeting room. He is seated at the large oval table, tapping a pen against his chin, as he stares at the row of screens on the wall in front of him. "I found it," he says as I drop into a chair beside him. Excitement glitters in his eyes, and it's good to see it.

He's been cool with me since we returned from Alabama. I asked him to stay with me at Van and Lauder's house, but he chose to stay with Abby and Kai instead. I haven't pushed him, because I don't want to upset him when I know he's still processing, but I'm not backing off either. I'm just giving him some space. For now.

"Look." He enlarges the screen nearest us. "That's how they got in. See there." My eyes follow the route they took, and I nod. "They snuck in under the firewall, and then they downloaded employee records and used legitimate logins at times when certain staff members were on vacation or on training or after they have left before the internal IT team had disabled their accounts."

"They've been snooping in plain sight. Man, I feel so dumb. Why didn't we think to trace employee logins against leave records?"

"It was simple but brilliant. No one would think to check those records unless they were tipped off."

"Do we know which employee logins they are using?"

"We don't," Xavier says, "and going through thousands of employee records will take too long. If we time this perfectly, we can plug the hole and then reset all the company logins simultaneously. At the same time, we will embed new alerts and an extra few layers of security. As an added precaution, I suggest we move banks because I wouldn't rule out some leak from the banking side. This was a dual attack. Security and finance."

"We should move everything to Barron to manage," I concur as the thought occurs to me.

"I think that'd be wise," he agrees. "We can trust Charlie to keep the money safe."

"Dad will be fucking delighted," I say as Anderson strolls into the room.

"I was grabbing some shit from my car, and I intercepted a delivery driver," Kai says, setting a slim rectangular box down in front of Xavier. "I signed for it. You're welcome. Also, Hunt?" He locks eyes with me. "Abby wants you at our place for dinner. The whole crew will be there."

"I'm in." I readily agree because it means I get to spend some downtime with Xavier. Anderson nods and walks off.

"I didn't order anything," Xavier says, looking perplexed as he picks up a scanning device and runs it over the box.

"It's safe," I confirm. "I ordered it for you."

His brow puckers as he grabs scissors and opens the box, removing the special edition fire-engine-red MacBook Pro with a shell-shocked look on his face. "Holy fuck." His Adam's apple bobs in his throat as he runs his fingers reverently over the smooth exterior. "How the hell did you get one of these?"

"I called in a favor. I know you've been pining since you lost yours in the explosion. It's no biggie."

"Thanks, man." His voice sounds choked.

"You're welcome."

"I'm still not fucking you," he adds, flipping the screen up and pressing the power button on. "I'm done having sex with married men."

I hate he's including me in that lineup, but technically, it's true. "It wasn't a bribe." I lean my elbows on the table. "I'm worried about you."

"Don't be. I'm fine."

"Are you really?"

"I made another mistake. It sucks that I chose the wrong guy again. Let another prick manipulate me, but I refuse to let a dead man destroy me. I'm moving on."

Ignoring my hurt at his words, because I know he's grouping me with that dick from his hometown and Jamison, I tell him what I've wanted to tell him for days. "I told Sydney I'm filing for an annulment." Either party being coerced into marriage is one of the five grounds for annulment in New York, so it should be a cakewalk, even if we have to stand in front of a judge, at a trial, and explain. My parents will throw a hissy fit if the news leaks that our marriage was an arranged sham, but I have zero fucks to give these days.

"Isn't that a little premature? We haven't located the missing money yet."

"I'm confident we'll find at least some of the money."

He cocks his head to the side. "Why annulment? Divorce is actually easier."

"Annulment means the marriage no longer exists in the eyes of the law. It's as if it never happened." I drill him with a look. "I want to remove all trace of it so when I get married for real it's my first marriage in every conceivable way."

Silence engulfs us for a few minutes, charged with a tense undercurrent that lingers in the space between us.

"What about the merger?" He swipes his finger across the keypad of his new Mac.

Trying not to take his apparent disinterest to heart, I let him steer the conversation wherever he wants or needs it to go. "It hasn't been finalized yet, so this can be quick and easy."

"I doubt your father will be pleased. Leaving your new wife a few weeks after you got married will look shady as shit."

"I don't give a fuck what he thinks. Or my mom. He should never have asked me to do it in the first place, and I should never have agreed."

"How did Sydney take the news?"

"She was a little upset. Her father is very controlling, and she thought I was sending her back to him."

He looks up from the screen. "She lived with her father?"

"Yep. He essentially had her in chains. I'm helping to set her free." I'm paying her the prenup settlement so she can get her own place and keep working at the gallery. Or go traveling like she originally planned or do whatever the fuck she wants with her life."

He chews on the corner of his mouth. "You have feelings for her."

I rise and walk to his side, placing my hands on his shoulders. "Not the kind you're thinking. She's a nice woman who's been dealt a shitty hand in life. I care about her enough to ensure she doesn't return to her prison. But if it's an issue for you, I'll completely wash my hands of her."

"It's nothing to do with me, Hunt." He shucks out of my hold.

"It is and it isn't." I shove my hands into my pockets, breathing heavily. "I'm giving you space because I know you need it. But I meant what I said. I love you, and I'm here for you. Whatever you need, it's yours."

"I've got something!" Charlie shouts from outside, effectively ending our conversation. But Xavier heard me.

We race outside, finding Drew, Anderson, and Lauder poured over Charlie's screen.

"What have you found?" I ask.

"The Cayman Islands account and a secret account of Denton's with the same bank. The sum of both accounts is only about half of what was stolen, but it should help."

"Damn straight." I slap Charlie on the back.

"Send the intel through to me and Hunt," Xavier says.

I rub my hands in glee. "It's time to clean out some bank accounts."

"CHAMPAGNE?" I QUIRK a brow later that night when Van hands

me a flute as we lounge around Anderson's backyard. The scent of grilled meat wafts through the air, and my stomach rumbles in appreciative anticipation. It's been an exhausting few days and it's good to just kick back.

"We're celebrating," she says, ruffling my hair.

I narrow my eyes at her.

"Knock that shit off, Hunt," Lauder growls.

I swear his eyes are glued to his wife, like he can't bear not to look at her every second of every minute of every hour. "You're as bad as Anderson these days."

"I heard that, dickhead." Anderson flips me the bird from his position at the massive outdoor grill.

"You were meant to," I call out before taking a mouthful of my drink.

"It's great we've cracked the Techxet problem," Drew says. "But celebration is a little optimistic. We still have Hamilton to deal with, and that'll be infinitely trickier."

"We have the recording. Maybe we should use that," I muse in between mouthfuls of champagne. That wouldn't be breaking the terms of my father's agreement with the elite. Though they aren't exactly honorable.

"It's not enough," Anderson says, coming over to the table and snatching his beer. "He'll weasel his way out of that. We need more."

"I wish we could use the intel my dad has, but it's too dangerous," I say. "We need to find something that implicates Hamilton on his own."

"I agree," Drew says. "He's playing a long game, and we're playing catch-up. I think we've taken our eye off the ball too much these past few months and we need to up the ante."

"The problem is finding the right dirt to bury him in," Lauder says, swatting Van on the ass as she moves past him to keep an eye on the grill.

"Let's put this one fully to bed and then turn our sights to Hamilton," I suggest.

"What did your dad say?" Charlie asks me, resting his chin

on Demi's shoulder. She's perched in his lap, looking content, with her arms draped around her fiancé. It still freaks me out how much she looks like her cousin Abby. If Anderson is still weirded out by it, he hasn't said anything to me.

"He's on board. He wants you to set up a meeting for early next week." I called Dad, to relay the good news, just before we left the warehouse to come here.

"Sweet." Charlie nods, and I know it's a major coup for him to land Techxet as a new client. It's a win-win for both sides.

"Did you talk to him about the other stuff?" Xavier asks.

"Yes. He's over the fucking moon." I don't mention how he tore into me for going after the elite when he specifically told me not to. He calmed down quickly though. It turns out Herman was refusing to adhere to his side of the agreement because he got wind of the security breach and he wouldn't invest until he had assurances his company and his investment would be safe. Although we haven't recovered all of Dad's money, depositing a large chunk considerably cheered him up, and he forgot his anger.

Xavier and I had spent the rest of the afternoon hacking into the Cayman Islands bank and figuring out how to move the money without detection. It was as easy as breathing in the end because their systems are shockingly lacking for a financial institute of their size.

"Earth to Space Cadet Hunt." Xavier flicks his fingers in my face. "You zoned out."

"I was just thinking." I absently thread my hands through my hair. "Dad wants us to attend a special session of the board meeting on Monday to present our report for the next steps. And he wants us to brief the CTO over the weekend."

"Sawyer!" Abby shouts out through the window. "Get your bodacious ass in here."

"Yes, ma'am." I get up, my thigh brushing Xavier's in the process, sending a jolt of heat through my skin. Bending down, I press my mouth to his ear. "Can I get you anything from inside?" I deliberately lower my tone, using a husky voice I know he loves.

A subtle shiver works its way through him, and I smile. He waves his tall glass of cider in my face. "I'm good. Go help my bestie."

"What's up?" I ask Abby when I step into the kitchen. Shandra smiles at me as she exits the room, heading outside.

"Help me with the salad." Abby hands me a knife and a large bowl filled with tomatoes. "Chop these."

"Do you boss Anderson like this?" I ask as I wash my hands in the sink.

"Everywhere but the bedroom." She grins as she slices a red onion into thin rings.

"Was there a reason you dragged me inside besides my stellar skills with a knife?" I ask as I start slicing tomatoes.

"I want to know what your intentions are toward Xavier."

Direct and to the point. It's one of the things I love about Abby. That and her loyalty to my man. "You're a good friend to him, Abby. I'm glad he has you. Especially now."

"He's been there for me more times than I can count, and you haven't answered my question."

I don't hesitate or falter with my reply. "I love him, and I want to be with him." She sets her knife down on the chopping board, scrutinizing my face. "I'm telling the truth."

She nods, smiling. "You finally pulled your head from your ass. That's great. Now what are you going to do about it?" Picking up the knife, she resumes slicing.

"Right now, I'm giving him the space he needs while planning ways to win him back."

"Go big or go home, Hunt." She waves the knife in my face. "And if you fuck things up again, I will use this on you. Your dick will be the first to go."

"Jesus Christ. You're definitely Drew's twin."

Her brows knit together. "What does that mean?"

I pop a tomato in my mouth, chewing it slowly as I watch Drew through the window. He's leaning back in his chair, giving off an air of casual indifference as our friends laugh and chat around him, but he's taking it all in. Not missing a thing. "Your brother has a lot of aggression inside him and a dark side I believe none of us have come close to seeing."

She sets the knife down. "Should I be worried?"

"I don't know."

She stares out at him. "I wish I knew what was going through his head, but he's so guarded. I actually think he's worse than you."

"I'm a changed man. Just watch and see." I waggle my brows.

"I really want you and Xavier to make a go of it, but only if you are all in, Sawyer. You can't hurt him again. I don't think he could handle more rejection."

"How bad is it? He's been quiet this week, and I know he's hurting."

"He's more freaked out about the shootout than hurt at Jamison's betrayal. I heard his body was pretty gruesome."

"It was, and I knew he was freaking out. He let me comfort him in the car, but the second we rolled into Rydeville, he shut me out."

She stops slicing onions to run her hands and the knife under cold water. I grab a tissue from the box on the window ledge and hand it to her.

"Thanks." She dabs at her leaking eyes. "He'll come around, Sawyer, and I think you've given him enough space. Now, you need to prove to him your love is the real deal. You've got to show him, beyond a shadow of a doubt, you are sincere, devoted to him, and planning to stick around for the long haul. He needs reassurance and commitment. Risking his heart on you again will take trust on his part, and you have to do the work now."

"I'm prepared to do whatever is necessary. I won't stop until he knows and trusts I am the man he needs me to be."

CHAPTER TWENTY-SEVEN

Xavier

I FINISH PRESENTING my report to the board and the CTO and reclaim my seat beside Sawyer. He squeezes my leg under the table and smiles. "You were fucking amazing," he murmurs.

"Thank you, Mr. Daniels," Ethan Hunt says, his brow puckering as he watches me and his son with our heads bent together. "That is excellent work. Russell tells me you have agreed to supervise the technical team to bring this project to a conclusion. Techxet is grateful for your expertise."

"I'll help," Sawyer says. "We'll get it wrapped up before we both need to head back to Massachusetts." Sawyer starts his sophomore year, along with our other friends, in two weeks.

Ethan Hunt frowns. "I assumed you'd transfer to West Lorian U. I'm not sure your new bride will relish the idea of living in Rydeville."

"I'm sure we don't need to discuss this in front of the board." A muscle pops in Sawyer's jaw. "I would like to talk to both of you after we are done here," he adds, his gaze dancing between his parents.

Surprise bubbles up my throat, because that's news to me. I assume he's going to tell them he's filed for an annulment. I can't see that going down well with Ava or Ethan.

"I was hoping you'd agree to relocate permanently to HQ," Russell Chalmers, the CTO says, swiveling in his chair to face me. "You have been a huge asset to this project, and you're a massive asset to this company. You are the smartest technical specialist we have on the team, and I see a very bright future for you within Techxet."

Sawyer jerks his head to mine, and I spot pride mixing with panic as he stares at me.

"Thank you for saying that. It's good to know I'm valued. I appreciate the offer, but this is only temporary," I tell my superior. "My life is in Boston and Rydeville."

Sawyer visibly relaxes, squeezing me under the table again. Ethan narrows his eyes. It's almost as if he can see through wood and he knows his son has his hand on my thigh.

"I know Justin will be happy to have you back," Russell says of my boss back in Boston.

"If that is all, I think it's time we wrap up," Warren Feldman, the CFO, says. "I have some more information to prepare before our three o'clock meeting at Barron Banking and Financial Investment Services."

"Good work, team," Ethan says, and I smother a snort. "Let's work to move our finances and secure our systems by close of business on Friday. Approve overtime where necessary, but get the job done."

Chairs screech as the board members gather their stuff and make to leave. I shut down my Mac and stand.

"Don't go." Sawyer tugs on my arm. "I want you to stay for this."

I arch a brow but say nothing, standing beside him.

"Let's move this to my office," Ethan Hunt says. His suspicious gaze is firmly fixed on me as the four of us leave the boardroom and walk the long hallway to the CEO's office. "Hold my calls, Magdalena," he says as we pass by the kindly older woman who is his right-hand woman in the office. Magda deserves the Nobel Peace Prize for putting up with Ethan's prudish, boring ass for so long. I don't know how she does it.

"Hey, Magda." I flash her a smile, stopping by her desk. Hunt's parents continue into the office, but Sawyer lingers.

"How did your date go last week?"

Sawyer smiles, amusement dancing in his hazel eyes.

"It was another washout." She rolls her eyes. "I think I'll be taking a back seat on the dating front for a while."

"Don't give up too soon," Sawyer says. "Your Prince Charming could be just around the corner or even right under your nose." He slants me with a pointed, flirty look.

"I'm taking you out for cocktails tonight," I say, deciding on the spur of the moment.

"*We're* taking you out," Sawyer corrects me. "If you're determined to steal the affection of my best girl, then I at least deserve a fighting chance."

Magda emits a tinkling laugh, patting Sawyer's hand. "Sweet boy. There is more than enough room in my heart for both of you wonderful charmers. I'm sure my old heart doesn't know what to do. And to think I was feeling a little melancholy today."

Sawyer leans down, kissing her on the cheek. "Then it's decided. Let's eat first. You pick wherever you want to go, and make a reservation in my name."

"Choose someplace snazzy, and I'll help you find some charming gentleman to sweep you off your feet."

"If only I was young again and you weren't gay."

"That's what they all say," I joke, taking her hand and kissing the back of it.

"Sawyer. We don't have all day," Ethan Hunt calls out from his office, the agitation clear in his clipped tone.

"What crawled up his butt?" I say, giving Magda her hand back. Her lips twitch as she fights a smile.

"The same old prejudice and impatience," Sawyer murmurs, placing his hand on my back and ushering me into the room.

Sawyer's parents notice, and they exchange wary glances as Hunt closes the door.

Ethan gives me a quick once-over, and though I'm wearing a suit, I can tell it doesn't meet his exacting standards. Maybe the vibrant purple color or the velvet lapels aren't his taste, or perhaps it's my new hair color. I'm enjoying a break from the Mohawk, but I still wanted to try something different. So, I came back early last night and got my hairdresser to come to my place. Now, I'm sporting the same messy bedhead style Sawyer seems to like, but my dark hair has been dyed a silvery gray with purple and blue undertones.

It's fucking fantastic, and I know I look like a million dollars. It's not my problem if Ethan Hunt is too blind to notice magnificence when he's in the presence of it.

"What's this about, Sawyer?" Ava Hunt asks, taking a seat beside her husband, across the table from me and her son. I set my laptop down on the table, resting my hands on top of it.

"I have filed for an annulment, and Sydney moved out over the weekend."

Shock splays across their faces. "Wasn't that a little hasty?" Ethan clasps his hands on the table in front of him. "You didn't even give the marriage a chance."

"Sydney's lovely, and I thought you two were getting along much better now," Ava adds, tucking her hair behind her ears.

"I don't love her, and I was forced into marrying her," Sawyer says.

"I know the deal has fallen through with Herman Shaw and there is no business reason why you must remain married to her, but you can't just cut the woman loose after only a few weeks of marriage. Sydney makes the perfect society wife, and she comes from good stock."

He is beginning to sound more and more like the old-money elite, and I can't fathom how someone like him produced someone amazing like Sawyer.

Ethan removes his cell, sliding it across the table to Sawyer. "Call Sydney up, and tell her you made a mistake."

"Why the hell would I do that?" A vein throbs in Sawyer's neck, and I can tell he's working hard to maintain his usual calm façade. "I have done my duty, and that is the last time I will let either of you force me into making a decision I don't want to make. I am done with pandering to you. Done trying to fight for a scrap of your love."

"Sawyer." Ava sucks in a sharp breath. "Whatever do you mean?"

Sawyer barks out a bitter laugh. "Come on, Mom. Let's have a real honest-to-God conversation for once in our lives. You and Dad have never loved me. Not in any meaningful way. I'm grateful for the life you have given me, but all you taught me was that intelligence, wealth, and reputation are the only measures of success in this life—and the only things worth aspiring to—when all I ever wanted was your love and your time. My inability to open up and share the truest parts of myself stems from my need to self-protect my heart, because locking up my emotions and focusing on the tangible things I could control were the only ways I could cope with your blatant neglect of me growing up."

"Sawyer, why are you saying these hurtful things?" Ava says, her eyes filling with tears. "We gave you everything you could want as a child including independence to make your own decisions."

So that's what we're calling it these days. Disgust coats the inside of my mouth, and I hate this for Sawyer. Sawyer's Adam's apple bobs in his throat, and I reach my hand under the table, giving his thigh a reassuring squeeze, to let him know I'm here for him and I'm proud of him.

"What is going on, Sawyer?" Ethan asks, his eyes locked on my hand under the table.

"I'm finally admitting my truths, Dad, and I'm sorry if the truth hurts. It's cliché but so fucking appropriate. I was so starved for love I didn't even realize when I found it, and I almost ruined the best thing to ever happen to me. All because I'm still trying to win your approval and your love. But no more." Sawyer grabs my hand, links our fingers, and pulls our conjoined hands up onto the table. "I am done playing this game your way. This is my life, and I'm living it the way I want."

Without hesitation or any prior warning, Sawyer grabs my head, pulls my mouth to his, and kisses me passionately. I don't let him down, and it's not just because I lose every brain cell in my head the second Hunt's lips fuse to mine. I know how much strength and bravery it took to do this, and I'm with him every step of the way.

"You've made your point," Ethan snaps. "This is a goddamned place of work, not a sex club," he splutters.

Sawyer breaks our lip-lock, threading our hands together again and placing them on top of the table. Ava Hunt stares at her son in complete shock. The look on Ethan's face is one of disgust and disappointment. He glares at me. "You're fired. Get the fuck out of my company."

I smile because his reaction is as predictable as me wearing superhero underwear.

Sawyer pierces his dad with a look of disdain. "You would fire the man I love. The man I'm *in* love with. The man I want to spend the rest of my life with. Just because he doesn't fit your vision for me?"

"Sydney is who you should be with!" Ethan thumps his fist on the table.

"I don't love Sydney!" Sawyer roars, straining across the table at his father. "I love Xavier." He pulls me to my feet. "I quit." He unclips his staff ID from his belt and throws it down on the table.

I silently add my staff badge to Sawyer's on the table. "You have my report. Russell knows what needs to be done to fix the breach. I'm willing to accept calls if anyone on the team has questions because, unlike you, I won't let my emotions and my personal feelings color my professionalism."

"Don't even think about withholding payment on the bonus Xavier was promised," Sawyer says. "You won't like what I'll do if you attempt to screw him over."

"You dare to threaten me?" Ethan glares at his son as tears spill quietly down Ava's cheeks.

"Stop it. Both of you." She rubs her fingers under her eyes. "Let's just sit back down and talk this through."

"No." A muscle pops in Ethan's jaw. "He's made his bed. Let

him lie in it," he snarls.

"Ethan, please." Ava pulls on his arm, pinning pleading eyes on him. "If Xavier is Sawyer's choice, that's good enough for us. Our son has impeccable taste, and we trust his judgement."

I wonder if she really means that or she's just saying what needs to be said to defuse the situation.

"Get out," Ethan says. "And don't come back until you've come to your senses."

Pain glides across Sawyer's face, and my heart hurts for him. I've been in his shoes. I know what it feels like. Forcing my anger aside, I eyeball Ethan Hunt, attempting to reach him, purely for Sawyer's sake. "Your son loves you. All he asks is for the same unconditional love in return. I might not be your choice for him, but it's not your decision to make or your life. At least trust your son to make the right decisions for him. I am willing to put this behind us because I love your son and I want him to be happy. Surely, we can agree on that much?"

"I'm not discussing this with you, and I'd like you both to vacate my office now." His cold expression matches his stone heart.

I grip Sawyer's hand closer as Ava sobs at her husband's side.

"Come on, Xavier. We know where we're not wanted." Without another glance at his parents, Sawyer strides out of the office, holding his head high with my hand in his. I'm tempted to slam the door, but I want to remain professional. I won't give that man any legitimate reason to criticize me.

Magda smiles broadly when she spots us, jumping up and rounding the table. She pulls us both into a hug. "I knew I was right about you two! I've seen the spark, and I prayed it meant what I thought it meant." Her smile fades a little when she sees the expression on Sawyer's face. "What's wrong?"

"Do you even need to ask?"

Sympathy splays across her face. "They're in shock. They'll come around."

They might not. My parents didn't. But Sawyer doesn't need to hear that now. He needs my support and my love, and he's got that in spades."

"I don't care if they do." Sawyer plants a swift, hard kiss on my mouth. "Xavier is all I need."

"I'm here for you." She squeezes my arm. "For both of you."

"Thanks, Magda. We love you too." I pull them into a group hug.

"Text me the dinner details," Sawyer says when we break apart. "We'll meet you there and tell you everything."

We separate to go to our offices to pack up our things, meeting ten minutes later in the lobby. I walk toward Sawyer, carrying a box, watching the commotion on the sidewalk through the large glass doors with interest. "What's going on out there?"

There must be at least fifty people congregated on the sidewalk directly outside the building, all looking up.

Laughter rumbles from Sawyer's chest. "I had almost forgotten." He jerks his head forward. "It's a surprise. Come on."

We leave our boxes with the receptionist for a few minutes, and I can't contain my happiness as Sawyer takes my hand, walking me out the door, uncaring about the attention we're receiving from people inside and outside the building.

The crowd parts as we approach, and a round of applause breaks out. Giddy smiles and inquisitive looks surround us as Sawyer walks me to the center of the sidewalk and slams to a stop. More onlookers crowd the sidewalk, and I spy people on the other side of the road looking up.

Sawyer stabs me with his gorgeous eyes, squeezing my hand. His whole face is alive, his recent upset all but forgotten. "I told you I'd fight for you and I won't stop proving how much I love you. I hope this goes some way toward showing you how much I care." He tips my chin skyward, pointing. "I think I look rather hot in spandex."

I'm rooted to the sidewalk in shock as I stare at the massive banner that runs along the entire side of the Techxet building. Written in big bold lettering is "I'm loyal to nothing, General. Except…the Bright One." He's signed his name underneath, so people are in no doubt who's behind the masked superhero. The reference is a spin on an iconic line from *Captain America*, quoted in one of the Marvel Universe comics. If I'm not mistaken, it's from *Daredevil* number two hundred and thirty-three. A proud, smiling Sawyer Hunt stands tall along the full length of the banner, dressed as Captain America, with his chest out, carrying the infamous shield against his impressive broad chest.

I burst out laughing at the sight of him in the tight costume, and I can't stop. I clutch his arm and double over, almost choking with laughter, conscious there are cameras capturing this moment but I couldn't give two fucks. You have to know Sawyer Hunt to know how big of a deal this is. The old Sawyer would have run a million miles from doing anything like this. Too scared to put his heart on the line in such a public way. This is going to be all over social media. Our friends are going to milk this forever. There will be no hiding from this. Sawyer would know, and he still did it.

My laughter dies, and I straighten up, turning around so I'm facing him. I clasp his face in my hands, fighting tears as a sudden rush of emotion sweeps through me. "You look fucking magnificent in spandex, and nothing says love like superhero love." Emotion glitters from his eyes, joining what he must see in my gaze. "I love you, Sawyer Hunt. You crazy, beautiful man." We move together, our mouths fusing as one, and we kiss as if we're the only two people in the world and we're not surrounded by cheering crowds underneath a giant-sized banner that outs us to the entire world.

I don't think life gets much better than this.

CHAPTER TWENTY-EIGHT

Xavier

"Which is the closest available meeting room?" I ask the receptionist, holding firm to Sawyer's hand.

"Uh. Let me check." She pushes her glasses up her nose as she checks the system. "3B is free for an hour."

"Perfect. Book us in," Sawyer says, as confident as I am that the news of our leaving hasn't been conveyed to all the relevant parties yet. "Keep an eye on our boxes," he adds, grabbing the key as we practically race across the lobby toward the meeting rooms.

Sawyer slams me up against the back of the door the second we enter room 3B, plunging his tongue in my mouth as he locks the door and presses the switch to close the blinds. I grip his shoulders, moaning into his mouth as we devour one another, grinding our erections together. I shove at his shoulders, pushing him off me. "I need in your ass right fucking now, Sawyer." Tugging the zipper on his pants down, I drive my hand underneath his boxers to get to his dick.

"Fuck." Sawyer hisses as my thumb sweeps across the precum beading his crown.

"Over the desk, Hunt." I push him across the small room, keeping my hand wrapped around his cock. When his butt hits the desk, I yank his pants and boxers down his legs and drop to my knees. His gorgeous dick bobs in front of my face like the most mouthwatering popsicle, and I dive in, feasting on his cock while I fumble with the zipper on my pants, desperate to stroke my aching shaft.

Sawyer rolls his hips, thrusting into my mouth as I suck him deep, the tip of his dick hitting the top of my throat. My tongue rolls around his piercings and I'm in heaven. "Goddamn. You look hot on your knees between my legs." Sawyer grabs fistfuls of my hair, using his hold to control the motion of his dick as he shoves it in and out of my mouth. My hand wraps around my erection, and I groan around Sawyer's length as precum seeps from the head of my cock. Carefully, he pulls out of my mouth, yanking me upright. "I assume you don't have lube, so let me get you ready." Lowering my pants, he chuckles when he sees the Captain America boxer briefs I'm wearing. "I chose the perfect superhero," he teases, pulling them down my legs.

"Any superhero would be perfect. You know I love them all. I'm super generous like that." I hiss as he cups my balls, running his tongue along them and sucking them into his mouth. "Suck me, man." I jerk my hips. "I need to be inside you, and we should probably hurry."

Sawyer smiles up at me as he pumps my cock in his hand. "If the banner doesn't give my dad a coronary, I think catching us fucking in one of his meeting rooms would do it."

"Enough about your dad. Suck my dick."

He flashes me a cheeky grin before he swallows my cock whole. I grab the edge of the desk to steady myself as he works me over, running his lips up and down my cock and sliding his tongue over my piercing while fondling my balls and running his finger along my taint. I'm close to nuclear detonation already because Sawyer's touch is just that amazing. "Enough," I pant, yanking my dick from his mouth. "Over the desk. Ass in the air."

"Yes, boss." Sawyer grins, and I grab his head, planting a brutal kiss on his mouth.

"I fucking love you."

"I fucking love you too." He kisses me one more time before leaning over the desk, jutting his ass in the air, and spreading his thighs wide.

I kneel behind him, spreading his ass cheeks and lowering my face to his puckered hole. My tongue licks a steady, impatient path all around his hole while I push two fingers in and out of him, getting him ready.

Sawyer grunts, his hand moving to stroke his dick as I line up at his entrance. "Are you okay to go bareback?" I ask because we've never done that before.

"Yes," he hisses. "Get in me already, Bright One."

"Impatient much, Drill Sergeant?" I tease as I inch my dick in his ass.

We both curse as I fill him up, and then there's no more talking. Sawyer stretches his arms along the top of the desk, gripping the far edge, as I slam in and out of his tight ass, struggling to maintain control. Fucking him with no barrier—physical, emotional, or mental—is my every dream come to life, and I never want this to end. But my dick has other ideas, and I already feel a familiar tingle building in my spine as my balls lift and tighten. Sliding my hand around his hip, I grab his hard-on and pump him in time with the strokes of my dick in his ass.

"Fuck, yes. Xavier. Damn that feels too good. I'm not going to last."

"I'm close too," I rasp, closing my eyes as waves of pleasure rip through my body. I pick up my pace, thrusting into him hard and deep, and he shatters on my hand the same time I deposit my seed in his clenching ass. I drape my body around him, uncaring how sweaty and hot I am, just needing to hold him like this as my dick softens in his ass. "I love you, Sawyer. You are it for me."

Sawyer motions for me to move, and I step back, letting him straighten up. He turns around, and the look of love and adoration on his face is everything I never dared to dream of. "You're my everything, Xavier. There is only you."

A loud banging on the door interrupts us. "Mr. Hunt and Mr.

Daniels. I'm here to escort you from the premises."

Sawyer grabs a handkerchief from the inside pocket of his jacket and hands it to me. He uses a second one to wipe my cum from his ass while I clean my hand. We tuck our dicks away and right our clothing as the thumping grows more insistent on the door. I move to open it, but Sawyer reels me back, smoothing hair off my face and closing my jacket button. "As much as I'd love my dad to know what we were doing in here, I won't have anything tarnishing your reputation. You have conducted yourself impeccably while Dad has acted like a prick. I won't let anything be taken from you."

"I'm loving this new you," I say, fixing his hair while he buttons up his jacket. "But I love the old bossy, moody, grumpy Sawyer too. All the parts of you fit me to perfection."

"Why, Xavier. That might just be one of the nicest things you've ever said to me," he teases, tossing my own words back at me.

I roll my eyes and grab his hands. "Let's get the hell out of here."

"DUDE, IT'S GONE viral," Abby says over FaceTime later that night when we are back at Sawyer's penthouse. I didn't particularly want to come here, but I didn't want to go to a hotel either. Not when we're trending on all the social media platforms and we're all anyone is talking about on entertainment channels. I couldn't stay at the apartment because Techxet owns it, so Hunt helped me to grab my shit, and we dumped it here before heading out to meet Magda for an early dinner.

"We know," Sawyer drawls, swinging his legs up onto the couch, his feet landing on my lap.

"I still can't believe you did it," Anderson says, grinning manically. "What have you done to my best friend, Daniels?"

"Shown him the light," I reply, rubbing Sawyer's feet as I sip my glass of shiraz.

"When are you guys coming back?" Abby asks.

"We're going to pack up Hunt's shit and do some house hunting this week, so we'll probably leave for Rydeville this weekend," I confirm. Since we returned from dinner, we have been busy making plans for the future, excitedly discussing options while we share a bottle of red wine.

"You can stay with us," Abby offers, and Anderson nods. "You know we have plenty of space."

"Lauder offered too," Sawyer explains, "so we'll probably move between both of you until we find our own place."

"You're moving in together?" Abby is practically bouncing all over the couch while her husband watches her in amusement.

"We are. We're going to sell my apartment in Boston and buy a new one, as well as look for a small business premises now we've decided to set up our own IT security consultancy firm."

"And we're going to look for a house in Rydeville so we can split our time between the two. At least until I graduate RU," Sawyer explains.

"I'm so proud of you, Sawyer," Abby says with tears shining in her eyes. "And I'm so happy for you, Xavier. You're getting everything you ever dreamed of."

"I am." I scoot closer to Sawyer, and he moves his legs, sliding his arm around me. I hold my hand up, showcasing the platinum band on my ring finger. "Sawyer gave me a promise ring and committed to me forever and ever and ever." I lean back, angle my head, and kiss him. Because I can and I want to.

Abby screams, and my eardrums protest. "This is fucking awesome. We've got to celebrate. Be back in Rydeville Saturday night. I'll plan it with Nessa and Shandra."

"Show me your hand, Hunt," Anderson says, leaning in closer to the screen.

My man smirks, holding his left hand up. "I've got one too though Xavier is insisting he's buying me a new ring."

"Well, duh." I slap his chest. "You can't buy yourself a promise ring from me, dumbass." I roll my eyes, jumping when he pinches my nipple, spilling red wine on the couch.

"For fuck's sake, Xavier. You're worse than a toddler." Now it's his turn to roll his eyes.

"Don't be a dick though I know it's your default setting. The couch is leather. It'll wipe off."

"You guys crack me up," Abby says. "But I'm so happy you're in love and together. We just need to fix Drew and Shandra and the whole crew is loved up."

"Babe." Anderson grabs her onto his lap. "You can't interfere. They need to sort their shit out in their own time and their own way."

Abby pouts, but she doesn't argue. We end the call and finish our bottle of wine as we continue making plans.

"SAWYER," I SHOUT, racing from the living room toward the bedrooms. "You have to see this."

He pokes his head out of his bedroom where he's packing his things. "Where's the fire?"

"Look at that." I slap a thick manila folder into his chest.

"What is it?" he asks, taking it from me and moving to the couch by the wall in his master suite.

"William Hamilton's demise." I shift on my feet and rub my hands together. "It's got tons of evidence we can use against him. Tax evasion. Sex trafficking. Drug deals. There's even arms deals he's done with overseas enemies of the US. That's treason with the potential for terrorism. There is no way they won't throw the book at him for this."

Sawyer's eyes pop wide as he skims through the bulky file. "Where did you get this?"

"It was in the box I took from the office yesterday, but I've got no clue how it got there. It wasn't in my stuff when I cleared out my desk."

"Someone must have put it there when we left the box with the receptionist."

"I'm guessing so." I had come to the same conclusion.

"We need to find out where this came from."

"For sure, but right now, we need to agree what to do with this."

"Let's call Lauder and Anderson."

I plop down beside him. "You're worried using this might force Hamilton to reveal the Montgomery murder tape?" It's my biggest fear, even if I'm excited to finally have some concrete ammunition we can use to hang that motherfucking bastard.

Sawyer nods. "I am, but we may have no choice. If Hamilton isn't taken down, he'll keep coming at us. At all of us."

"I agree," Anderson says ten minutes later when we're on a group Zoom call with Jackson. The girls are present too. They're not happy. Understandably so. I don't like the risk either, but it seems like there is no other option.

"Why not use this to force Hamilton into submission?" Nessa says. "Between this, the evidence your father has, and the recording you guys taped, there is more than enough to force him to toe the line. Tell him to quit as president and walk away and you won't hand his ass to the authorities."

"That won't work, beautiful." Jackson circles his arm around his wife's shoulders. "He'll just be more determined to come after us."

"Lauder is right. This intel is too dangerous to make him aware of its existence. The only thing we can do is hand it over to the authorities," Anderson says.

"And it's the right thing to do," Sawyer adds. "This guy needs to pay for his sins. The stuff in the file is disgusting. Especially the sex trafficking. He has sold thousands of kids and forced others into prostitution and kiddie porn. He has to be stopped."

"What if we went to Keven Kennedy?" Abby suggests. She's been deep in thought. "Give him that and tell him about the tape. Explain the circumstances. Maybe you can make a deal that keeps you out of jail."

Sawyer, Jackson, and Kai exchange knowing looks, silently communicating as tension bleeds into the air.

"I think we should give the evidence to Kennedy but say

nothing about the tape," Jackson says. "We'll put him in an awkward position if we mention it, and there may be nothing he can do."

"I agree with Lauder. I say we take our chances," Anderson says.

"We could break into his place after he's arrested and see if we can find it," I suggest. "I'm betting his buddies will dump him the second this goes down. He'll be more vulnerable, and it should be easier to get into his office and his home."

"I doubt we'll find it in there," Kai says. "We know from past experience these guys never leave stuff lying around where anyone could find it."

"We have to take the risk," Sawyer says. "If it is disclosed, we'll lawyer up and use the media to paint Montgomery as the villain he was. There would be outrage if they sent us down for it."

Anderson and Lauder nod. "I think that's the smartest play."

"You would still be arrested, and you might be sent to prison to await trial," Abby says, her voice thick with fear.

"That's a chance we have to take, babe." Anderson wraps his arms around his wife. "It's time to do this. This is bigger than us."

"This is the best way to protect everyone," Jackson agrees.

"Then we're doing it," Sawyer says, and I slide my fingers through his. I don't like they are having to take this risk, but I see the logic in their strategy.

"I'll make the call to Kennedy," Anderson says as Abby swipes at her eyes.

I blow her a kiss, touching her pretty face on the screen. "It will be okay, bestie. None of us have fought this hard for it to end like this. No matter how it goes down, it will be all right. We'll make sure of it."

CHAPTER TWENTY-NINE

Sawyer

"I LIKED THAT last place," Xavier says, throwing himself down on the couch in his Boston apartment, where we are currently living.

My cell vibrates with a message, and I pull it out as I kick off my sneakers and sit down. "Me too. The rent is good, and the area is up-and-coming."

"Plus, it's only a few blocks from here." We have decided to concentrate our efforts on finding a new business premises and a house in Rydeville. We can use Xavier's apartment until we have the time to buy a new one. Right now, our priority is getting the business up and running, and I'll be returning to school next Monday. Magda has resigned from her position at Techxet, and she's going to come and work for us part-time so she can enjoy semi-retirement. We're putting her up in a hotel until she's found a place to call home in Boston. We're both thrilled she accepted our offer without any hesitation, having no permanent ties in New York. "Turn on CNN," I say, reading my message from Anderson. "The news has broken about Hamilton."

Keven Kennedy visited us in New York along with two of his colleagues, and we handed them the evidence. We hadn't heard anything until last night when he sent us a group message to say an arrest was imminent.

Xavier turns on the TV, flicking through various news channels, and it's the headline on all of them. Hamilton is also being linked to the recent murder of Ronald Murtagh in the Otisville Correctional Facility. That news hit the headlines a few days ago. Maybe I'm cold, but I feel no remorse. That guy dug his own grave.

"Now we wait," Xavier says, turning off the TV. Tossing the remote aside, he crawls into my lap. "I'm scared."

"Don't be." I cup his cheek. "We'll handle whatever comes our way. Worst-case scenario, I grovel to Dad and get him to hand his evidence over in exchange for making the case against us go away."

"Would he do that?"

I nod. "Perception is everything to him. You know that. Can you imagine how horrified he'd be if I was arrested for murder and my face splashed all over the news?"

"He might wash his hands of you," Xavier softly says because he knows Dad hasn't made any effort to reach out to me in the week since we left his office.

"Mom won't let him," I say. "You know she wants to make amends."

My mother reached out to me a couple of days before we left New York, and I met with her for lunch. She apologized and begged me not to give up on Dad. She has promised to work on him. We actually had a really good conversation, and she listened to me. I don't know if she understands fully where I'm coming from, but she's willing to try, and that's good enough for now.

Dad is being a typical stubborn ass and digging his heels in. I cannot see him ever changing his mind. Especially when the board has just removed him as CEO in a shocking, unexpected move. They are unhappy with his mismanagement of the fraud and the security breach and furious at him for how he dealt with Xavier and me. He is still staying on. For now. In a new role as head of project development, as a conduit between IT and sales, focusing on new product and service lines. This will be a huge blow to him, and I wonder if he'll sell his shares and set up something new. Time will tell, I guess.

"Try not to worry," I add, smoothing the creases in his brow. "I'm not thinking about it, and you shouldn't either. Let's just live our lives, and we'll handle it when the time comes." I grab his hips and graze my teeth along the column of his neck. "I can think of better things to do with our time," I purr, thrusting my pelvis up, my cock thickening behind my jeans.

"Me likey what you're thinking." Xavier grabs the hem of his shirt, pulling it over his head. He flings it on the floor. "Naked fun time is my favorite pastime."

"I've noticed," I drawl, popping the button on my jeans as he climbs off me to remove his jeans, boxers, and sneakers. "You can't keep your hands off me." I flash him a smug grin.

He props his hands on his hips, and he looks too funny standing in only teeny-tiny Batman briefs. His messy silvery, purple, and blue hair is a mess of waves tumbling over his brow, and I can't wait to grab it as I fuck him hard. "Excuse me, Hunt." He shoves his briefs down, and his heavenly cock springs free. "It's *you* who can't keep your hands off *me*." He arches a brow as I shuck out of jeans and boxers and grab the lube packet from my back pocket. I have taken to carrying them with me everywhere we go now. Irrespective of who initiates it, we are pretty sex-crazed at the minute.

"This is an equal relationship." I sink onto the couch, pulling him on top of me. "In every way. Sex included." I drag his lower lip between my teeth. "Our grabby hands are a mutual thing."

Xavier beams at me as he swipes the packet from my hand and tears it open. "It is, and I love how much more agreeable you are these days."

"I still hate your messy shit all over the place," I remind him because we argue daily about his untidiness. "I'm trying to be less controlling, but he's got to meet me halfway. I groan as he lowers his mouth over my dick, running his lips up and down my hard shaft and licking my piercings.

He looks up at me with his lips hovering over the tip of my dick. "You love messing in my shit."

My face puckers. "You did not just go there."

He chuckles as he lathers my dick in lube. "I did, and don't pretend you're grossed out," he adds, straddling my hips and gripping my dick. "Not when you're hard as a rock at the prospect of fucking my ass."

He guides my dick to his ass and sinks down on me. "Fuck, Bright One." His hole tightens around me, and I'm seeing stars. Xavier holds himself still on top of me, and I don't move, wrapping my arms around him as his head falls to my shoulder, and we embrace, savoring the feel of one another.

The only thing better than filling Xavier's ass is him filling mine.

"Love you," Xavier whispers, lifting his head and claiming my lips in a soft kiss.

"Love you too." I thrust my hips up. "I'd love you more if you moved," I tease, digging my hands into his waist and rocking my hips up.

"So fucking impatient." Xavier slowly moves up and down on top of me as I roll my hips in sync with his motion.

"When it comes to you? Always." I slam my lips against his as he bounces up and down on top of my dick, and we get lost in one another as we have so often since we reunited.

"ARE YOU EXPECTING company?" Xavier asks a few hours later as we're tangled together on the couch, watching a movie. We went another round in the shower with Xavier taking my ass this time, before drying off and changing into sleep shorts.

"Nope." I remove his limbs from my body and stand, walking to the dresser and grabbing my gun. "Stay there. I'll check who it is."

I peer through the peephole, surprised to see Keven Kennedy standing outside our apartment. I let him in and lead him into the living room, apologizing for our state of undress. I put my gun away and sit beside my boyfriend.

"No need to apologize," he says, perching his butt on the arm of the leather chair. "And I'm sorry for dropping by so late, but I didn't think this should wait."

"Okay." Xavier takes my hand in his, understanding, like I do, this could be a turning point.

Keven hands me a small brown envelope. "Hamilton tried to bargain with that tape. I assume you know what I'm referring to."

I nod, unsurprised.

"It's not as bad as it looks," Xavier blurts, his voice trembling a little.

Yeah, I'm pretty sure it is. Lauder was a crazed animal as he literally ripped Montgomery to shreds.

"There were extenuating circumstances," Xavier continues, panic evident in his tone. "Montgomery was a corrupt bastard and a sick pervert. Vanessa was his bio daughter, and he lured her overseas and attempted to rape her. The guys rescued her, and it was self-defense. He would've killed them if they hadn't killed him."

Keven clears his throat. "I don't doubt any of that, but it still makes for pretty gruesome watching." Sympathy splays across his face. "We know what he did to Dani Lauder and countless other victims. That's why my boss turned a blind eye when I pocketed the evidence and walked off with it."

"What do you mean?" I'm not sure I'm following. "Are you not here to arrest me?"

He shakes his head and stands. "That doesn't exist, and I've never seen it."

"Thanks, man." Relief floods my body as I rise, pulling Xavier with me. "We owe you so much."

"What if there are other copies?" Xavier asks, worry still etched on his face.

"My team is handling all the technical aspects of the case. If anything else is uncovered, I'll be the first to see it, and it will mysteriously disappear too." He drills me with a look. "Burn it, and heed my advice. Steer clear of the elite and stay out of trouble. I can't guarantee my boss will give you another free pass if anything else should surface."

This isn't the first time we've had some explaining to do or the first time Keven has helped us out. "We can't thank you enough, Keven." I slide my arm around Xavier. "If we can ever do anything for you, you only need to ask. I know Anderson and Lauder would say the same."

"I know how easy it is to get trapped into doing shit, and it can be hard to break the cycle. I also think I'm a good judge of character. I know you're good men, and Rick is a good friend of Kyler's. We stand by our friends, especially in times of need."

"We appreciate it."

Keven cocks his head to one side. "I heard an interesting rumor. That you have left Techxet and you're setting up a private consultancy?" His gaze drifts between us.

"We are," Xavier says, arching an eyebrow. "Are you interested in joining us?"

My eyes pop wide. Keven has mad technical skills, and the three of us working together would be a dream team.

"Not now. I like my work with the FBI. Maybe in the future." Keven shoves his hands into the pockets of his pants. "Would you guys be open to working with us, on special projects, from time to time?"

I try to temper my excitement.

"Does a bear shit in the woods?" Xavier says, and I roll my eyes.

"What my partner means is we would be open to exploring opportunities to work with the FBI."

"Cool. I'll let my boss know. We're pretty understaffed most of the time, and occasionally we hire outside tech help. It would be good to have you guys to call on."

"Whatever you need, we're here," Xavier says, and I nod.

"One last thing before I go," Keven says, walking toward the door. "Where'd you get all that intel on Hamilton?"

"We don't know," Xavier says. "Someone left it with my stuff at Techxet."

"Well, whoever it was, he or she did all of us a huge favor. The intel is solid, and there's no way Hamilton is wriggling out of this. He's going down for good."

"That is the best news I've heard in ages," Xavier says.

"Take care, and thanks again for bringing this to us. We appreciate it," I add.

We say goodbye and let Keven go.

"I want to know who gave us that intel," Xavier says, reading my mind.

"We need to hack into the camera feeds at Techxet. I want to see who placed it in your box."

"You call Anderson and Lauder while I get working on that."

I grin. "Bet Dad didn't think about that when he was firing you." Xavier came up with the new security system, and we both know how to get into the system undetected because he created the new security firewalls. And that's if they are even installed yet.

"Best thing your dad ever did for me," Xavier says, pecking my lips as he grabs his Mac and heads to the island unit, hauling his ass up on a stool.

"Truth." We are living our best lives now, and the last layer of stress is now lifted.

I move into the living room to call our friends and their wives from my burner cell, giving them the good news.

"Hunt. Get over here stat. You need to see this," Xavier shouts as I end my call. I stalk to the kitchen and lean over his shoulder. "Is that who I think it is?" my boyfriend asks. He has the screen frozen on an image of a guy with cropped blond hair. He's turned around from the reception area, staring straight into the camera with a savage grin on his face.

Shock splays across my face. "Argon put the file there?"

Xavier nods as I absently run my fingers up and down his arms. "He waited for the receptionist to take a bathroom break, and he snuck in and placed the file in my box. We dropped the ball with this guy."

"Who the hell is he, and why was he interning at Techxet?"

"He's only a kid," Xavier says, enlarging the screen a bit more.

"Hang on a sec," I say as all the blood drains from my face. "He had blue eyes and glasses on when we met him. Now he's got brown eyes and no glasses."

"Contacts?" Xavier muses.

I stare at him, that sixth sense I had about him still lifting the fine hairs on the back of my neck. And then it hits me. "No fucking way."

"What?" Xavier turns to me as I race to my messenger bag, pulling out a notepad and pen.

I climb up on the stool beside my boyfriend. "Put his image into Photoshop and change his hair to dark brown," I say as I write his name down on the notepad.

ARGON SANDERON.

"Holy. Fuck." Xavier's spine stiffens as we both stare at the image of the dark-haired intern. "How did we not see this before?"

"Because he disguised himself and kept out of our way on purpose. Look at his name. Tell me what you see."

Xavier's eyes pop wide as he stares at me. "We need to go to Rydeville."

"Right now," I agree because this cannot wait.

CHAPTER THIRTY

Sawyer

"What the fuck is going on?" Kai asks, looking part perplexed, part scared, and part pissed, as he answers the door to us at two a.m.

"We discovered something," Xavier says, pushing past him. He glances down at his sleep pants. They are black with red lips patterned all over them. "Cute PJs." He smirks.

Anderson flips him the bird. "My wife bought these for me. I wear them to please her."

"Pussy." My lips twitch as I step into his house.

"You dare to throw shade at me, General?"

I roll my eyes. "Guess I asked for that one." We turned up to the restaurant in Rydeville on Saturday night to find all my friends and their significant others wearing T-shirts with an image of me dressed as Captain America on the front, and on the back, the shirts read "I love you, Bright One." They also had a full-length roll-up banner on display at the table, which was a smaller version of my banner.

Fucking assholes.

They are never going to let me forget this. But I'll handle it. Because I got the guy. And that's all that matters.

"What's happened?" Abby asks, rubbing sleepy eyes as she

emerges in a red knee-length silk robe.

"They have something to tell us," Anderson says, slinging his arm around his wife's waist. "Apparently, it couldn't wait until morning."

"It can't," I say, following Xavier into the living room. Kai flips the switch on the wall, and the room is bathed in light. We sit down at the dining table and Xavier powers on his Mac.

"You should call Rick," I suggest. "He'll want to hear this."

Anderson frowns, taking my cell and placing the call to his brother without questioning me.

By the time we have a sleepy Rick staring at us through FaceTime, Xavier has the screenshot loaded on his Mac.

"This guy is Argon Sanderon," I explain, showing them the image of the blond-haired student. "He was interning at Techxet over the summer."

"I remember you mentioned him at the hotel," Anderson says. "He was the one Jamison let into the apartment."

"Correct," Xavier says. "He's also the one who gave us the file on Hamilton."

"What the fuck?" Rick says, sounding more alert. "Why would a kid have that kind of information? And if he was working with Jamison, which is the implication, why would he squeal on Hamilton?"

"Both good questions," I say. "And—"

"We don't have answers to them yet." Xavier cuts across me, and I glare at him. "Keep your hair on, Drill—"

I slam my hand over his mouth to shut him up. "Focus, Daniels." I'm already a laughingstock among my friends. If they hear his pet name for me, I will never live it down. Never. I'm learning to relax more and to go with the flow, instead of controlling everything, but I still have limits.

"Show them the next image," I tell Xavier as he switches pictures.

"He's been wearing a disguise, and I'm willing to bet he dyed his hair that blond color." I bring my phone in closer to the screen so Rick can see. "Look close. Who does he remind you of?"

Abby spots it first. "Oh my God." She grabs Kai's arm, looking up at him with tears in her eyes. "He looks like you!"

"Look at his name." Xavier flashes it on the screen.

"It's an anagram," I explain.

Rick is deathly silent, and Kai's face has turned pale. He grabs the back of the chair to steady himself. "I don't believe it." Silent tears stream down his face, and he does nothing to hide them from us. "It's our brother," he rasps in a hoarse voice. "It's Rogan."

Want to find out what the two missing Anderson brothers have been up to? Find out in *The Hate I Feel* available now in the *Hot Summer School Nights* anthology. This story will be extended and released at a future date within the Rydeville Elite series

Drew is the last book in the series, releasing sometime in 2022. Subscribe to my newsletter or join Siobhan's Squad on Facebook for updates as I have them. Type this link into your browser: http://eepurl.com/dl4l5v

ABOUT THE AUTHOR

USA Today bestselling author **Siobhan Davis** writes emotionally intense young adult and new adult fiction with swoon-worthy romance, complex characters, and tons of unexpected plot twists and turns that will have you flipping the pages beyond bedtime!

Siobhan's family will tell you she's a little bit obsessive when it comes to reading and writing, and they aren't wrong. She can rarely be found without her trusty Kindle, a paperback book, or her laptop somewhere close at hand.

Prior to becoming a full-time writer, Siobhan forged a successful corporate career in human resource management.
She resides in the Garden County of Ireland with her husband and two sons.

You can connect with Siobhan in the following ways:
Author Website: www.siobhandavis.com
Facebook: AuthorSiobhanDavis
Twitter: @siobhandavis
Instagram: @siobhandavisauthor
Email: siobhan@siobhandavis.com

BOOKS BY SIOBHAN DAVIS

KENNEDY BOYS SERIES
Upper Young Adult/New Adult Contemporary Romance
Finding Kyler
Losing Kyler
Keeping Kyler
The Irish Getaway
Loving Kalvin
Saving Brad
Seducing Kaden
Forgiving Keven
Summer in Nantucket
Releasing Keanu
Adoring Keaton
Reforming Kent

STANDALONES
New Adult Contemporary Romance
Inseparable
Incognito
When Forever Changes
No Feelings Involved
Only Ever You
Second Chances Box Set

Reverse Harem Contemporary Romance
Surviving Amber Springs

Dark Mafia Romance
Condemned to Love

RYDEVILLE ELITE SERIES
Dark High School Romance
Cruel Intentions
Twisted Betrayal

Sweet Retribution
Charlie
Jackson
Sawyer
The Hate I Feel
*Drew^*

THE SAINTHOOD (BOYS OF LOWELL HIGH)
Dark HS Reverse Harem Romance
Resurrection
Rebellion
Reign
The Sainthood: The Complete Series

ALL OF ME DUET
Angsty New Adult Romance
Say I'm The One
Let Me Love You

ALINTHIA SERIES
Upper YA/NA Paranormal Romance/Reverse Harem
The Lost Savior
The Secret Heir
The Warrior Princess
The Chosen One
*The Rightful Queen**

TRUE CALLING SERIES
Young Adult Science Fiction/Dystopian Romance
True Calling
Lovestruck
Beyond Reach
Light of a Thousand Stars
Destiny Rising
Short Story Collection
True Calling Series Collection

SAVEN SERIES
Young Adult Science Fiction/Paranormal Romance

Saven Deception
Logan
Saven Disclosure
Saven Denial
Saven Defiance
Axton
Saven Deliverance
Saven: The Complete Series

*Coming 2021
^Release date to be confirmed
Visit www.siobhandavis.com for all future release dates. Please note release dates are subject to change based on reader demand and the author's schedule. Subscribing to the author's newsletter or following her on Facebook is the best way to stay updated with planned new releases.

Made in the USA
Monee, IL
20 July 2021